Praise f

Clandestine O

"Through this fascinating novel, Diana Block brings to life stories about radical history that will educate and engage today's activists. Her portrayal of a woman in solitary confinement rings true to experience, offering a raw view of the struggle for resilience under daunting circumstances. Through flights of imagination, the novel gives us hope for political transformations in the future."
   —Sarah Shourd, author of *A Sliver of Light: Three Americans Imprisoned in Iran*

"Diana Block has accomplished what a number of writers have tried unsuccessfully—capturing the profound revolutionary spirit of the political movements that emerged from the 1960s. *Clandestine Occupations* is also the first work of fiction set in that era to center women, not just one strong female character. It is a work filled with suspense, intrigue, ideas, and love. Nothing else has come near illustrating the slogan of the time, 'the personal is political.'"
   —Roxanne Dunbar-Ortiz, author of *An Indigenous People's History of the United States*

"Diana Block creates a vivid and engaging tapestry of political passions interwoven with the intricacies of personal relationships. *Clandestine Occupations* takes us into the thoughts and feelings of six different women as each, in her own way, grapples with choices about how to live and act in a world rife with oppression but also brightened by rays of humanity and hope."
   —David Gilbert, political prisoner, author of *Love and Struggle: My Life in SDS, the Weather Underground, and Beyond*

"In evocative yet unsentimental prose, Block transports us into the world of radical activism, clandestine organizing, feminism, persecution, and prison. A gripping read for both those familiar with the 1970s or new to its rich history of political organizing."
   —Victoria Law, author of *Resistance Behind Bars: The Struggles of Incarcerated Women*

"Diana Block once again challenges our understanding of the ethical essence of revolution. Beyond political theory and practice, the moral dilemmas and turmoils are constant and consistent. Where does your loyalty lie, how does your dedication confront obstacles? These are the questions found in these pages as Diana searches for a just balance in human relationships and politics. *Clandestine Occupations* captures and occupies the heart and spirit, teaching us what it means to be genuine and sincere in revolutionary life and love."
   —Jalil Muntaqim, political prisoner, author of *We Are Our Own Liberators: Selected Prison Writings*

"Diana Block's novel *Clandestine Occupations* is an engrossing, deeply moving, page-turning feminist thriller: a walk on the *noir* side of society's leftist edges of hideouts, prisons, pseudonyms, betrayals, and loyalties. At the same time it is an emotional exploration of relationships: mother/daughter, gay/straight, in jail/outside jail.

"Block writes in a compelling authentic voice as she follows six characters beginning in 1986 and projects into the immediate future up to 2020 through four decades of their intertwining lives. Each person's story reveals another piece of the suspenseful plot as the protests of the past inform the present (and even the future).

"You cannot stand outside this novel. It demands that readers reflect on our own lives and the intimate changes we made, and are making to the swiftly moving global flow of history. *Clandestine Operations* helps us examine our personal and political interconnections and in spite of it all our surviving capacity for love."

—Nina Serrano, prize-winning poet, 2014 Pen Oakland Josephine Miles Award for excellence in literature

"At the crossroad of the personal and the political, Diana Block's new book is the first major novel taking us to the world of the women who in the 1960 and '70s opted for clandestine struggle. Powerfully written, it is an uncompromising denunciation of social and institutional injustice, and an honest confrontation with the dilemmas we must face as we encounter it in our daily life. It is also a story of female and intergenerational solidarity bringing us voices we cannot ignore. Read this book."

—Silvia Federici, author of *Caliban and the Witch*

"In this poignant and moving novel, Diana Block writes a story, rich in complexity and engaging to read, that interweaves people and issues too often ignored in the literature on prisons and radical history. Her writing—exploring the intersections of gender, sexuality, race, and class—gets us to feel the dilemmas and dreams of women forced to make tough choices. She writes with an intimate knowledge of prison life, mothering in clandestinity, and activism, and her characters jump out as real and textured. Like Schenkkan's *Kentucky Cycle* or Sayles's *Lone Star*, Block's stories intertwine across generations, race, and difference in complicated and unexpected ways."

—Diane C. Fujino, professor of Asian-American Studies at the University of California, Santa Barbara, and author of *Heartbeat of Struggle: The Revolutionary Life of Yuri Kochiyama*

"Diana Block's novel shows why well-written fiction may be the most honest and profound way to recount history. *Clandestine Occupations* does just that, projecting from inner lives to outer events, and in the process illuminating our understanding of both. This is a lovely and necessary book."

—Laura Whitehorn, former political prisoner and editor of *The War Before: The True Life Story of Safiya Bukhari*

"*Clandestine Occupations* is a triumph of passion and force. A number of memoirs and other nonfiction works by revolutionaries from the 1970s and '80s, including one by Block herself, have given us partial pictures of what a committed life, sometimes lived underground, was like. But there are times when only fiction can really take us there. A marvelous novel that moves beyond all preconceived categories."

—Margaret Randall, author of *Sandino's Daughters* and *Che on My Mind*

Clandestine Occupations

An Imaginary History

Diana Block

PM PRESS
2015
★

Clandestine Occupations: An Imaginary History
Diana Block © 2015
This edition © 2015 PM Press

ISBN: 9781629631219
Library of Congress Control Number: 2015930896

"Clandestine Kisses" by Marilyn Buck, from *INSIDE/OUT: Selected Poems*, reprinted by permission of City Lights Publishers

PM Press
P.O. Box 23912
Oakland, CA 94623
pmpress.org

10 9 8 7 6 5 4 3 2 1

Cover: John Yates/Stealworks.com
Layout: Jonathan Rowland

Printed by the Employee Owners of Thomson-Shore in Dexter, Michigan. www.thomsonshore.com

For
Luba Simon Block, 1915–1977
Marilyn Buck, 1947–2010
Jalil Muntaqim, 1951 and still going strong!

And for all the ancestors, comrades, friends, lovers,
daughters, sons, prisoners, and freedom fighters who
inspired this imaginary history.

Clandestine Kisses

by Marilyn Buck,
for Linda and her love

kisses
bloom on lips
which have already spoken
stolen clandestine kisses

a prisoner kisses
she is defiant
she breaks the rules
she traffics in contraband women's kisses

a crime wave of kisses
bitter sweet sensuality
flouting women-hating satraps
in their prison fiefdoms
furious
that love
can not be arrested

From *INSIDE/OUT: Selected Poems*
City Lights Publishers

Timeline Highlights

1970   Luba, Cassandra, and Rahim meet in Cuba on the Venceremos Brigade

1973   Sage moves to San Francisco from Chicago

1975   Uprising organization formed

1976   Cassandra is arrested for the first time

1977   Rahim is arrested

1978   Cassandra escapes from prison

1978   Sage starts visiting Rahim at San Quentin

1979   William Morales, Puerto Rican political prisoner, liberated from prison

1979   Assata Shakur, Black Liberation Army political prisoner, liberated from prison

1982   Rahim transferred from San Quentin to Pennsylvania prison

1983   Sage leaves Uprising

1983   Joan moves to Chicago from Indianapolis

1984   Joan meets Reynaldo

1984   Sage meets Brooke, her life partner

1984   Sage starts working at Hanover Foundation

1984   Luba AKA Lynne meets Belinda while living underground in Los Angeles

1985   Luba in Chicago on a brief break from her underground life; meets Joan

1985   Puerto Rican Macheteros celebrate Three Kings Day with gifts to community

1985   Luba gives birth to Nick and escapes FBI encirclement

1986   Cassandra recaptured in Chicago; Luba and her collective placed on 10 Most Wanted list

1994   Joan and Luba encounter each other in Pittsburgh writing class

1995	Luba surfaces with Nick and other collective members in Chicago
1995	Luba returns to the Bay Area
1996	Unshackled Women organization formed
2005	Rahim in SF County Jail facing charges from 1974 cold case
2007	Maggie sees Luba at a parole hearing in Sacramento
2007	Maggie meets Rahim as a hospital patient
2008	Charges against Rahim dropped; he is sent back to Pennsylvania prison
2009	Anise visits Cassandra in prison
2010	Cassandra dies a couple of weeks after "compassionate" release
2011	Occupy movement begins
2014	Israeli attack on Gaza, Ferguson uprising, Black Lives Matter movement is born
2019	#BreaktheBracelet goes viral, and the Urban Maroon movement is born

Birth Years

Cassandra	1948
Rahim	1949
Luba	1950
Sage	1951
Belinda	1952
Joan	1961
Maggie	1965
Nick	1985
Anise	1988
Gordon	1989

Contents

MISSING—
BELINDA
1986

At first I wasn't worried when Lynne disappeared from my life. She had disappeared before and returned. It was August in Los Angeles, and all the people who can get away pack their bags. If I could, I too would escape from the broken backs, the torn meniscuses, and the arrogant doctors of the Ortho ward at Arcadia Memorial Hospital where I put in my mind-numbing sixty-hour weeks. I figured Lynne must have gone to visit her family with her new baby. I wouldn't have given it a second thought if it weren't for the envelope hidden in my basement that I had promised to safeguard for her.

Lynne had called me right after her baby was born in the beginning of August. I knew he was born on August 2, that her labor was five hours long, and that the baby's name was Alex. *Alex is my favorite uncle*, she explained, even though I hadn't asked about the origins of his name. I bit my tongue and didn't say, *If uncle Alex is such a favorite, why haven't you ever mentioned him to me before?* which was what I was thinking. With most people I didn't give a shit and just said what was on my mind, but I had come to be more careful with Lynne. She deserved that consideration.

Lynne liked that I was blunt. About a week after she started working evenings as a unit clerk on the Ortho ward, she came up to me as I was doing my charts.

I heard what you said to that doctor, she began in her serious, husky voice.

Already eavesdropping on confidential nurse-doctor conversations? I kidded, not sure where she was coming from. But she wasn't put off.

Dr. Stanwyck was accusing that elderly Black patient who just had back surgery of manipulative behavior because he wanted more pain meds.

I interrupted her.

Oh, yes, young Dr. Stanwyck. Just finished med school and he thinks he's the supreme authority on pain and manipulation. But sweetie, that's my specialty. So I told him that poor Mr. Williams needs his meds or he isn't going to be able to heal correctly. I stopped myself before I turned it into a rant.

Weren't you worried you'd get in trouble—telling a doctor that you knew better than he did?

Oh, it's okay. If they fire me, I'll just go back to being a waitress. Almost as much money and less stress.

Lynne laughed, and when she did her mouth relaxed and she stopped being such a super-solemn chick. It made me want to get to know her even though it was against my rules to get too friendly with anyone at work.

I had noticed her the first day she started the job. She was wearing dangling amethyst earrings and bright purple pants underneath her required striped uniform top. Her hair was reddish and cropped short, almost like she had chopped it off herself (something I often did instead of wasting money on a haircut). Altogether she had a radically different look from our last unit clerk, Tammy, who had been strictly pastel, fake pearls, and dark roots eclipsing her ultrablonde waves. I could have easily ignored Tammy's constant silly chatter, but I couldn't stand how her voice changed from slurpy to shrill when she commanded the Mexican orderlies to run errands that were really in *her* job description. So it wasn't a big loss when Tammy got pregnant with her third child and decided that it would be cheaper to stop working and stay home to take care of her kids.

After our first talk about back pain and doctors, Lynne and I couldn't seem to find any small talk groove to get us to the next step in our acquaintance. Lynne seemed to always be mulling over something momentous in her head during her spare moments between answering call bells and transcribing doctor's orders. Once I commented that she was the first unit clerk I ever knew who read long foreign novels in the break room. She immediately looked uncomfortable, almost guilty, and mumbled something about having majored in Latin American literature in college, so I dropped it.

One time she asked me why I always wore a white nurse's cap when they were no longer required. It seemed to her that the caps had sexist associations.

The nurse's cap originally derives from the nun's habit. I wear it to remind myself that I am eternally committed to an equally sacred profession. I watched amused as Lynne seriously began to turn this answer over in her head. Before she could reply, I switched it up.

Actually, it's my version of a witch's hat, and I wear it to promote an alternative form of healing in this bastion of Western medicine. Now she was looking frustrated, so I decided enough was enough and started to laugh.

Sweetie, I just wear it to keep my prematurely gray mop of hair in place, I offered in a conciliatory tone. This time she chuckled. Still, I wasn't sure I wanted to get to know the kind of person who claimed the moral high ground about a nurse's cap.

But a few months after she started the job, when I saw her dancing at the staff Christmas party she blew away all the pop psychology character theories I had been busy constructing about her. Staff Christmas parties were the one work-related social function I made myself go to each year. I avoided the department parties, held in the hospital conference room, where nurses, doctors, clerks, and orderlies were all supposed to intermingle like equals and forget who really ordered who around. After the uncomfortable party icebreakers, where we were obliged to partner off with a member of a different vocational sector, each group quickly gravitated toward their own segregated occupational zone. The staff parties, however, didn't include the doctors and the venue rotated from one person's house to the next each year, although I had made it clear that my house was out of bounds.

That year, the party was at Juan's house. Juan was the orderly I liked the best. He never complained when you asked him for help moving a patient, even when it was time for him to clock out, and he was always willing to help translate a patient's requests from Spanish to English if you needed him to. Most of the nursing assistants and clerks thought he was very cute. Even though I warned each of them that he had way too many *novias* already, it didn't stop them from flirting with him at every opportunity. But Lynne had never expressed any interest in Juan, so I was a little surprised when forty-five minutes into the party, before anyone had a chance to get really plastered on the huge assortment of booze spread across the table, I looked away from Imelda, the nurse I was talking to, and caught a glimpse of Lynne dancing with Juan. I tried to get back to my conversation with Imelda, but my eyes kept wandering back to Lynne.

She was wearing her signature purple pants, but in place of the uniform top she had on an aqua and purple flowered Hawaiian shirt, which might have looked loud and stupid on someone else, but somehow she was able to bring it off. Instead of looking like she was trying to figure out the world's problems, she was totally absorbed in the beat of this old disco song, shaking and rolling her hips like this was what she had been longing to burst out and do every day while she was hunched over, transcribing notes on the Ortho ward.

I was trying to figure out whether she was dancing for him or dancing for herself—which to me is the only way to really, truly dance—when the song ended, and before I knew it she had come over, inviting me to dance too. Even though I pulled back she kept insisting. It wasn't like women never danced with women at our parties. There were so many more women than men you had to get over the girl-boy formula if you wanted to dance at all. Everyone knew that I wasn't a dancer, and usually by the time they were all drunk enough to let loose on the dance floor, I would be out the door. But Lynne didn't know my rules and might have thought I was against women dancing together or something if I didn't dance with her, so reluctantly I let her draw me into the expanding circle.

The whirling motion, the hammering beat, the sexy flash of Lynne's body moving in her purple pants somehow fueled my own body's movement until we were all breathlessly vibrating and panting out the words of the song together—*I will survive, I will survive* . . . But then the music stopped and Lynne walked over to Imelda to try and pull *her* into the next dance. I knew I had to leave before I did something really foolish.

Where are you going so early? Lynne caught me as I was trying to get out the door.

My true loves are waiting for me to take them out for a walk, I explained, trying to keep it light.

You have dogs?

Five at last count.

My God, I can hardly imagine having one.

You'll have to come and meet them sometime. As soon as I said it, I realized that somehow Lynne had tricked me into violating another one of my rules.

Over the next couple of weeks, I found myself talking more easily with Lynne in between medication rounds and charting and trying to keep the patients calm and pain-free. We talked about the party and how drunk and stupid people had gotten, especially Juan, who was trying to get every one of the nursing assistants into bed with him simultaneously. We talked about the head nurse, Clara, and how she was giving each nurse more patients than our contract allowed, but no one except me seemed to want to protest this abuse. We talked about music, and I confessed that I didn't really like disco or rock.

Jazz is what I really love. I have hundreds of albums and whenever I have any extra money I go out and buy another record.

Lynne looked a little surprised.

Really? she said. *I like jazz too, but not that many people in this part of the world seem to be into it.*

I could have been stopped by the peculiar way she said *in this part of the world,* as if we were cohabiting an alien territory, but instead I found myself repeating the invitation that I had previously made.

You should come over and listen to my records sometime.

Lynne seemed startled by the invitation, now repeated in our everyday work environment. But after a moment's pause, she replied,

Yes, that would be cool.

Soon after that, Lynne disappeared for the first time. Of course she had an alibi. She told the head nurse that her father had just died and she needed to go back east for the funeral. After a week she called and said she needed to stay away longer and deal with his papers. When she still wasn't back after two weeks, Clara was ready to fire her, but I persuaded her to wait a little longer, given Lynne's superior transcription skills. Just when I was on the verge of getting bitter that I had put myself out for someone who didn't even have the workplace etiquette to keep us posted, Lynne reappeared.

I wasn't sure what excuses she gave Clara, but she immediately dived into the staggering pile of accumulated doctor's notes. She attacked the typewriter keyboard with a vengeance and told the rest of us that she was really okay, since she hadn't been that close to her father anyway. But when I looked over at her beating the keys with her fingers and scraping her teeth back and forth over her lips until they were chafed and almost bloody, I wondered what family drama had taken place on her trip back east. She had never been a mellow girl but now she seemed about to boil over.

Looks like you could use a little musical relaxation, I commented one day as she was rubbing her sore hands. Then I invited her over to my house for the third time. If this didn't work, I swore I wouldn't ask again. But Lynne surprised me and suggested we get together the following Saturday afternoon when neither of us was working.

I spent Saturday morning trying to tidy things up a little, which is hard to do when you rent an old leaky house that the landlord never wants to repair, have five dogs that run the place, and rarely have anyone over who might care at all about what it looks like. Lynne seemed to overlook the residual mess, though I thought I saw her wrinkle her nose slightly when she first walked in, reminding me that dog smell is impossible to remove by a surface morning cleaning. I had put my babies out in the back yard for the time being, since I gathered that Lynne wasn't much of a dog person, but I hadn't thought about the lingering odor.

Lynne immediately zoned in on the scattered Picasso and Matisse posters that I used to cover the cracks in the walls, and the dozens of pictures of my honeys, from the time they were puppies, that covered the rest of the available space. At first I thought her questions about each picture were just polite, but when she seemed to be genuinely interested I couldn't help myself and launched into the story of how I got each dog.

Consuela is my last, I explained when I got to the end of the list. *I wasn't going to get her at all, but one day I was driving by the shelter and some greater power made me pull over and go inside. And there she was—half-blind, her poor black fur standing on end in sorry tufts, cowering when anyone came near. She had just been found in some filthy apartment when her owner died, and God only knows what he had been doing to her to make her scared like that. I knew as soon as I saw her that this was fate and she needed to be with me and my other girls.*

I glanced over at Lynne and for a minute I thought I had lost her with my talk of fate and a greater power.

Why Consuela? Your other dogs all have Irish names— Bridget, Erin, Megan, Sinead?

Consuela is for my Puerto Rican grandmother, whom I never met. Figured I had recognized my Irish side enough, might as well give some honor to my father's ancestry even though he was a wicked bastard.

You're Puerto Rican? Lynne sounded like she was choking.

Well, I don't usually claim my Puerto Rican half. My Irish mother's gene pool somehow gave me this light skin and green eyes, and the wild black curls that came from his side have been covered up by the gray. My father has been missing for so many years I can hardly remember him now. But yeah, he helped make me and name me, so I do have Puerto Rico in my sangre.

Wow! Lynne said, still sounding like she was short of breath. *I never would have guessed. That's amazing!*

Suddenly, I felt very angry. I hardly ever told anyone about my father, since when I did people usually said something stupid like *What part of Mexico is Puerto Rico in?* But here was Lynne, someone I was beginning to feel okay about, and her reaction sounded ignorant.

Because I speak English without an accent and I'm a nurse, not an orderly?

Lynne turned red and immediately tried to make amends.

I'm sorry, I didn't mean it like it sounds. It's just that growing up in New York, I knew lots of Puerto Ricans and I miss them. Out here, I haven't met any Puerto Ricans, so connecting with you and then finding out you're Puerto Rican, well, it feels like serendipity or something.

When Lynne mentioned her past, it always sounded a little off, like she wanted to say more or she wished she had said less. But I wasn't one for probing, and I didn't need any more apologies. In a few minutes, the entire afternoon would combust if we couldn't move on.

Well, one Puerto Rican I really love is Tito Puente, so how about we listen to him?

We made our way back to my bedroom where I had my stereo and all my albums. I could see Lynne carefully taking in the space—the colored fabrics I had hanging on the walls, the posters of Coltrane and Mingus, the lava lamp, and a small purple and yellow *vejigante* figure, which was one of the only mementos from my father that I had managed to hang on to over the years. We settled down on the shag rug among the pillows, and I lit one of my large collection of incense burn-ers. Lynne's eyes kept drifting back to the misshapen vejigante with its hollow eye holes and five cracked papier-mâché horns jutting out of its head.

I don't know whether a vejigante is a clown or a devil or a little of both. I used to imagine that it was a protective spirit that my father deliberately left to watch over my brother and me after he split, but he probably just forgot it was here, he took off so quickly, I explained. *Sometimes when I come home from work and have had it dealing with arrogant people all day, I sit down in front of the lava lamp with Consuela in my lap and the other doggies around me, and I summon the vejigante's powers until the perfect hex emerges. I contemplate how I could use it if I wanted to.*

I thought I saw Lynne flinch. The part about the hex was going too far for her.

Just kidding, I laughed. But I wasn't.

I lit a joint and handed it to Lynne. For a moment she looked worried, as if we were in high school and the principal might walk in, find us, and all hell would break loose.

It's okay if you'd rather not. I'm used to smoking alone. Sometimes I invite the doggies but they decline to partake.

Lynne took a few tokes and then handed it back to me. I put on Tito Puente's *Mambo Diablo*, which I had recently bought, and quickly began to lose myself in the maze of tim-bales, vibraphone, bongos, congas, trumpet, flute, and piano. I could tell that Lynne too was getting inside the music, her left hand tapping, her head nodding, her usually hunched shoul-ders vibrating rhythmically. I could imagine going over to her, taking her hand and leading her into a fierce mambo where the sound merged into our moving bodies and we let the music guide us where we wanted to go.

My father played the congas.

I hadn't meant to say this out loud, but all of a sudden the image of him sitting in our living room, banging on the drums with wild, uncontrollable energy, was too vivid to keep to myself.

It's one my best memories of him. He started to teach me once. Not sure how old I was, six or seven maybe. My mother was at work waitressing and he began to show me how to tap out the beat. I was just starting to feel like I was getting the hang of it when my mother came home, tired and angry as usual, and said it was giving her a headache. They started to fight and that was it for the congas. When he finally left a year or so later, I kept expecting to see the congas back in the corner of the living room where he kept them, but they were gone for good. All he left was the vejigante.

Did you ever meet your grandmother, Consuela? Lynne asked cautiously.

No. But my father would show me pictures of her and the house where he grew up in some village in PR. He would point to the flag that was flying on top of the house and say, That's my bandera, not the fucking stars and stripes. Our Puerto Rican bonita bandera.

I hadn't thought about any of this for so long. I couldn't believe it was coming out of my mouth now.

Was he an independentista?

That stopped me. Of course I knew the word—someone who wanted Puerto Rico to be independent. I had done a paper on the independence movement for some class in college and learning all that stuff I never knew about Puerto Rico blew my mind. When Lynne said the word, independentista, a picture immediately popped into my head of Lolita Lebrón being arrested in Washington, DC. I had spent hours staring at the photo while I was supposed to be doing my report. She was fiercely beautiful even in that terrible moment, wearing a tailored suit and pillbox hat. I couldn't believe that she and three Puerto Rican men had gone into Congress, unfurled a Puerto Rican flag, and started to shout and shoot at the assembled lawmakers.

It was totally incongruous that this impeccable lady had just stood up in front of all those old white men and interrupted their tea party. But that was the point—no one saw it coming. Those crazy independentistas were able to get the white guys to stop whatever bullshit they were talking about. They made the world pay attention, if only for a few minutes, to the fact that Puerto Ricans didn't want the U.S. to keep controlling their land, their water, and the air they breathed. They didn't want to be a fucking U.S. colony anymore.

Even with policemen on both sides of her, grabbing her arms, even when she knew she was going to prison, Lolita looked cool and unflinching. I kept looking at the picture to try and solve the puzzle but somehow I never could. Lolita was beautiful and brave, but she was *loca*. I could understand being that angry, but I couldn't wrap my mind around risking my life for some ideal like independence, especially when she must have known damn well that shooting up Congress may be a showstopper but it wasn't really going to make Puerto Rico be free.

Lynne probably had a different take on the whole situation. She pronounced the word *independentista* like she was used to saying it, like for her and her friends it meant something familiar and real instead of some foreign, fantasy concept. She made me realize how little *I* really understood about Puerto Rico, and I started feeling mad all over again.

Well, my father always talked about how fucked up the yanquis were. But he moved here, married a drunken Irish yanqui, and only talked about how cool freedom was when he was full of booze. He sure as shit got his own freedom when he left us. Walked out after one of their endless drunken brawls and he didn't come back to give us history lessons when we got older. But it sounds like you know much more than I do about Puerto Rico and independence, probably from all of your independentista friends.

As soon as I said it, I wanted to take it all back. Lynne was looking disoriented and her teeth were rubbing across her lips.

You're putting words in my mouth, she protested.

I didn't mean it that way, I mumbled but couldn't find words for anything more.

The music had ended and the needle was scratching purposelessly back and forth. We were on the verge of sinking into terminal disconnection when I heard the sound of the dogs barking happily outside.

Do you want to meet my babies? I asked, grasping at straws. To my relief Lynne said, *Sure.*

Everything was better out in the sun with my buddies, as it always was. They came bounding over to greet us, no questions asked, no complicated explanations needed about why I had put them out in the yard for the past couple of hours. Just unconditional joy at seeing me and meeting Lynne. They seemed to sense that Lynne might be easily overwhelmed by their doggie buoyancy, so they calmly sniffed around her, giving her a chance to find her balance with them. She let them smell her hand and pet each one tentatively.

I'm kind of timid around dogs, she explained, even though it was more than obvious.

I can tell they like you anyway, I reassured her. Lynne sat down in the grass and Consuela quickly went and sat in her lap. Lynne began to slowly stroke her as if she understood exactly how Consuela needed to be touched in order to make all her pain disappear.

Have you ever had any pets? I asked, suddenly aching to know much more about who Lynne really was, why she was nervous around dogs, and how a person like her had come to be sitting in my Monrovia backyard.

Growing up we had a couple of cats. The first one jumped out of our fourth-story window and was never found again. The second one kept wandering over to our neighbors' house where they fed her delicious Puerto Rican food instead of food from a can, so after a while we just let them keep her.

She stopped abruptly, probably because she realized that the conversation had somehow drifted back to Puerto Rico. This time I wanted to hear more.

So your parents had a lot of Puerto Rican friends also?

Not exactly friends. We lived in a building on the Upper West Side where gradually most of the white Jewish families moved out and Puerto Rican families moved in during the fifties. My father would complain, like most of our bigoted neighbors, that the Puerto Ricans were taking over the neighborhood.

She glanced at me to see if I was offended again, but I motioned for her to keep going.

It wasn't until much later that I understood that all these Puerto Ricans had been pushed out of their villages and off their island by the U.S. plan to industrialize Puerto Rico. My parents couldn't afford to move anywhere else, and our neighbors were all very friendly, so eventually my parents loosened up and became cordial. Especially when the Torres family fed our wayward cat.

What did your father do?

It was Lynne's turn to cut the conversation off abruptly, even though it was a simple question.

He was a bureaucrat, a paper-pusher, was all I could get out of her. I tried a few more by-the-book questions about her childhood that she pretended to answer without telling me anything. After some more stilted conversation, she told me that she had to go pick up her roommate from work. Before she left, she made a special point of saying goodbye to each dog. Finally, she turned to me.

Thanks so much for having me over, Belinda, she said earnestly and reached over to give me a hug. It only lasted a second, but it felt more-than-tender. It made up for all the afternoon's missteps and mistakes.

That night I had a dream that Lolita Lebrón was teaching me how to play the congas. I knew this had to be a sign, but I didn't dare speculate about what it signified.

At work, I kept looking for little ways to show Lynne that I liked her without overstepping those invisible boundaries between coworker friendship and something more. I made sure there were sharpened pencils with sturdy erasers in the ward clerk's pencil cup before she came in for her shifts. I reminded her when it was time for her to take a break, even when the orders were piled high in her in-basket. I helped her interpret the most indecipherable doctor's handwriting. Over the years, I had made it my business to defy the elite aura of mystery created by illegible doctor handwriting, and my acumen in divining their scribbles had become legendary.

One day, I noticed on the staff rolodex that Lynne's birthday was coming up on March 1. When I saw that Lynne was scheduled to work that day, I decided to buy her flowers, even though this was a step beyond my other small gestures of appreciation. I dragged myself out of bed that morning a half hour early so that I could stop by a local flower vendor that I passed each day on the way to work. I picked out a gorgeous bouquet of purple irises that made my heart pound and put them in a plain brown shopping bag so they wouldn't attract unnecessary attention on the ward. As soon as I saw Lynne walking into the locker room, I grabbed the bag. Before I could be overcome with shyness or embarrassment, I strode in, pulled out the irises, and wished her a happy birthday.

I had expected her to blush, to be surprised, to demur, and to finally be pleased that the flowers were so pretty and I had remembered. I hadn't expected the look of pure panic that passed over her face at the words *happy birthday*. It was as if I had said *you're fired* or even *you're under arrest*. I watched as she struggled to regain control over her face.

I almost forgot it was my birthday today. My roommate wasn't up yet, and I just don't make a big deal of birthdays anymore.

But these flowers are totally beautiful. Purple is my favorite color. They're perfect. You shouldn't have.

At that moment, I knew I shouldn't have. I also knew that the rest of what she said was bullshit. People don't just forget their birthdays. Even I, who don't put stock in most holidays or celebrations, expect that my mother will make it through her alcoholic haze to remember the day she birthed me, and that my brother will call from whatever flophouse or jail he happens to be in. A person has to have a dark secret reason and a calculated plan to erase their birthday from their memory. Up until then I had thought that Lynne's secrets were quirky rather than dark. Now I wasn't sure. But I knew that the hospital locker room wasn't the place to explore this mystery, so I just excused myself.

I happened to see your birth date on the rolodex a couple of days ago, so when I passed by a flower vendor this morning, those irises just jumped out at me. Sorry if I took you by surprise.

We busied ourselves looking for a vase large enough to hold the bouquet that Lynne then placed prominently on display in the corner of the nurse's station where she sat. I listened as she enthusiastically credited me each time someone walked by and commented on the beautiful flowers. And when several other nurses and assistants suggested that we take her out to lunch, she graciously accepted the invitation and seemed to genuinely enjoy the whole occasion. Over the pizza, Lynne laughed as people shared funny stories of birthday surprises or weird birthday calamities. She even came up with a brief story of her own about how she broke her leg just before her sixteenth birthday, ruining all her plans to wildly celebrate sweet sixteen. The lunch made me feel less guilty about spotlighting Lynne on her birthday. But I felt further away than ever from deciphering who she really was.

After the birthday fiasco, I figured I should back off. I prided myself on being able to psych out where most people were coming from. I could cut off a young resident right before he launched a disdainful diatribe about how fat people brought their back problems on themselves with my statistics about how fast food was the real villain behind obesity. And I could definitely discern last night's binge behind the veteran nurse's crazed rant against all the incompetent people who had caused *her* medication errors. But Lynne remained illegible and that was unsettling.

Still, a couple of weeks later when Lynne asked if I wanted to go see the movie *Missing*, I said yes before I could remind myself to hesitate. She explained, in a teacherly tone, that the movie was based on a true story about the disappearance of a left-wing American journalist in Chile after the military coup that took place on September 11, 1973.

Normally I never went to political exposé-type movies, but I didn't want her to think that I was totally apathetic when it came to politics. I made myself read the newspaper most days and vaguely followed the daily recap of global wars, coups, assassinations, and insoluble corruption. I knew Reagan was up to no good with the contras in Nicaragua and I had had conversations with one of the Salvadoran orderlies about how scared he was for his family back in El Salvador because the right-wing government, backed by *los Americanos*, was killing off everyone who didn't support them 100 percent. I had even heard a little about the dictator who had taken over Chile, Augusto Pinochet, from an orderly who had fled that country. But why use my precious free time to see treachery and ugliness magnified a hundredfold on the big screen? I said yes to Lynne not only to clear my name and get another chance to hang out with her. I had to find out why she wanted to see this particular movie with me.

It started out like an ordinary movie date, with popcorn and Coke, though Lynne only had water, divulging that she hated all soda pop. This seemed to me to fit perfectly with all her other eccentricities. Before the previews began, we talked about work and she asked me how each of the dogs was doing. We especially dwelled on Consuela, who had developed a mysterious ailment that made her listless and lethargic. It felt natural, even relaxed, to be sitting next to each other, chatting and laughing. When the lights dimmed and the previews began, I felt a twinge of gloom because I knew we could never progress to holding hands during this kind of movie.

There was no subtle lead-in to the meat of the film. Menacing soldiers out for blood, military trucks rampaging boisterously through Chile's streets, random brutal shootings of ordinary people just trying to get back home safely—all the violent horrors that I try so hard to protect myself from were immediately blasting me full force in the face. Men fighting, men making war. The bravado in my father's voice when he would come back from a stupid drunken brawl in a bar and proclaim that he had beaten the other guy to a pulp because the fool had taunted him that Mexico was a real country while Puerto Rico was nothing but a sorry-ass, teeny-weeny American island, owned hook, line, and sinker.

To me, it was all testosterone, ego, and mindless pummeling. But I knew that Lynne wouldn't have brought me to see a macho war movie.

I resolved to concentrate and get into the story line, or the purpose of this movie date would be lost for both of us. Charles Horman, the lefty journalist working in Chile, had disappeared right after the coup. His father, Ed, a patriotic American, flew down to help Charles's wife Beth find him. Slowly Ed and Beth began to understand that they wouldn't get any help from the American embassy in their search for Charles because the American government was 100 percent behind the cover-up and the Chilean coup itself.

Ed and Beth were looking through mountains of piled dead bodies in the morgue, lifting the corners of sheets that revealed the tortured remnants of faces, the stumps of deliberately mutilated legs and hands. Having lost hope of finding Charles alive, they at least wanted to find his dead body. My hands were clammy and I could smell the grease putrefying at the bottom of the popcorn bag. All of a sudden, Lynne began to breathe hard and fast, maybe hyperventilating. I put my hand on her arm and whispered, *Are you okay?* It took her a few seconds to gasp, *It's just so horrible.* Then she got up quickly and went to the bathroom.

When she returned about ten minutes later, she seemed to have gulped down her emotions and was able to watch the rest of the movie more calmly. But it was hard for me to focus any longer on the movie's mystery. Was Lynne related to Charles Horman in some way? Did she have a brother or sister who had been in Chile at the time of the coup and was missing ever since? Why had Lynne wanted me to see this movie with her?

At the end, Ed confronts the young, arrogant U.S. embassy representatives with proof of America's complicity in the coup. The reps callously defend their actions as necessary to preserving the American *way of life.* They accuse Ed of caring only because he is personally involved. If he didn't have a personal connection, they taunt, he would be sitting at home watching TV, just like all the other millions of oblivious Americans.

I didn't watch much TV, but I knew that I was one of those millions. Where had I been on September 11, 1973? In a stuffy classroom? Waitressing in a fancy Beverly Hills restaurant where the big tips were the only thing that kept me from walking out for good at the end of each day? Regardless of where I was, nothing about Chile had filtered through my own daily frustrations at that time. Even now I only was in this theater, watching this movie, because I was personally connected to Lynne.

As we walked out after the movie, we were surrounded by intense conversations. One woman in a flowing, flowered skirt was declaring loudly to a group of friends,

It makes me furious that the papers always lie to us! They're telling us the same kind of cover-up shit now about what's going on in Nicaragua and El Salvador!

Another woman, wearing a T-shirt that proclaimed *U.S. Out of El Salvador!,* was scolding her boyfriend, *You're so cynical. What's the point of seeing a movie like this if you don't think anything can be done to change things?* I sympathized with the boyfriend. All I wanted to do was go home, gather my doggies in a tight circle, light a joint, and forget everything that I had witnessed in the past couple of hours.

Human beings are just corrupt and deceitful. That's why I pin all my hopes on animals, I commented to Lynne, hoping that this light spin would deflect a deeper discussion about what we had just seen. I half expected her to chastise me in the same tone that the woman had taken with her boyfriend. But Lynne sounded more wistful than irritated when she replied.

I don't think the people who were trying to build a new society in Chile were corrupt and deceitful. After a pause she added, *But I understand what you're saying. Sometimes seeing a movie like this can make things seem hopeless.*

It was a warm, fresh April night and a full, golden moon was just showing its gorgeous face. In another month or so the overheated, stale-aired LA summer would take over and all the possibilities of this moment with Lynne would be lost. I suggested we go pick up the doggies and take them for a walk in the park. Lynne agreed.

The dogs scampered up and down the moonlit slopes, except for Consuela, who was still recovering from her doggie virus and lingered near Lynne and me, eavesdropping on our conversation. I couldn't shake the movie's heavy aura and despite myself I needed to talk with Lynne about it.

So what do you think can be done to stop coups like Chile from happening over and over again? I asked, trying to make the question sound curious rather than challenging.

Lynne stooped down and began petting Consuela.

Well, I don't think there's any one thing. People write their elected officials and sign petitions, they go on marches and demonstrations, and that's all fine. But to me, you can't end a government like Pinochet's in Chile, or Reagan's for that matter, unless you are prepared to fight. You know, there are clandestine guerrilla groups in Chile now that are doing just that.

For some reason her answer triggered some buried fury in me.

But how can they ever win against these fucked-up governments with all their power? Reagan and Pinochet are so sure of themselves they don't even give a shit when a movie like this comes out and tells the world how evil they are 'cause they know nothing will stop them. Don't get me wrong, I think people who fight for what they believe in are very courageous. But if they just end up missing, killed, or in prison, what good can that do?

Lynne didn't answer right away. She just kept tenderly stroking Consuela while she looked up at the brilliant orange moon, searching for an answer.

I think people have to be willing to be killed or go to prison in order to make the kind of revolutions that need to happen in this world.

Her voice was cracked with emotion. I flashed on the photo of Lolita Lebrón. Was Lynne's striped uniform top as much of a camouflage as Lolita's tailored suit? Was Lynne really fierce and crazy like Lolita?

She must have heard my silent speculation or realized that she had accidentally crossed some forbidden line.

Don't worry, Belinda, I'm just blowing off steam, she tried to reassure me. *The movie and the moon have made me kind of loopy, opened up thoughts and feelings I usually keep to myself.*

Then randomly, without any introduction or lead-in, I blurted out my own secret.

You know, I'm gay, I announced. Once the words were out, I realized that I wanted Lynne to accept the truth about me minus embroidery—my saga of Irish–Puerto Rican Catholic repression, my gnawing fears of exposure or my twisted history of rejection.

Immediately, Lynne stopped stroking Consuela and put her hand firmly on mine.

Thank you for telling me, Belinda. I kind of had a feeling you might be. You know, I'm gay too.

I couldn't say that I had had a feeling about her. More it had started as a windy wish that had turned into a driven desire that I couldn't admit to myself. A fervid fantasy that after all the uncertainty and murkiness between us we would at some point reveal ourselves to each other and everything would shift into place.

My next question should have waited a week, a month, or perhaps even longer, but it had a will of its own.

Do you have a girlfriend?

Her hesitation signaled the answer before she said it out loud.

Well, yes. I mean we just started seeing each other, and I'm not sure where it's going totally. But, yes. How about you?

Whether she was telling the truth or buffering rejection, my moment of euphoria had been upended.

I'm between girlfriends right now, I answered lightly. In another minute we might have fallen back into the strained pattern of our relationship, but Lynne grabbed my shoulders and looked straight at me.

Belinda, I am so glad that I met you and that we have been able to be who we are with each other. Your friendship means so much, trust me!

My eyes were starting to water, so I just nodded. I might never sort out her fibs from her facts, but on some gut level I did trust Lynne.

When Lynne asked me to have tea with her after work the following week, I wasn't even hoping that she had broken up with her new girlfriend. After our *Missing* date, I had allowed myself one good cry to purge all the subterranean pipedreams that had been percolating since I first caught sight of her in her purple pants. Then I decided, uncharacteristically, to accept Lynne's seriousness, her quirkiness, her gayness, her political convictions, and even her mysteries.

When, in the snugness of a booth at Denny's, she asked me to keep some papers for her at my house, my heart started to race. She explained that she was working on the fringes of the Sanctuary Movement, which was helping political refugees who had left El Salvador and other parts of Central America avoid being murdered for their politics. Her group was finding homes where people could safely stay while they applied for political asylum. They also needed a place to store information about the refugees that wasn't likely to be searched. She had thought of me.

Everything clicked into place. Lynne must have asked me to go see *Missing* to gauge where I was at about such political issues and whether I could be trusted. Somehow, in spite of all my barbed questions and cynical defenses, I had passed the test and she had decided to ask for this favor. The request made me tingle with an energy that went beyond my feelings for Lynne. This was a simple thing I could do to help people in need. It wasn't a dramatic shot at Congress or a futile phone call to legislators in whom I had no faith. It was an inconspicuous but useful way I could channel my Irish–Puerto Rican rage instead of just screaming curses at my hapless vejigante.

Lynne was saying that there was no pressure and she would understand if for any reason I couldn't do this. I interrupted to tell her that I was happy to take it on and thanked her for having enough confidence in me to ask. When she handed me the sealed manila envelope, I had already figured out the best creviced corner in my crowded basement to hide this information until whatever time she wanted it back.

I thought that I was making progress in solving the Lynne mystery, but she shook it all up again one day after our shift had ended when she told me she was pregnant. I had noticed that she was gaining some weight, but I assumed it was stress, which was why most of the female staff owned a collection of pants in varying sizes. Through the maze of brainteasers spinning in my head, I heard Lynne calmly describing her ticking thirty-five-year-old biological clock, her yearning for a child, and the sperm bank trip that had been successful the very first time. It took all my self-control not to ask whether she was planning a solo-mom affair or taking her new girlfriend along for the motherhood ride.

Instead I just mumbled, *What a world to bring a baby into.*

The subject of babies always tore me apart. They were so beautiful, so buoyant, so trusting, so utterly unprepared and undeserving of everything this world threw at them. What made Lynne think she could do right by a baby? A lesbian on a unit clerk's salary, who stayed away from her job for weeks at a time and had high ideals about political refugees. How could she pretend to offer stability or security to a baby?

Lynne put her hand on my arm. *Belinda, this was a very hard decision for me, a long time in the making, but now I feel really good about it. I don't expect you to understand or agree with it, but I really need your support at work. I know everyone else around here is going to act weird since I'm not married and don't even have a boyfriend.*

And just like that, all the fork-tongued words melted away in my mouth.

I can't think of anyone who would make a better mother than you, I told Lynne as I hugged her tight. I wasn't lying either. If I put aside my charged emotions and the canned wisdom about security and stability, I believed that Lynne Rogers would figure out a way to be an amazing mother.

Once Lynne went public with the baby news, I became her ardent defender. When some people began snidely joking about the fertile Ortho water that caused all of our unit clerks to become pregnant—with or without a man to aid the process—I barked at them so ferociously that they backed off. They soon switched to killing her softly with endless comments on the progress of her stomach, speculations about how long her labor would be, and bustling plans for a baby shower where blue was the theme-driven color for everything from booties to banners, since Lynne knew that she was going to have a boy. I was offended by all of it, but Lynne was exceedingly gracious and seemingly grateful for the good wishes and the manly little blue outfits that she received in abundance.

I was determined to get Lynne something special, something that wasn't blue. After searching for weeks, I found a Central American crafts store in Pasadena that had a beautiful multicolored weaving that I could picture hanging above the baby's crib. On my way out of the store, I stumbled over a table with an assortment of small painted boxes. Each box was filled with six tiny Guatemalan worry dolls. After the store owner told me the legend of the dolls, I knew I had to include them in my gift for Lynne and her baby.

The dolls are supposed to remove worries from sleeping children, I explained to Lynne when I gave her the presents. *Children tell a worry to each doll when they go to bed at night and then place the dolls under their pillow. By morning the dolls have absorbed all their fears.*

Lynne held each doll for a long moment before carefully placing it back inside the box. It seemed like she was confiding in the dolls already.

When Lynne called me to announce Alex's birth in the beginning of August, she assured me that she would come over to my house the following week. We wanted to introduce the baby to my doggies soon after he was born so that he would never have a chance to absorb dog anxiety from his mother. I planned to ask her then whether she still needed me to keep the envelope.

New mothers are very busy, so I wasn't worried when I didn't hear from her the next week. After two weeks, I could feel a knot of anxiety starting to gnaw at my insides. I unearthed the scrap of paper with Lynne's phone number from under the bills and nursing magazines piled on my desk, asked myself one more time whether I should intrude on her new life, and then picked up the phone and dialed the number. I wasn't entirely surprised that the phone was disconnected. I tried several times, listening to the disembodied automated message again and again. I had no other hint of Lynne's whereabouts.

When we first started getting to know each other, I had asked her where she lived. She had told me Van Nuys, or maybe it was Sherman Oaks. At the time, it had seemed like thirty miles was a long distance to drive for a unit clerk job in a small Arcadia hospital. I preferred to circumscribe my geographic boundaries, along with the rest of my life, so when Lynne and I got together it was on my end of the world. Now I couldn't remember a single clue that Lynne had given me about her neighborhood—no street name or grocery store or nearby park. But even if I had known one of those obscure landmarks, could I comb the streets hoping to bump into Lynne and her baby out for a walk? Could I wait all day, dogs in tow, in a tawdry Van Nuys park expecting that Lynne and Alex would eventually show up?

Then I remembered the name of the hospital. Countless times, other staff had asked Lynne where she was going to have the baby, forgetting the answer as soon as she had given it so that they had an excuse to ask again in order to comment on

Humana's relative merits and the possible risks of Lynne's plan to have the baby in the hospital's newly established natural birthing suite.

I devised a clever scheme to call Humana Medical Records posing as an official representing Arcadia Hospital's Personnel Department. I authoritatively asked for Lynne Roger's current phone number and address, explaining that we needed to contact her as soon as possible about an urgent insurance issue. She had moved since her maternity leave without updating her records. I almost started screaming when the Medical Records clerk, and then the supervisor, refused to even confirm that Lynne had delivered her baby there and insisted that I needed to put the request in writing before they would even tell me the next step of the request procedure. Even though I knew that this was the appropriate protocol, I had hoped that the sincere life-and-death urgency in my voice would convince this Medical Records Department to transgress a privacy rule that I, at most times, believed was sacrosanct.

I wasn't ready to go to Arcadia's Personnel Department. Entangling Lynne in our hospital bureaucracy might mean that she could never safely reappear. But every time I had to ask the substitute unit clerk to redo a transcription because of some stupid mistake, every time I glanced at the baby shower picture hanging on the bulletin board, which Lynne had reluctantly agreed to pose for, I scoured my brain for new ways to find her.

I was wandering through a Van Nuys park with the dogs sniffing for Lynne's scent. Suddenly she was banging on a door trying desperately to get to us and I was fumbling helplessly with a knob that wouldn't turn, until the banging woke me up. The dogs were barking excitedly, so I realized the summoning noise was not just inside my head. It was eight on a Sunday morning, and no one should be battering my front door at that hour even if the bell wasn't working. Unless it was my brother. It couldn't really be Lynne.

Who the fuck is it? I shouted in my nastiest, sleep-deprived tone that I had learned at my mother's knee.

FBI. The word made me pull my robe tight and lose my grogginess instantly.

We're sorry to bother you at this hour, Miss Murphy, but we need to talk to you about your friend Lynne Rogers.

My hand reached for the doorknob. Did they know where Lynne was? Had they found her in a ditch? Then I heard one of them tapping his foot impatiently and that pissed me off. I took my hand off the knob.

I don't know anything about Lynne Rogers, except that she's a secretary where I work, I said through the door, but my voice had lost its mean edge.

Miss Murphy, you may be interested to know some of the things that Lynne Rogers was involved in that have put her and other people in danger. We need to talk with you in order to make sure nothing terrible happens to her or anyone involved.

It sounded like a script from a grade-B cop movie. Their motives were pure and they only wanted to help.

You'll have to come up with something better than that, I spat out sarcastically.

Miss Murphy, do you know that your coworker's real name is Luba Gold?

I opened the door then, but only a crack. With all the mystery morsels that Lynne had dropped here and there, with all her quirkiness about her family and her birthday, somehow I had never questioned her basic identity. If I sat the FBI down in my living room, would I end up learning more about Luba Gold than they would about Lynne Rogers? Since I knew nothing, could it really hurt to talk with them?

They thought they had me and escalated their attack. One of them leaned in toward my face peering through the door and asked in a stage whisper, *Have you ever heard her talk about her connections to Puerto Rican terrorists?*

Everything reeled, spun, flipped. Independentistas, Chilean guerrillas, Salvadoran refugees. I could confess that I had talked about all of this with Lynne Rogers and, yes, these discussions had fired mind-altering connections for me. But these probably weren't the kind of connections the FBI was asking about.

The longer we stood exchanging words at my doorstep, the closer I was to betraying Lynne. Consuela was beseeching as she rubbed up against my leg. I thought of Lynne stroking Consuela's fur so kindly, so lovingly. I pictured Lynne's fiery face as she stared up at the blood-orange moon and told me that sometimes people had to be willing to go to prison and even be killed for what they believed in.

I mustered my most authoritative, expertly informed nurse's voice.

I have nothing to say to you. I don't want to talk to you. Go away now. I slammed the door shut before I could change my mind

That caught them by surprise. They thought they were reeling me in, but I had spat out the bait. For a few moments they were quiet, probably exchanging silent coded looks. Then one of them said in a more polite voice, *Okay, Miss Murphy. We're sorry we disturbed you so early on a Sunday morning. Just think about what you might have heard. We're leaving our card in your mailbox. Call anytime.*

A few minutes later, I heard their car pull off. Who knew when they would come back with more ammunition in their bag of tricks?

After they left, I went on some type of clandestine auto-pilot, as if I had been preparing for this day of reckoning for months. I pulled on my jeans, grabbed some hot dogs from the refrigerator, got the sealed envelope Lynne had given me from its hideaway in the basement, rounded up the dogs, and piled us all into my truck. I drove nonstop, zooming past Pasadena, trying not to speed through Sherman Oaks, Van Nuys, and Woodland Hills. We finally reached Topanga Canyon Road, and as we wound our way down toward the beach I checked my rearview mirror constantly, although I had no idea what I would do if I thought someone was following me down the curvy two-lane road with nowhere to run but off the side of the cliff.

Occasionally on a hot summer day when I didn't happen to be working, I would bring the dogs to this beach for a special treat. I had even thought about coming here with Lynne. For a while after we got there, I let my honeys romp around, burrowing into sand tunnels and jumping giddily with the waves. Then I barbecued the wieners and put the envelope and everything inside of it into the fire.

Consuela whimpered and hovered around the fire as if I were burning part of Lynne. My heart twisted. Was I doing the wrong thing by destroying the envelope that Lynne had asked me to safeguard? At various times since Lynne had disappeared, I had wondered whether she remembered the envelope. I had questioned whether the envelope even contained any significant information, since she never referred to it again after she gave it to me. I even briefly thought about opening it, but instinctively I rejected that option. The envelope was the repository of our mutual trust. I had no good reason for knowing its contents.

Consuela stuck her paw toward the edge of the fire as if to drag the envelope back to safety. I yanked her back. If I took this as a sign, if I pulled the singed envelope from the flames with the crazy hope that someday I could hand it back to Lynne, where could I possibly hide it? Now that the FBI was stalking my house, burning the envelope was the only possible way to avoid betraying Lynne.

I buried the ashes deep inside a cavernous hole that the doggies helped me dig in the sand. This was no fancy, finessed cover-up, just one step toward protecting Lynne and baby Alex. I knew I had to do more.

On the drive back, we passed a woman with a kid on the side of the road standing next to their broken-down car. Were Lynne and baby Alex standing on some roadside, waiting for a dangerous hitch? Were they holed up in some sleazy LA motel, sneaking out only to the corner 7-Eleven for formula and sandwiches, scared to go any further? Or had they escaped to some distant, magical place where people were welcoming and the FBI could never find them?

When we got back home, I did two loads of laundry to cleanse the smell of burning ash from my clothes and the beach blankets, then scrubbed the house from top to bottom to get rid of the rancid FBI odor that had snuck in when I opened the front door. When I went out to the back yard to collect the dogs to feed them dinner, their eyes glinted red with the sunset, casting a charmed glow. Then I knew what more I could do.

I urged the doggies through their evening meal more quickly than they would have liked and ushered them into my room. I carefully lit all of my many incense burners, releasing a strange mixture of scents that almost made me dizzy. I turned on the lava lamp, put *Mambo Diablo* on the turntable, and sat down with the dogs in front of my makeshift vejigante altar. I watched the lava bubble until its supernatural shapes multiplied on the insides my eyes. I gathered my breath, emptied my conscious mind, drew the vejigante's devil-clown energy into my own and summoned a hex that would stop the hunters dead in their tracks.

I repeated the same ritual for seven nights and then I pared it way down. Before I went to sleep, I simply closed my eyes and pictured Lynne living in the mountains of Puerto Rico with Alex, some carefree dogs she had come to love, and her independentista friends. Then I crossed off one more day on the *Jazz Greats* calendar that hung by the side of my bed.

At work, I quietly took down the picture of Lynne at the baby shower from the bulletin board. When people came to me whispering conspiratorially that Elena had heard from Clarissa, who was friends with Martha in Personnel, that some FBI agents had come around asking about Lynne Rogers, I advised them pointlessly not to be tattletales. I steeled myself for the inevitable return of the FBI to my house. I prepared myself to withstand their questions. I would refuse to cooperate no matter what they threatened.

One recent morning, a year after Lynne had disappeared and I had almost stopped anticipating another FBI thud on my door, I noticed a short article in the *LA Times*. According to the article, eight fugitives had just been put on the FBI's most wanted list because they were part of a conspiracy to help a Puerto Rican woman terrorist escape from prison. The eight had somehow managed to evade an FBI encirclement in the San Fernando Valley in August 1985. After searching for a year without any leads, the FBI had arrested a co-conspirator, Cassandra Bridges, on the outskirts of Chicago and were escalating their search for the rest. One of the eight was Luba Gold, who was thought to be traveling with a small child.

Every day that passes, I thank the vejigantes, the witches, the jazz spirits, the worry dolls, and my magic dogs that Lynne, AKA Luba, and baby Alex are still among the missing.

AKA—
JOAN
1995

I WAS SITTING IN MY UNIVERSITY OF PITTSBURGH CREATIVE WRITING CLASS, HOPING that Jane, the instructor, wouldn't call on me to read my story, when Luba walked into the classroom. Of course, I didn't recognize that it was Luba right away. I hadn't seen her for ten years and her hair was now meticulously neat and platinum blond, totally unlike the tousled reddish cut she had worn back in the eighties in Chicago when I met her. Still there was something vaguely familiar in the serious set of her face and the way her teeth were scraping back and forth over her lower lip as she handed Jane her add-on slip. And when she asked Jane if it was okay to join the class late, the huskiness of her voice made me shiver.

Perhaps it was that imperceptible quiver that made Luba look over toward the back row where I had deliberately stationed myself for each class session. Or maybe she was just casing out the room to see who was in it and whether it was really safe for her to stay. Regardless, she looked straight at me, and in that split second our mutual recognition was complete.

I could hear the panic crackling through her throat when she told Jane that she had made a mistake and quickly slid out the door.

I wanted to run after her to assure that her secret was safe with me. To tell her I was so, so sorry for all the trouble I had caused her. But a shrill of cautionary voices inside my head urged me to sit still. The only thing I could do for Luba now was to let her get as far away from me and my damaging aura as possible.

I tried to concentrate on the story a young woman in the class was reading but my ears were throbbing from the sound of Luba's voice. I had started this class because *my* story was rotting, mute inside of me. I was searching for some gadget that could help me pry it out. But so far Jane's writing prompts had not done the trick. Our first assignment was to write about a big, significant move that we had made some time in our lives. I began quickly enough, long before the assignment was due. My father's neatly ordered rows of guns and rifles mounted on our living room walls. The constant, dull whir of my mother's sewing machine, fabricating a wardrobe I never wanted to wear. The closeted gray classrooms of my Catholic girls' high school. The close-minded canon of my Indiana college professors. These were the details that I was able to type out easily to explain why I desperately needed to move from Columbus to Chicago.

On the very last page, I described the call from my high school best friend, Francis, a month before my college graduation in 1983, inviting me to share her Chicago flat. The story concluded with my daring decision to accept her invitation, despite my father's stern disapproval, but with my mother's sneaking support.

I got my paper back with Jane's pointed question scribbled across the top, *What happened after you moved?* I had evaded the heart of the assignment. After all this time, I still couldn't dig up the words to describe the move that changed my life.

As soon as Jane finished giving us the next writing assignment, I rushed out of class, a siren howling in my ears. I didn't stop running until I reached my bed at home. All of my gagged memories of that long-ago move were now wailing through me, and goose bumps were blowing up my arms and legs.

There were only a few times in my life when the pressure in my ears had erupted onto my skin. Once was when I got off the Greyhound bus in Chicago and headed for Francis's Lincoln Park apartment for the first time in 1983. The muggy June heat and the crush of the El only seemed to make the bumps worse. But once I made it up three flights of stairs and walked into Francis's flat, my ears and my skin quieted down.

The place was dilapidated but not dingy. Shelves with rows of dog-eared books were balanced precariously on milk crates, and the cracking plaster walls were covered with colorful posters of freedom fighters from El Salvador, Nicaragua, and Puerto Rico. In the middle of the floor of my bedroom-to-be was a beautiful crazy quilt, spread across the double mattress like a tempting invitation. The noise in my ears mellowed to a tingling hum and my gnawing anxiety about moving to Chicago floated guiltlessly away through one of the many chinks in the tall, open windows.

How long did that thrilling tingle last? A few months at most, as I biked all over Chicago, began a job as a part-time book-keeper, and cut my hair, abandoning the long, straggly ponytail that I had worn since elementary school. Late at night I would bump into Francis in our bright orange kitchen, and sometimes we would have a beer together. I didn't see much of her since she was busy learning how to be a car mechanic and working with a group called Amigos, which supported independence for Puerto Rico and freedom for Puerto Rican political prisoners.

I had seen the movie *West Side Story* a couple of times, and there had been a Puerto Rican girl named Lolita in our high school. Lolita was very quiet but surprised everyone when she got the highest SAT score of our senior class. I didn't know much else about Puerto Rico, so I wondered why Francis, who everyone now called Frankie, had decided to put all her spare time and energy into working for the independence of this small island. When Francis asked if I wanted to go to a meeting of Amigos, I eagerly said yes.

This isn't about charity, Francis warned me when I told her I was excited to be able to help in some way. *It's about solidarity.* I considered asking her what the distinction meant, but something in the way she pronounced the word *solidarity* reminded me of the nuns at our old high school, solemnly lecturing us about *purity*, *sanctity*, *fidelity*, *charity*. Asking *them* a question about these exalted concepts never went well, so I learned to keep my mouth shut. Unlike Francis who, in those days, liked to question everything.

When we got to the community center where the Amigos meeting was held, Francis quickly introduced me to a few people who greeted me politely and then went back to their animated conversations. When Francis left me to set up the projector for a slide show, I busied myself looking at the pictures of lush Puerto Rican landscapes and portraits of Puerto Rican heroes who had fought for independence. I was staring at one of Lolita Lebrón, realizing that my brilliant high school classmate must have been named for her, when a woman came up to talk with me.

Frankie told us that you have been involved in the Sanctuary Movement, she said expectantly. I explained that I hadn't done very much, only helped collect food and clothes for a church that was providing shelter for Salvadoran refugees. She looked disappointed and, after making some excuse, walked away leaving me to wonder what exactly Francis had told these people about me. I resolved to pay close attention to the slide show in order to make up for my lack of knowledge and experience.

The slide show was packed with information. It described the centuries of conquest that Puerto Rico had suffered, the many historic battles and courageous people who had fought for freedom, and the importance of building solidarity with the armed struggle for independence. According to the slide show, this struggle was now growing tremendously, not only on the island of Puerto Rico but inside the continental borders of the United States, where half the Puerto Rican population lived.

By the end of the slide show, my ears were pounding with the sound of stories I had never heard before. One in particular replayed in my head. Alicia Rodríguez had been arrested just a few years before, in 1980, and charged with the intangible crime of seditious conspiracy because the government had no evidence to connect her to any of the dozens of political bombings they believed she had participated in. To keep her from telling her side of the history in the courtroom, the judge had ordered her mouth stuffed with handkerchiefs. Tape was then wrapped across her lips to make sure that she couldn't utter a word. When Alicia was unable to speak, she began to hum loudly, furiously, persistently. Finally, the judge banned her from the courtroom. The trial proceeded without her seditious presence.

Alicia and the other Puerto Rican prisoners were courageous and committed beyond belief. I couldn't imagine having the passion and strength to do what they had done. Still, I couldn't silence a nagging whisper in my head questioning whether bombs were the best way to go about winning independence for Puerto Rico.

After the slide show, Pedro, who was chairing the meeting, asked the group for feedback. People quickly offered well-thought-out critiques focused on strengthening the points about armed struggle and the need for solidarity. When Pedro finally turned to me and asked what I, as someone new to the group, thought about the slide show, I had no idea what to say.

I was really moved by the women prisoners, I began cautiously. When I saw heads nodding in agreement, it gave me a little confidence and I pushed on.

The women were all so strong and brave. I kept wondering whether they had any children and, if they did, what they were feeling about being separated from their kids. Maybe it would be good to include something about their children in the slide show.

I was glad that I had come up with a concrete suggestion until I saw that Pedro was wrinkling his forehead like my father did when he was irritated. Francis jumped in quickly to express the group's concern about my suggestion.

We can't talk about their children. It's a security issue, she said in a patient tone that made me want to crawl under my chair. *It could be dangerous for them and their kids.*

I nodded my head along with everyone else, kicking myself for not having understood this obvious problem. Pedro moved on to summarize the discussion about solidarity.

We need to give people many options, he said firmly. *And we need to make it clearer that solidarity is not only about education and demonstrations.*

Later that night, Francis and I sat in our cheery orange kitchen drinking beer and making a shopping list for the week. Suddenly she put her arm around my shoulder.

I know that this is all new for you, Joanie, she said in the affectionate manner I remembered from our teenage years. *It was all new for me too a little while ago, but I've learned so much from Pedro and the other Puerto Rican compañeros. Not just about Puerto Rico but about collective commitment and revolution.*

I could see how this was a logical, easy step for Francis. She had always been passionate about her own beliefs, but it was a lonely passion. Now she had found a community that gave her zeal a larger meaning. I had no doubt that she was prepared to defend these new commitments to the hilt.

I know that different ideas can be hard for you to deal with sometimes, Francis went on. I stopped her before she could open up the part of our past that I did not want to talk about.

I want to help, I really do. The slide show really upset me. Puerto Ricans have suffered so much, I had no idea. I just need to know what I can do to be useful, I declared.

My Secret Saint Joan, Francis said tenderly, throwing her arms around me in a bear hug.

I was never sure when she used this nickname whether she was just teasing or she truly saw something in me that I didn't see in myself. I admired Francis from the very first day of ninth grade at St. Teresa's when Sister Marie pointed out the wrinkles in her navy school uniform. Francis asked, in her chiming voice, why wrinkles should matter to anyone. I looked down at my own flawlessly ironed uniform and realized that I had always wanted to ask my mother that question as I watched her painstakingly press the creases of my skirt and shirt until they disappeared.

Maybe because it was the first day of school, Francis got off with just a reminder not to waste everyone's time with nonsensical inquiries and to make sure her uniform was ironed in the future. At the end of the day, I searched her out, even though I was usually very shy, and asked her if she wanted to walk home together.

Pretty soon we were best friends and sharing everything. Francis told me how her mother died when she was seven. She knew her father loved her but sometimes she couldn't help but resent how often he had to work late at his job at the Catholic Worker house. Sometimes he didn't get home till eight or nine at night. But when he explained, apologetically, that he couldn't turn away the poor souls who needed his help so badly, she would always forgive him. To her, he was the most saintly person she knew.

I told Francis how different my father's religion was. Memorizing catechism, attending every mass, following all the rules and going to confession faithfully was what being a good Catholic meant to him. Every Sunday after mass, he would meticulously clean his gun collection, and I came to believe that this was an unstated part of his religion as well.

I never quite understood why my father had given in to my mother's wish to name me after Joan among all the saints. He held the name against me whenever he could, blaming it for all of my small rebellions. But Joan of Arc was my religious rock. I read about her, was inspired by her, prayed to her. I wasn't courageous like her but I did hear voices, like St. Joan had. When I shared this with Francis, she gave me a puzzled look, and for a minute I was sorry I had confided in her. Then she smiled and gave me a hug. *You are my Secret St. Joan*, she said and the nickname stuck.

When Francis and I occasionally cut afternoon classes to sneak into R-rated foreign movies, I felt brave and unruly. Sometimes we would go over to the Catholic Worker house afterward, where Francis and I helped serve food in their large dining hall.

I don't know how I would make it through high school without my Secret St. Joan, Francis would tease after one of our afternoons out.

One day in eleventh grade, after we had gone to see a foreign movie about Italian peasants fighting for their land, Francis abruptly told me that she had kissed a girl and it felt amazing. She was looking to me for understanding, like she had offered me when I shared my secrets, but my ears were screeching and my arms were breaking out in goose bumps.

Does this mean you're gay? I stuttered stupidly without looking her in the face.

I guess so, she answered flatly and changed the subject to our homework assignment for the next day.

We didn't talk about her being gay again until she was discovered making out with a girl in a stall in the school bathroom in the middle of our senior year. I called her the night after she was suspended and told her I would do anything I could to support her. She thanked me and said that she had discussed it with her father and they had decided that it was best if she went to live with some cousins in Chicago to finish up high school there.

My father made me pay for my open loyalty to Francis after the scandal. He always knew that she was a bad apple, he said, and forbade me from having anything to do with her while I was living under his roof. So I saved my quarters and called Francis from phone booths all over Columbus until I went to college in Indiana the next year and continued our long conversations from my dorm room phone.

During one of those conversations, Francis mentioned that she had heard about a church in Indianapolis that was helping provide sanctuary for people who had been tortured in El Salvador for their political beliefs. I started going by the church on the weekends, helping to collect food and clothing and other donations in my spare time, and getting to know the women, men, and children who had taken refuge in the sanctuary.

I believed in their cause. I wanted to help. But when two of the Sisters who were heading up the Sanctuary work were arrested on charges of harboring fugitives, I stopped going to the church. It was a cowardly decision, but I knew my father would never forgive me if I were arrested and didn't graduate because I was aiding *foreign terrorists*. I never told Francis that I had stopped helping the sanctuary effort.

Once I started working with Amigos, my aimless, rambling bike rides around Chicago were quickly replaced with long, focused meetings each day after I finished my bookkeeping job. I sat at information tables in the park. I wheat-pasted flyers on lampposts and buildings at two in the morning, while others kept watch for the police. I explained to people at educational events how Puerto Rico was a colony where farmers were being pushed off their land, women were being sterilized, and naval training maneuvers were making the land toxic. The political prisoners were defending their island nation from constant attacks that would never stop until Puerto Rico was independent. When I proclaimed that the prisoners were freedom fighters not terrorists, I almost believed it.

People began calling on me to help out whenever there was a pressing need. Sometimes I was asked to drive miles to deliver a package to someone who lived outside of Chicago. Other times I was asked to sit on the front steps of someone's apartment while a meeting was going on and observe who was coming in and out of the building.

More and more the discussions at our meetings were about the importance of clandestine struggle. People constantly referred to the *need to know* principle as the foundation of security. Each person only needed to know what was necessary to fulfill their responsibility, no more. That was fine with me because I didn't want to know what was in the packages I was delivering or why I had been asked to watch the comings and goings of so many ordinary people in an apartment building. I just wanted Francis, Pedro, and the others to see that I was trustworthy and willing to make sacrifices for freedom.

We were all so busy that I hardly saw Francis except at an occasional meeting. She had given up her job as a car mechanic and spent almost all her time working with Pedro and Amigos. People in Amigos called me when they wanted my help but rarely to hang out and have a beer. The double mattress in my room, which had looked so inviting when I first moved to the flat, was only a place where I tossed and turned each night. In my disturbing dreams, our living room posters of freedom fighters proudly holding their rifles were replaced by row upon row of overloaded gun racks. Their menacing weight threatened to bring the whole house down.

One night, I was sitting at a party on the side of the room, sipping my beer and watching everyone else dance, especially Francis and her new girlfriend, Carlita. Amigos had held a large demonstration that morning to support the political prisoners and everyone seemed to think it was a big success. Now they were putting aside the weeks of work that had gone into planning the demo and were dancing like the freedom of the prisoners depended on how frantically they moved.

I was drained. I had scoped out the march route backward and forward from early in the morning and now my arms, legs and mind felt limp. I knew if I tried to dance, I would move like a robot, mechanically twisting to the beat but deaf to the rhythm's pulsing throb.

If only I were a lesbian, I thought for the hundredth time, maybe it would be easier to fit in. Or if I had studied Spanish instead of French in school. Or if I could write lyrical poems for the prisoners, instead of stuffing envelopes, standing on corners, and delivering mysterious packages. Drinking a couple of beers had unleashed the envious voices that I usually could keep quietly contained in a corner of my head.

When Reynaldo sat down next to me, I thought for a minute that he had mistaken me for someone else. I had seen him before at a few events, but that morning I had specifically noticed him at the demonstration. He had stood a little to the side, just watching. He wasn't holding anything—not a flag, a banner, or even a camera. He looked like he wasn't totally sure what he was doing in the middle of the angry, chanting crowd.

Sometimes it's good to find a quiet place to just take it all in, he said as he sat down, and right away I liked that his voice was soft and deep and he looked directly at me when he spoke. I answered that I kept waiting to grow out of my high school shyness at dances but, sadly, it hadn't happened yet. Reynaldo chuckled as if he had the exact same problem. Then he asked me where I had gone to high school, and before I knew it I was telling him stories about my life in Columbus and even how I met Francis in her wrinkled uniform on the first day of ninth grade.

So she's always been an agitator, he commented.

Not exactly an agitator, I said. *But definitely a free thinker, always asking questions about everything.* Then I added something that I had not even thought out loud to myself.

But lately she never seems to question anything that Pedro says, and that makes me a little worried. Reynaldo nodded as if he understood this too.

We left the party and went for a long walk through Humboldt Park. For the first time since I had moved to Chicago, I didn't feel nervous or out of place walking in a Puerto Rican neighborhood, because I was with Reynaldo. I asked him about his childhood, and he told me he had been born in Lares, the city where the great uprising against the Spanish took place in 1868. He learned the history of the rebellion as soon as he could understand words. Although *El Grito de Lares* had been crushed very quickly, for his mother and father the spirit of resistance lived on in the blood of the people. No surprise that Lolita Lebrón had been born in Lares.

His parents sent him to live with his aunt and uncle in Chicago for high school because they thought he would be able to better learn how to fight the monster if he was educated in its center. But once he began to attend a Catholic school, he quickly learned to forget all about colonialism in order to succeed. He even refused to speak Spanish with his aunt and uncle for a couple of years, his own foolish gesture of rebellion.

Now that he was done with school and working at his uncle's insurance business, he wanted to reconnect with the independence movement, but it was more challenging than he expected. He completely respected the dedication of the compañeros in Amigos and the amount of work they did. He just wasn't sure about their support for violent struggle. When he tried to raise questions about this strategy and why it had never succeeded in the past, no one wanted to discuss it. Everyone deferred to Pedro's opinion and that in itself made him uncomfortable. Pedro's charisma seemed to quiet even the strongest voices.

How clever Reynaldo was to recognize my field of confusion, planting the seeds of treachery right from our first conversation. He named the doubts that had been lurking in my mind since my very first meeting with Amigos. Yet he was careful not to move too fast. He didn't even ask to come home with me that first night, as most men would have. Maybe he knew that our brief kiss at the door would awaken more desire than a night full of kissing might have. The crazy quilt was dancing in anticipation as I lay down quivering on top of it. The sound of Reynaldo's voice, like a simmering lullaby, soothed me into the best sleep I had had in months.

The morning after Reynaldo first stayed over, I was bubbling with excitement. I couldn't wait to tell Francis how happy I was that I had finally met someone I really liked who was also committed to the independence movement. But I could tell right away by the squint in her eyes that this was not good news to Francis.

Reynaldo is very new to the work, she began in the controlled, patient tone she often used nowadays, especially at Amigos meetings.

Isn't it good that new people are getting involved? I responded quickly.

People aren't sure where he's coming from. She used the anonymous word *people*, but I knew she meant Pedro.

Just because he questions Pedro's opinions doesn't mean there's a problem with him, I snapped back.

Francis looked shocked. *Is that what you think this is about, asking questions?*

The hurt and indignation in her voice made me stop for a minute. In all the years I had known her, Francis had been right about everyone. She knew instantly which nuns had hearts of muscle and blood underneath their starched habits and which ones had chests of iron where their hearts should be. She knew that my father's ice core would never melt and that my mother would always come to my defense even if she did it secretly. She saw courage and strength in me that I couldn't see in myself.

I was just getting ready to apologize for snapping at her when she put her arm around me.

Maybe I'm being too hard on Reynaldo, Joanie, Francis offered. *He has volunteered to do childcare for all our events for the next month,* she added.

I was glad that we had avoided a standoff, but I realized that if I wanted to protect my growing feelings for Reynaldo, I should keep them to myself.

There were many things I loved about Reynaldo—his soft voice, his slow hands, the way he listened intently to most everything I had to say, and his willingness to open up with me.

He confided in me about his own struggles to express himself, his guilt about having stayed away from the independence movement while he was in school, and the political misgivings that kept him up at night. Why didn't Amigos listen more to the community's concerns about daily survival instead of just pushing their own radical agenda? Could the goal of independence or revolution ever justify violence and the destruction, injury, and loss of life that would inevitably result? Were Pedro and the other Puerto Ricans leading Francis and the other young white members of Amigos down a dangerous path by exploiting their guilt about being white and privileged?

Reynaldo articulated the concerns that I had felt but had been unable to name over the past year. Francis, as always, was so sure of what was right and wrong, but wasn't it possible that she was just a pawn in a scheme that was way beyond her understanding or control?

Secret plans were being hatched within Amigos before my eyes. When I arrived at our meetings, the clump of people that had been standing outside in an intense huddle would greet me and then scatter quickly. Once, after a meeting, instead of biking home to meet Reynaldo as quickly as possible, I went down to the end of the block and watched from a recessed doorway as Francis and Larry walked to the opposite corner of the street toward a phone booth. After looking around several times, Francis went in the booth and made a call, while Larry stood and watched.

It's like they are playacting, I told Reynaldo that night.

Amateur playacting, Reynaldo agreed. *But the consequences could be extremely serious*, he added solemnly.

That was the first time I heard the iron core within the soft shell of his voice. It was also the first time he got annoyed with me when I suggested that maybe I should leave Amigos since things were getting so crazy. No, he disagreed. It would be more constructive to make notes of what I was observing and hearing instead of leaving.

I must have looked disturbed, because he added quickly in a gentler tone,

If Francis gets in too deep, you may be able to help pull her out.

This was the logic that became my justification. I was going to save Francis from the trap of Pedro's charisma. And Reynaldo was the navigator who charted our course forward, though at the time I thought we were a team, figuring it out together. Once we started, it became harder and harder to turn back. Whenever a whisper inside me would question something we were doing, I would hear Reynaldo's reassuring answers, his deep, wise voice lulling over my groundless worries.

We discussed which things from the meetings were important to note down and which were clutter. We developed a simple code to write the notes in so it wouldn't be obvious what they were about if the notebook were discovered, even though I hid the notebook in a file cabinet at my bookkeeping job. At the end of each week, we reviewed what I had written and dissected its meaning.

I didn't really mind that a lot of our time together was taken up discussing the possible plots that Amigos was being drawn into or that we spent less and less time going for walks or bike rides or even events together. Our relationship was cemented by our shared political purpose, and for a time that felt good. But when Reynaldo mentioned that he wanted to get closer to Pedro in order to find out more about the plans that were being developed, I got upset.

This is becoming so deceptive, I complained.

How is this different from taking notes about meetings? Reynaldo argued. Before I had a chance to try and figure out my own muddy reasoning, he took me in his arms.

This is all new and confusing for me also, Joan. But the more we find out about their plans, the more I feel committed to stopping any real harm. I began to say that so far we hadn't really found out anything concrete when Reynaldo continued.

Maybe I can influence Pedro to move in a nonviolent direction if I work more closely with him. I can be charismatic too, right Joan? I had to agree with that as his calm hands stroked my concerns away for the moment.

I thought Reynaldo would be upset when Francis asked me not to bring him over to the flat while Luba Gold was staying with us. Luba was an older Amigos leader visiting from California. According to Francis, she had some big decisions to make in her life and needed to be in a woman-only space for reflection and support. But Reynaldo was very pleased by the news that I would be getting to spend time with Luba, whom he had heard about from Pedro.

Luba could be a key piece to the puzzle we are trying to solve, he stated earnestly. He asked me to take extra care to record all my conversations with Luba in my notebook.

People in Amigos talked about Luba with a certain awe, so I expected her to be gorgeous like the pictures of Weather

Underground leader Bernardine Dohrn or tall and striking in a tough way, like Francis had now become. When I finally met Luba, I was relieved that she looked rather ordinary. She was just about my five-foot-four height and her reddish hair seemed like she had cut it herself, with curls straggling down her forehead every which way. Her voice was low and husky, and her mouth could shift in a split second from a thin-lined worried frown to a wide, welcoming smile.

There was another thing about Luba that I wrote down in my notebook, even though I didn't think it was the kind of observation that Reynaldo cared about. She wore a beautiful pair of amethyst earrings that peeked out from under her curls every day. When I asked her if the earrings had special meaning for her, she bit down on her lip as if to stop herself from saying something she might regret. But she went on anyway to explain that a former lover had given the earrings to her.

My girlfriend, Isabella, was a curandera, healer of sorts and believed that amethyst had protective powers. Even though we're not together anymore, I keep her in my life by never taking the earrings off. I waited for her to say more, but she was clenching her teeth back and forth over her lip, and nothing else came out of her anxious mouth.

I was relieved that Luba didn't want to discuss our political work or the many debates that were preoccupying Amigos. Instead she talked about the novels she was reading and the poetry she was trying to write in between her organizing work. When she asked me about myself, I told her about my family, St. Teresa's high school, and a little about my long, somersaulting friendship with Francis, though I was more careful about what I shared than I had been with Reynaldo.

Sometimes at three or four at night I would wake up and hear Francis and Luba talking in hushed, tense whispers, and I realized that they must be avoiding heavy conversations when I was around. Oddly, I felt glad for this exclusion, even though I knew Reynaldo would be disappointed that my notebook contained little besides the titles of Luba's most beloved books and lines from some of the poems that she recited to me. One night, I woke up to the sound of Luba talking out loud. She must have forgotten that I was on the other side of the wall, or maybe at that moment she didn't care.

I know that people wanted me to come to Chicago because they are worried about me. They think I may be emotionally shaky, not entirely reliable. I'm okay but I can't keep on moving back and forth between over and under whenever someone decides I'm needed for something else. It's driving me crazy and it doesn't make political sense.

I couldn't hear Francis's reply and had almost fallen back to sleep when once again I heard Luba speak. *It can be so hard sometimes. There's this woman, Belinda, whom I've met in my other life. I really like her but I know it can't go anywhere on a personal level. I can try and figure out if she can be helpful to the work but nothing beyond that. Believe me, I am making a lot of sacrifices, but there are limits.*

Again, I couldn't hear what Francis was counseling in response but it didn't seem to calm Luba down. When she spoke again, her voice was cracked with sobs. *I can give up a lot of things, but I can't give up having a child. That shouldn't have to be the choice.*

Her words kept me up for the rest of the night. Reynaldo probably would have been interested in this conversation, but I didn't write any of it in my notebook.

It wasn't until I sat in a meeting with Luba that I saw how commanding, even fierce she could become. It was a long meeting focused on the latest action by Los Macheteros, one of the Puerto Rican underground groups. A year and a half before, Los Macheteros had expropriated $7 million from a Wells Fargo Bank in West Hartford, Connecticut, and no one had ever been arrested for this astounding action.

Just recently, on January 6, 1985, the day Puerto Ricans celebrated as Three Kings Day, the group had dressed up as the Three Wise Men. The Wise Men had distributed dolls, bikes, cash, and food in poor neighborhoods in Connecticut and Puerto Rico to the delight of parents and children. A couple of days later Los Macheteros called the press to explain that they had used some of the money liberated from Wells Fargo to give back to the community.

Everyone at the Amigos meeting agreed that it was a bold public action, but some people questioned whether it was too risky and a violation of clandestine principles to appear in public, even in disguise. As the debate heated up, Luba's mouth became a wired streak across her face. She chewed furiously on a piece of gum, or maybe she was just eating up her own gums. Finally she spoke in a strident, snapping tone that had little resemblance to the mellow hum of our private conversations.

Who are we to second-guess Los Macheteros? They have to be faceless, but why should they remain nameless also? People need to know that Los Macheteros aren't just a group of greedy terrorists taking money for their own self-interest like the media makes them out to be. If clandestinity doesn't serve the political purposes of the movement, we end up secure but buried alive.

No one in the room had much more to say after that.

A few days later, on her last night in Chicago, Luba surprised me again when she suggested that the three of us throw the *I Ching* together. When I first moved in with Francis, I had been curious about the thick gray book sitting on an end table next to a ceramic ashtray holding three coins. *It's the Chinese Book of Changes*, Francis told me briefly in response to my question. Then she added, as if she were teaching a five-year-old, *It's a non-Western way of understanding the cosmic forces at work in the world.*

In high school when I had been wrestling with questions of faith, Francis had urged me to give up what she called the *crushing crutch* of traditional Catholicism and its *mind-numbing rituals*. By the end of my first year in college, I had officially forsaken the Catholic Church. Now I was skeptical of all cosmic forces, Western or otherwise, but it wasn't a subject I wanted to debate with Francis.

Luba and Francis moved the *I Ching* and the ashtray with the coins to the long coffee table in the middle of the living room. They lit some candles, rolled a few joints, and set pillows down on the floor in a ceremony that seemed familiar to both of them. Luba must have noticed a shadow of doubt cross my face.

It's just a way to help us to stop and reflect about where we are in our lives and the choices before us, Joanie. Her voice had regained its husky tone and her eyes looked misty even though she hadn't taken her first toke. *It will be interesting, you'll see.*

Francis began. She threw the coins with care, shaking them for several seconds in her hands, then tossing them precisely, as if the correct gesture could determine how they would land. Once she and Luba figured out which hexagram the coins had spelled out, Francis turned the pages quickly until she got to number 49 in the book. She read the title *Ko, Revolution*, and let out a low, happy whistle. Her voice shook as she pronounced the hexagram's Judgment.

Revolution. On your own day you are believed. Supreme success. Furthering through perseverance. Remorse disappears.

To me, it sounded like an elaborate fortune cookie prophecy, and I almost laughed out loud at the comparison. But Francis didn't see it that way.

This is really an amazing throw, she said excitedly and went on to read how revolution should only be undertaken after people had tried to bring about reforms without success, when there was no other way left open. If you believed in yourself, then others would believe in you and that was key for making revolution. Luba was nodding energetically in agreement and Francis shot her a long, conspiratorial look. I had all I could do to keep from having a stoned giggling fit.

Luba threw her coins with a careless fling, as if it didn't matter to her what hexagram they would yield. But when she began reading the lines from hexagram 3, I could hear the quivering crack in her voice.

Difficulty at the Beginning. Times of growth are beset with difficulties, but these difficulties arise from the very profusion of all that is struggling to attain form. Everything is in motion: therefore if one perseveres there is a prospect of great success, in spite of the existing danger.

I was changing my mind. The *I Ching* was more like a powerful poem than a fortune cookie. The words ripped through you, making meaning from formless thoughts and feelings that were brewing inside. There were tears sparkling down Luba's face, reflecting the glimmer of her amethyst earrings.

This is just how I've been feeling. So much is going on. So much that is pushing me forward, pushing me to take risks and make changes. But when I wake up in the middle of the night, the difficulties seem so complicated, so insurmountable. I'm afraid of everything and I don't know if I'm strong enough to take it all on. But the hexagram is saying that it's always natural for new beginnings to be hard. You can move through it if you're committed and do it on your own terms.

Francis looked uncomfortable. *Luba*, she said in a cautionary tone that broke Luba's trance. *Boy, I'm really more stoned than I thought I was*, Luba apologized. She turned quickly to me. *Your turn, Joanie. Let's see what the* I Ching *has to say to you.* I tried not to hear an unspoken challenge in her words.

As soon as I slung the coins from my hands, I felt a wave of free fall fear like I used to experience when I jumped off the high dive at our school gym. As Luba and Francis figured out which hexagram I had thrown, I thought about bolting to the bathroom. Too quickly they handed me the book, telling me I had gotten hexagram 9. I fumbled with the pages until I found the page where the hexagram's Judgment began. The title leaped out at me, *The Taming Power of the Small.* I began to tremble all over, though I was determined not to let the tremors enter my voice.

The force of the small—the power of the shadowy—that restrains, tames, impedes . . . a configuration of circumstances in which a strong element is temporarily held in leash by a weak element.

What set of sinister coincidences had landed me on this page, with this pointed Judgment? Was this reading a set-up meant to trap me and push me to divulge my shadowy role using my small notebook and foolish codes? Panicked voices were shrieking in my ears, but Luba and Francis were urging me to continue. Somehow I pushed on.

The power of disinterested truth is greater than all the obstacles. It carries such weight that the end is achieved, and all danger of bloodshed and all fear disappear.

The Judgment had somersaulted and now my voices were chattering madly. Maybe the *I Ching* was saying that I wasn't small and treacherous. Maybe my weakness was a righteous strength that I was using to protect those who were too headstrong to know when fear was a signal telling them to stop. Was I exploiting my weakness or turning it into strength? Not a fortune cookie or a revealing poem, the *I Ching* was a bad trip that I couldn't escape from.

Francis and Luba looked worried.

Joanie, what's going on? Is it the pot? Don't worry, you'll be okay. Just focus on our voices. We love you. You'll be okay. They were trying to talk me down, like friends, like sisters, like comrades, and at that moment I was infinitely grateful to them. Gently, they led me to my room and tucked me in under the crazy quilt.

The next morning, as we were driving Luba to the airport, she vowed she would never again throw the *I Ching* while she was high. Francis promised she would only buy pot that she knew was organic. I told them not to worry. I had always gotten a little freaky when I was stoned. Still it had been a fascinating experience, I assured them.

The signs were there, urging me to renounce my path. I could have walked away then before any real damage was done. Instead, I emptied my mind of prophecies, shut up my clandestine voices and trudged forward on the two-faced track that Reynaldo and I had mapped out. Reynaldo was away, traveling with Pedro more of the time. I threw myself stubbornly into all the many events, marches, and rallies that Amigos continuously had planned. I filled up my little notebooks with scribbles that I hoped someday would reveal something useful and important.

Occasionally, when Reynaldo was in town, we took a little time to sneak away and ride our bikes through the blossoms that managed to bud during springtime in Chicago. Only then my mood lifted. The relief was temporary, because I knew that we couldn't go on like this indefinitely. We were heading for a climax, I just didn't know when it would occur or what it would be.

When Reynaldo got back from a two-week trip to the West Coast, he asked me to meet him in a coffee shop in the Loop where we would be unlikely to bump into anyone we knew from Amigos. He was deliberately calm and slow as he told me that he had learned on the trip that a fanatical underground collective in the LA area was planning a large terrorist action soon that could endanger many innocent people.

I must have looked as if I were about to faint, because he reached over and held me firmly by my shoulders while he whispered intensely to me across the table. *We have a chance to intercept their plans, Joan. Pedro has given me responsibility for communicating information to their collective. We can give them the wrong information and keep them from being able to carry out their destruction.*

I waited for the punch line, which I knew had to do with me. *I need you to be the one to make the phone call, to be an anonymous voice, without an accent, that points them in another direction. This is your chance to make a difference, to prevent enormous damage, to help in the most significant way.*

Dozens of questions buzzed through my head. What was this dangerous action supposed to be? Who was this mystery collective? What wrong information would I be giving them? And how had Reynaldo magically maneuvered so that Pedro was now trusting him with communication of this sort? The charisma he boasted about must have been effective.

I knew Reynaldo would be irritated if I began to ask him any of this. Anyway, how could I back down now? What would it mean about my stated desire to shift things away from violence, if I weren't willing to make this one small telephone call?

I was glad that we only had a week to prepare. Less time to worry about whether I would look stranger in a blond or a black-haired wig. Less time to map my route out of Chicago on the Greyhound bus to a town in Michigan where I could change my clothes and put on my wig in the bus station restroom and walk to a nearby college to make the call. Reynaldo had already checked out a well-situated set of phone booths on the second floor of the student center where I could make the call in privacy, leave without a trace, and get quickly back on the bus. Less time to wonder about all these very complicated plans and why they were all necessary in order to make a simple phone call. Unless there was more to this than I understood. Or less, and this was simply a test of my commitment. I didn't need to know the answers. I didn't want to know the answers. I just wanted do my part and get this over.

The rest of the week was spent writing my phone script and practicing how to disguise my voice and my anxiety. *Your voice is good—soft, plain, Midwestern—but sometimes when you're nervous it fades away. You need to be able to speak clearly and firmly even though you will be under a lot of pressure. Even if you are asked questions that you can't answer*, Reynaldo coached. And so I rehearsed the brief instructions—date, time, meeting place, and the firm, polite refusal to give any more information than that, which was easy as I had nothing more I could give.

Reynaldo dropped me off at the Greyhound station at six the morning of the call. It was a chilly, barely light late April morning. The station was empty, as we had hoped it would be, even though I had a good cover story about going to visit some friends from college if by bad luck I happened to run into someone I knew there. Reynaldo hugged me tight. *I know this is hard for you, Joan, but it is a measure of your true solidarity. Next time will be easier.*

It wasn't until I was safely situated in a seat in the back of the bus, after carefully scanning the station for any familiar or suspicious faces, that I allowed Reynaldo's last words to register inside my head. I didn't want it to get easier.

Everything went like clockwork. The bus was on schedule, though we had allowed plenty of time for possible delays. I changed my wardrobe and put on my wig in the bathroom stall, then followed our mapped out route from the Greyhound station to the college, switching directions a few times, stopping to put on more lipstick as an excuse to use my hand mirror to see if anyone was following silently behind me. I arrived at the student center with an hour to kill, so I read through the silly women's magazines I had brought with me to keep from looking at my watch. Ten minutes before the time set for the call, I went upstairs to claim a phone booth. There was only one other person occupying a booth, which left several empty ones for me to choose from.

Things were going as they should, and I was handling these maneuvers correctly. For the first time since I had heard about this plan, I felt a wisp of confidence flit through my chest. At 1:00 p.m. exactly I dialed the number that I had memorized and also had written in code on a scrap of paper buried in my wallet. When no one picked up by the eighth ring, I put the receiver down. My feel-good bubble had instantly evaporated. Had I messed up the phone number or the time? Was there anyone on the other end expecting a call or was this just a test to see what I was or wasn't willing to do? Worse still, had I entered some twilight zone and would soon be encircled by cops and carted off to jail for my unknowing part in some grand terrorist conspiracy?

I had fifteen minutes to wait in this airless box before I could try the call again, according to the rules. The ominous echo of those eight long rings was drowning out the calm monotone of my prepared script. I began to read the graffiti scrawled across the walls of the phone booth. There were the usual array of names and hearts with arrows piercing through them. There was a lover's curse—*Jimmy R., may you die a slow painful death for how you hurt me*—and one predictable antiwar demand, *U.S. out of El Salvador Now!* After reading the ones at eye level, I noticed some words scribbled in a top corner of the booth.

You better think, think about what you're trying to do to me . . .

It was the beginning of an Aretha song that Francis and I had danced to over and over again in the privacy of her bedroom when we first became friends. The plea, scribbled in a meaningless phone booth doodle, began to repeat like a cracked record in my ears.

I had given up believing that the voices I heard were visionary after I took my first psychology class in college. But no matter, they still were my sporadic companions. I had forcibly silenced them since I met Reynaldo. Now they were enveloping me in full force, demanding, begging *think, think, think, think.* I couldn't shut them off. They were rocking my body and shaking the walls of the booth. Finally, fifteen minutes had passed, and I picked up the phone to dial the assigned number once again.

This time someone picked up on the second ring. *This is Sue*, I said in the soft modulated tone I had been practicing for days. *This is Pat*, a woman's muffled voice answered. My breath caught. For some reason, I had assumed that Pat would be a man. But there was no time to think this wrinkle through. *How's the weather there?* I continued with my script. *Chilly and wet*, she answered the cue correctly in an equally controlled tone. I went ahead and gave her the date, time, and the place, Miami, with professional authority.

Are you sure about this? Now she sounded alarmed. *I thought our vacation plans were for the Northwest.* I was firm when I gave the answer that Reynaldo and I had prepared. *Yes, there has been a change of location, but everything else is exactly the same. We are relying on you to be there.* For a few seconds there was silence on the other end. I imagined that she was breathing in and out to stay calm. When she finally spoke, her voice was less muffled, huskier and cracked with tension. *All right, we'll be there. I don't get why it has changed, but we'll be there.* Then she repeated the date, time, and place back to me as the instructions required.

As soon as she hung up, I knew for sure that the person on the other end of the phone was Luba Gold. I also knew that Luba Gold was not a terrorist fanatic, despite all the allegations Reynaldo had made about the people I would be misleading. For a split second, I considered breaking all the rules and calling the number back to beg her to forget the whole thing. Instead, I shoved the door of the phone booth open and gulped in the smoke-filled air of the student lounge. I rushed past students, blindly absorbed in their conversations about school, exams and gossip, and made my way out to the street. I reversed the steps that had brought me to the student center and arrived back at the bus station just as planned.

My arms and legs exploded in goose bumps as I waited on line to buy my ticket for the next bus back to Chicago. My head pounded relentlessly. I hadn't decided anything by the time I got to the counter, but the ticket I bought was for Columbus, Ohio.

I told my parents that I had broken up with my boyfriend and needed to leave Chicago. I told Francis that I had broken up with Reynaldo and needed to move back home. I wrote Reynaldo and assured him that everything had gone as planned, but I couldn't ever see him again. I expected a rush of accusatory questions from all of them, but my parents were too happy to have me back to ask me much of anything, and Francis said she thought it was for the best. She even offered to ship me my stuff. Reynaldo never wrote back. Maybe he decided that he would cut his losses by not badgering me, hoping that I wouldn't betray my own betrayals.

I found a job as a bookkeeper at St. Ignatius hospital and moved into an apartment a couple of miles from my parents' home. On the weekends, I biked endlessly around Columbus and I joined a choir at a neighborhood church. I wasn't looking for God. I couldn't go to confession. Filling my ears with majestic choral sounds was the only way I could quiet the roar of reproach that thundered through my skull day in and day out.

Pedro may have been an arrogant leader advocating a questionable path, but had I ever once tried to argue with him to his face? Francis may have been overinfatuated with revolutionary action, but who was I to anoint myself her guardian? Luba had freely chosen the risk-studded road she was on, but how dare I point her in a false direction that could lead her to a deadly cliff? And Reynaldo, Reynaldo who appeared one night and instantly became my smooth-voiced, slow-handed savior, rescuing me from loneliness and uncertainty, had Reynaldo ever really cared for my well-being, or for Francis's safety, or Puerto Rico's future?

A little over a year after my phone booth call with Luba, her name jumped out at me from a small, random article in the newspaper. Luba Gold and seven other people had been put on the FBI's ten most wanted list for their role in a conspiracy to help a Puerto Rican woman prisoner escape. Their conspiracy had been foiled by an FBI sting operation in Miami but eight adults, including Luba and a baby, had somehow managed to evade capture in California's San Fernando Valley. Failing to find the eight after a year's search, the FBI had just arrested a co-conspirator, Cassandra Bridges, on the outskirts of Chicago.

My first reaction was surprising relief. Luba was free. I had not put her in prison. She had outsmarted Reynaldo, who I now concluded must have worked for the FBI. Which meant that I, in my mixed-up, envy-love desire to protect Francis and the whole Amigos crew, had also been working for the FBI.

For weeks I stopped sleeping. I hardly ate, I couldn't sing, and I couldn't hear any of my voices. Luba was free now, but for how much longer? I had made her, a baby, and seven others into most-wanted fugitives. I had driven Cassandra Bridges, whoever she was, into jail. How could I ever forgive myself for the harm I had caused?

One day I saw a flyer on the library bulletin board advertising a hotline for battered women. I began to volunteer, listening to many, many women's stories that somehow shed

light on my own. My truth was too terrible to share, but helping others was a way to atone for my crime.

At some point, I met George, a social worker who also
sang in the choir. He was a little awkward but very kind. I
couldn't confess what I had done even to him, but slowly I was
able to accept that he loved me, or at least the part of me that
he knew. When George got a chance to work at the University
of Pittsburgh Medical Center in their newly opened AIDS
unit, we both eagerly accepted the opportunity to start our lives
together in a new place. I got an accounting job at Pitt, found
a community chorus to sing with, and began volunteering for
the local AIDS Women's project. Still once or twice a week,
in the middle of the night, I would hear a phone ringing from
inside an empty phone booth. When I couldn't stand its fearful
chiming anymore, I would jam open the booth and wrench
the receiver from the phone. Dreadfully, I would hear Luba's
husky voice on the other end, asking me to accept her call from
prison.

I tried therapy but it didn't help. Creative writing was one
more failing effort to push my story out before it damaged
my insides permanently. I never went back to the writing class
after Luba appeared and then disappeared so quickly that
sometimes I thought I had imagined the whole episode. Still,
after seeing her, I began to write. Hour after hour, locked in my
study I covered the pages of my notebooks with raw, uncoded
confession, yanking out the invisible handkerchiefs that I had
stuffed down my own throat and stripping the tape from across
my lips. And as I wrote, the jangled voices that had shrilled,

pounded, and sung until they had fallen silent for years chan-
neled themselves loudly and furiously into words on the page.

Six months after I quit the writing class, there was a front-
page article in the *Post-Gazette* about a group of people who
had surrendered to the FBI in Chicago after years of living
underground in Pittsburgh. One of them was Luba Gold, who
was accompanied by her nine-year-old son, Nicholas. I had accepted that an astonishing turn of fate had allowed our lives to
cross for one split-second, lifesaving, clandestine moment in
the creative writing class. I never expected that another miracle
would make it possible for us to connect in real life.

I looked up the address of the law office representing
Luba that was named in the article and wrote her a letter. I
reminded her of the time we spent together in Chicago and the
night we threw the *I Ching*. I sent a check to support her and
her comrades. At the very end of the letter I mentioned that
I had recognized her when she had entered the Pitt creative
writing class. I told her that I had quit the class right after that
and reassured her that I never would have done anything to
expose her identity. I mailed the letter right away, before any
doubts could discourage me from what I knew I should do.

Surprisingly, she wrote back quickly. Her short note
thanked me for the check but even more for being sensitive
to her situation. She mentioned that Francis was among the
group of people supporting her and helping to take care of
Nick. They would be staying in Chicago for a few months. Her
surrender had been part of a negotiated agreement with the
state, but the final court decision about each of their cases was
still to come. She suggested I may want to come to Chicago.

Part of me desperately wanted to accept Luba's warmth and openness and rush to be reunited with her and Francis. But I knew that her warmth would freeze quickly once she discovered the role I had played. Instead, I returned to work on my writing, shaping it into this story that others could read and learn from. Someday I will have the courage to send it to Luba. Someday, after my name and role have been revealed to the world through the FBI's Discovery documents. After Reynaldo and his group of FBI snitches have given their official testimony and exposed my collusion with their crooked sting. When there is nothing more left to uncover, I will disclose my side of the truth and hope for Luba's forgiveness.

CAGED—
SAGE
2005

SOMEONE HAD METICULOUSLY SCRATCHED A TINY, WHIMSICAL HEART ON THE PLEXIGLASS barrier. I stared at it, waiting for Rahim to come out. I wondered who had dared to take a key or a nail file from her handbag—I had to assume it was a woman—and defiantly, but quietly, etch a trite but true memento of connection that could be seen on both sides of this transparent, impermeable separation wall. It could have cost them their visit and all future visits. Maybe it had.

I was still trembling inside from the violent search of *my* bag fifteen minutes before. Wadded-up tissues, scraps of post-its, herbal pill bottles, Preparation H wipes all strewn across the counter as the young Latino guard carelessly searched for the culprit metal that had appeared dark and menacing on the x-ray screen as the bag rolled down the belt. Finally, he found the change purse filled with quarters that I had quickly gathered from various tables, desks, and counters in my house at the last groggy minute before dashing out the door at six this Sunday morning. I had suddenly remembered that years ago I always needed quarters for the vending machines when I visited Rahim at San Quentin. Foolishly, I hadn't even realized that at SF County there would be bulletproof glass between us on this visit. No chance to share the crummy junk food that had greased the wheels of conversation during those long-ago encounters.

I could have asked one of the other people who were already visiting Rahim—Luba, Chloe, Maxine, Brian—what the procedure was in County Jail, what I should expect, at least logistically, but I didn't want to draw attention to my decision (which was still uneasy and wavering) to visit Rahim again, after so many years of resentful silence.

What right does she have to be resentful? He's the one who's been locked in a cage all these years! I could imagine the contempt coating Maxine's words, though she would never say this directly to me. It wasn't that I resented Rahim, himself. When I tried to explain the intricate complexity of my emotions to Brooke, she listened patiently in her best clinical, bedside manner through an hour's worth of meandering, fragmented rationales about the old days, the organization, the strident political lines and divisions until she firmly put her arms around me.

Sage, honey, you don't have to go back there, through all that again. You haven't seen the man for twenty-three years and now he's right here, down at 850 Bryant. It's just about saying hello. Sensible, practical and, as she well knew, impossible for me to do on those clean and simple terms.

Still, I had gone ahead and called Chloe. She was keeping a schedule since there were only a few visiting slots each week and many family, old friends, and new young activists who wanted to see Rahim now that he had been absurdly hauled back to the Bay. Chloe gave me an early Sunday morning slot that was the only one available, and even though Sunday morning was my one day of the week for sleep-late indulgence, I didn't try and hold out for a later time. Now that I had made up my mind, sort of, now that I had started picturing Rahim twenty-three years older, I needed to see him soon, to look at his face and see how it had emerged through two more decades living inside a cell.

Chloe, who had always been one of the least judgmental people in Uprising, started to ask me, as she probably asked all the many people who called to schedule visits, whether I needed help getting to the jail by six thirty in the morning.

Sorry, Sage, I almost forgot that you have lots of experience with prison visits.

Our conversation had been happily impersonal and present tense until that moment. I quickly thanked her for scheduling me in and hung up before I would feel forced to comment on the vast gap between then and now.

I knew I wouldn't be able to entirely skirt the gap with Rahim. When I saw him last in 1982, his name was Clarence. He hadn't become Rahim until he was shipped away from San Quentin, back to a prison in Pennsylvania to serve time for another so-called conspiracy. In the seventies, they had railroaded him through one whirlwind trial after another before anyone in the movement really knew what was happening. From Pennsylvania, he wrote to me about how the other Muslim brothers had helped him choose the name Rahim, meaning compassionate and kind. I liked the name, even though our correspondence had become mired in the same battles I was having with all the other people I had called my comrades for years. Having changed my own name, I understood why he had chosen Rahim. Not, as he explained, because he thought he *was* compassionate but because this was what he truly aspired to be.

After I stopped writing, after I had begun to put the envelopes with the return name Rahim Jackson aside in a tall pile (until I finally decided to throw them out, unopened, in one desperate batch), he remained Rahim to me. This morning, I felt almost sacrilegious when I wrote "Clarence Jackson" on the visiting form as Chloe told me I must do if I wanted to get in to see him.

Of course they know that he goes by Rahim, but they won't do him the favor of calling him by anything but his slave name, she had explained ruefully.

The heart wasn't the only hieroglyphic carved on the smeared plexiglass. But try as I might, I couldn't decipher any other meaning from the patchwork scratchings that seemed to serve as the historical record of the thousands of anguished, fraught visits that had transpired in this booth. Perhaps they were simply the imprint of nails, screeching like chalk across blackboard, releasing the sweltering tensions that could not be expressed in a half hour conversation over tape-recorded phone wires. This much I remembered—prison visits cooked emotions until they threatened to boil over in a sizzling, uncontrollable mess.

I was starting to time travel back to that long ago San Quentin visiting room, when his hand appeared in front of me, pressed against the glass. I had always marveled at how perfectly trimmed Rahim's nails always were in an era when most of the straight white men I knew disdained nail clippers and cuticle care. Before I had a chance to place my hand up against my side of the glass to complete the greeting, Rahim was carefully wiping off the mouthpiece of the phone on the sleeve of his garish orange jumpsuit. He motioned to me to do the same. It seemed like a token effort to ward off the horde of germs that must be lurking in every overheated air particle of this stuffy corridor, but I dug in my bag and quickly wiped the phone with the wad of tissues that had survived the guard's search.

Sage, it's great to see you! Been a while, but you look good as always. I like the shorter hair.

And there it was, twenty-three years melted gently down into *a while*. His voice as deep and fluid as it ever had been. I stuffed down the reflexive self-consciousness that his compliment sparked despite its intentions (my hair too short, its streaks too gray), and looked at him. Most definitely, *he* looked good. A little gray, that ironically universal symbol of age, across all color lines, but no middle-aged pudge, no slackening muscles. At least not on first glance, as I tried to assess him in sideways glimpses and not look straight at him the way I often stared at people unconsciously. *You're always mugging people,* my daughter would reprimand me. *You're gonna get yourself hurt that way if you don't watch out.*

You look better than good, Rahim! Don't know how you've managed it!

All that working out with state-of-the-art equipment us prisoners get at taxpayer expense. He smiled and I remembered the way his voice was always carefully modulated and sonorous, counterbalancing his acid descriptions of all the horrors that were transpiring around him.

Actually, I haven't even been able to work out in this joint. They have me in my cell twenty-three hours a day with only an hour to walk around in a circle. That's what passes for PE here, driving up my blood pressure. But don't get me started or that's all we'll talk about.

Your blood pressure, Rahim, is it really a problem? You know my partner, Brooke, she's a nurse and she knows many doctors at SF General, and if you're having a problem, well, maybe she can get you some more help.

Thanks, I'll remember that. Especially for some of the other brothers in here. Diabetes, asthma, gunshot wounds, not to mention madness—most of them could use some outside intervention for sure.

Rahim had never been one to dwell on the personally painful. The big-picture problems—the reasons why so many Black men—and of course some sisters too—were locked up. The prisons as koncentration kamps for Black folks. COINTELPRO and the attacks on the Black Panther Party. These things he used to talk about for hours. And I had listened voraciously, wanting desperately to understand. But not just to understand. Wanting to be a vocal messenger to the world outside, convincing *them*, all the *thems*, to listen up, become educated, do something.

He glanced quickly down at his watch and I realized that the minutes for this visit were rapidly ticking away.

I want to hear about you, Sage. Tell me what's going on in your life. How old is your daughter? Anise, that's her name, right?

When I first heard it, I thought—two healing herbs, Sage and Anise, perfect.

Who had told him about Anise? Probably Maxine. Why hadn't I been able to break my stubborn silence and write him myself about the birth of this baby girl who I had yearned to have even back when I was visiting him? What could I say now to sum up Anise who wasn't the perfect, feminist teenage woman that I had fantasized she would become?

Well, she's seventeen—beautiful and smart in her own way. Right now we have a lot of mother-daughter stuff going on. The usual pattern, I guess, but challenging just the same. I should have thought to bring a picture to show you. I'm sorry.

No worries. Bring it next time. And one of Brooke also. I'm really happy, Sage, that you found someone that was right for you and you've been together all this time.

The tears began to burn up the insides of my eyes. In the last letters I ever wrote him, I had told Rahim about meeting Brooke. I had to let him know that even while I was moving away from all the history we had shared, I was moving toward something else and someone else. I knew that he would be less hurt by the relationship I had found on the outside than by the abandonment of our common vision. After all, we had stated and restated the obvious many times: he had a life sentence and I was a lesbian. But our vision of change, we thought we would share *that* forever. Until, little by little, it became too un-compromising, too demanding for me, while he and the others were still carrying it forward as if the world hadn't turned, as if we could still hope to overturn the mammoth, entrenched, twisted system that we all lived and breathed under.

Now Rahim was being kind, reminding me of the side of him that I had repressed, along with most of the memories that didn't fit my acrid picture of the past. I was disoriented by his generosity. No wonder I had anguished over the decision to visit him even once. Already, he was talking about next time. And now, since I was seeing and hearing him separated only by a plexiglass wall, I knew there had to be a next time.

Yes, Brooke is wonderful. She genuinely cares about people concretely, not in some abstract, politically dogmatic way—you know she never has been really involved in politics—but straight from her heart. She was the one who said I had to come see you.

As soon as the hurtful words bolted out of my mouth, I knew I had catapulted us back to a time when every misspoken phrase, each misinterpreted sentence in a letter became a stepping stone toward the precipice that ended in complete silence.

You mean you were thinking of not visiting me? When I'm right here at 850, just down the block from your Noe Valley hood? Nothing abstract about that. If you're looking for concrete, well here I am.

Ten minutes into the visit and I had almost succeeded in fracturing his studied, steady cool. I wanted to screech my nails across the plexiglass. Instead, I dug a pit into my arm.

I didn't mean it like that, Rahim. I knew it would be hard to see you, hard for both of us. And here it is being very hard, already. You still locked up. Having to think again about everything back then. It wasn't automatic, for me, sorry. It was a decision I wanted to make carefully, and Brooke helped me with that. You remember, I've always had that nervous nellie side of me.

He gave a little laugh, and I could tell that he too wanted the conversation to move away from hurt and mistrust.

Yeah, I remember that side, for sure, Sage. But I also remember another side. How you used to talk back at the guards when they yelled at the little kids running around in the visiting room. I was the one had to tell you to tone it down unless you wanted to get all of us thrown out of visiting for good.

I started to say that speaking out like that wasn't the kind of thing I had ever been nervous about. Talking loud, challenging things that were in front of my face—these used to be the things I was comfortable with, the entitlements my lawyer father and teacher mother had groomed me for from the time I was a little girl. No, the danger line that I couldn't cross had to do with actions that were covert and required secrecy, that demanded I mask my voice to serve a subversive purpose. I glanced at my watch. Only ten minutes left and we hadn't even talked about why Rahim was here, back again in San Francisco. Fifty-five years old and facing another ugly courtroom battle.

Yeah, those guards at Quentin were certainly a piece of work. So arbitrary and mean to kids who had so much to deal with already. I just couldn't stand by without saying something. We can talk more about all of that next time, next weekend. But please, before I have to leave, tell me what's going on with your case and how I can help.

Across the phone wire, I could hear him take a deep, deliberate breath.

You probably know the basics, already. Since 9/11, with the blessings of the Patriot Act, all sorts of cold cases from the sixties and seventies are being reopened with the help of Homeland Security money. Not enough domestic terrorists out there to prosecute, so why not go back in time and drum up drama about police officers being killed by crazy, bloodthirsty Black Panthers? They drag me back out here 'cause I was a Panther when all that shit went down, and I've already been framed for a couple of murders, so why not try for a few more? What an easy target.

When I first saw the article in the *Chronicle*, I thought it was an eerie, twilight zone mistake. Clarence Jackson was being extradited back to San Francisco from Pennsylvania to face charges in the 1974 murder of a police officer.

This can't be happening, I said out loud, before I realized that Anise was toasting her Pop Tarts on the other side of the kitchen.

What can't be happening? she asked, immediately interested in any drama going on, especially something that bothered me. I began to explain that I used to visit Clarence Jackson, who now went by the name Rahim, when he was at San Quentin back in the seventies. While I didn't know all the facts yet, it sounded like the FBI was either making a stupid mistake or trying to frame him. Anise interrupted me scornfully, as she often did these days, her dark black curls vibrating with angry energy.

Of course they're trying to frame him. You're always so careful to give them the benefit of the doubt, Mom. Just a few weeks ago, my friend Antwon was pulled over for nothing. Didn't stop the correct number of feet from the stop sign or some bullshit. Right away they had him up against the wall and before he knew it they were searching the car, without a warrant, and they found some weed. Now he's got to go to court and it's gonna fuck up everything for him.

I started to ask her for more details, since she had slipped and told me a story that she had obviously been keeping secret until then. But before I could say anything she slammed out of the house.

Over the next couple of weeks, every time I picked up the paper or turned on the local news, there was another sensational story about the violent history of the Panthers. None of the stories had a direct link to Rahim, but pictures of him wearing his Panther beret were plastered, in grungy newsprint style, next to ones of Panthers with guns. One day in the lunchroom at work one of my younger colleagues, Beth, pointed to an iconic one of the Panthers standing disciplined and defiant at the Capitol building in Sacramento, carrying their rifles.

They seem so macho, so into guns, she commented in an offhand way. Before thinking about it, I launched into an explanation. The Panthers were simply exercising their Second Amendment right to bear arms, like the Klan and other right-wing groups did all the time. They were making a point about double standards and Black people's rights to self-defense. Besides, the media was just using these pictures to slant the story and bias Jackson's trial.

Words and phrases came tripping out of my mouth as automatically as they had twenty-five years ago. Until I noticed the bewildered confusion on Beth's face. She was reacting not only to the content of my speech but to the political diatribe coming out of my mouth. Nowadays, when I wanted to engage in a political discussion, I was very careful not to lecture, to be sensitive to where the other person was coming from, to give the person space to respond and not ram my opinion down their throat. Or I avoided the discussion altogether, which was usually easier.

Sorry, I didn't mean to come on so strong, I apologized. *I just feel like sensationalism can distort the truth. Like with gay marriage. The way the media represents us, you would never know that we are regular folks with children and families.*

Beth was glad to move on to a topic where we had more common ground, and I was relieved as well. I needed time to think through my talking points, time to regain my balance, time to figure out if and when I would tell my coworkers that I knew the man who was being accused of such heinous crimes.

What's been so beautiful, Rahim was continuing to answer my question about the case, *is how so many of the OG's—Panthers, lawyers, and all the folks who are still around from Uprising—are all stepping up to my defense. And lots of young people starting to get involved too. You probably have reservations about the old group of people, Sage, but I'm sure there's some way for you to plug in.*

I had been worried that he would try and get me to join the defense committee. When Rahim believed in something, he took it seriously to the nth degree. He might understand that someone else was hesitating and unsure, but he was determined to use every persuasive tactic possible to change their mind. But there was no way I could sit down in a room with Maxine or Luba to debate strategies and tactics as we used to do for hours upon hours in the old days.

I thought I might be able to help with fundraising in some way. That's my job, you know, development director of the Hanover Foundation.

That's just what we need, Sage. I had heard that you were working with Hanover and hoping that you would step up that way. Actually, I have some ideas I want to run by you.

Rahim's mind was moving fast as usual with plans and plots. Sometimes his ideas had been brilliant, sometimes they had been one step away from insane, but always their flow was buoyant, abundant, unstoppable. I wasn't ready for *this* discussion either, so I was relieved when the guard yelled out that the visiting session was over.

In the adjoining booth, I could hear a woman sobbing, *Baby, we haven't figured anything out, and I don't know when I can get someone to watch the kids and make it down here again.*

I could see Rahim's facial muscles twitching almost imperceptibly, and even though he was the consummate professional when it came to prison visits, I knew that he was wrestling with a cloud of frustration at yet another unnatural, forced ending to a conversation that had just started buzzing.

Send me a letter with your ideas. We can discuss them when I come again, next week.

This time when he pressed his hand against the glass I immediately pressed back. Then I quickly walked toward the elevator before I got sucked into the throbbing whirlpool of interrupted emotion that was overflowing the corridor.

I was trying to follow the diagram filled with color-coded lines and boxes projected on the screen at Hanover's annual retreat. I had forgotten about the retreat when I promised Rahim I would visit him the following weekend. So I had to ask Chloe to ask Luba, who was scheduled to visit him that weekend, to let Rahim know that I wouldn't be able to come. I would have preferred someone else besides Luba as the liaison between Rahim and me, especially since the message was one of cancellation, which could easily be interpreted as deliberate withdrawal. But the only other people visiting on Saturday were his family, and it certainly didn't make sense to involve them in messaging of this kind.

Rahim, on the other hand, had been true to his promise. I had received a letter filled with fundraising ideas, which he had put together in superb outline form in the crafted calligraphy that was a hallmark of his writing. It had always given me pleasure to gaze on the flowing, intricate shapes of Rahim's letters, whether they were personal letters or manifestos. Until the day when the insistent intent of the words overwhelmed the quiet beauty of their shapes.

The thought of Rahim's letter, which I had hastily skimmed, with its bursting stream of ideas—people to contact, events to plan, raffles, auctions, even door-to-door canvassing—made it difficult for me to concentrate on the geometrically contained flow chart on the screen. The color coded boxes and arrows represented each step in the updated process of soliciting a donation from someone in our wide donor-advised granting circle. I myself had initiated the new process but had asked my assistant, See-Ming, who was much more skilled than I was at translating concepts into graphs and charts, to develop the final version.

How could I reconcile Rahim's fountain of possibilities—*it can't hurt to try some of these, can it, Sage?* he had prodded in his letter—with the rigorous process Hanover followed in deciding to approach a donor or evaluating the cost-effectiveness of a grassroots fundraising strategy?

When I first came to Hanover as a development assistant in 1984, soon after I left Uprising, this was one of the things

I appreciated most—the clarity of their guidelines. They made asking for donations and granting them into a science with a transparent methodology. They also showed their appreciation for the people who mastered these development skills.

In Uprising, I had been one of the people considered *good at fundraising*, but the recognition was always a double-edged sword. I was someone who could cross over into the world of wealth and finance, use my white, solidly middle-class background to identify and communicate with radical rich people who supported Third World liberation struggles and white anti-racist, anti-imperialists. This became my niche in the organization, which complemented my part-time job bookkeeping that paid for rent and groceries.

In the beginning, the niche was challenging but fulfilling. The circle of donors was wide, and I only had to explain our latest project confronting the Klan and right-wing gay-bashers or supporting prisoners at San Quentin, and people would agree to give—not millions or even hundreds of thousands, the kind of numbers that Hanover dealt with, but enough to support our projects and contribute substantially to the Third World groups we were working with closely.

Over time, the pool of willing givers began to evaporate. And the people who would consider supporting us had more and more questions. What exactly did we expect to achieve? What kind of accountability did the Third World groups have for the funds we gave them? Was their money really going for armed struggle? When were we going to start putting some much-needed emphasis on helping a Democrat win back the White House instead of focusing only on radical, fringe issues?

Some of their questions were picky and demanding, but some of them started to be my questions as well. Maxine accused that they were organizing *me* more than I was organizing them. I argued that Uprising was becoming too out of touch with the rest of the world's reality.

The sun was streaming through the panoramic windows of Hanover's conference room overlooking the Bay. See-Ming had completed the presentation and was competently handling the flurry of questions, delving into the reasons behind each step of the new process. She was articulate and focused. No ghosts trapped in the bowels of 850 Bryant to discombobulate *her* mind and make her doubt the meaningfulness of the metrics and matrixes on the wall.

I had always been something of the resident radical at Hanover. When I applied for the job, I told them just enough about my background with the Panthers and the antiapartheid movement to demonstrate my connections with *the community* and leftist donors, which was what they were looking for at the time. But the story that branded my Hanover identity had to do with my name. When I presented my Social Security card with the name *Ruth Greenwald* printed on it, I had to offer some easily comprehensible explanation about why my resume had *Sage* as my first name.

Ruth was always too biblical for me. So I had a name-changing ceremony and chose Sage. But I never went through all the paperwork to make it legal. So my card still says Ruth. The story got around and Ron, Hanover's executive director, made a standing office joke of it.

Now we're out on a limb for sure having someone with an AKA in our development department. The joke always made me flinch, since I had so carefully avoided a bona fide AKA. The real roots of my name change were more hallucinatory than mandatory.

A few months after I moved to San Francisco in 1973, after hours of smoking hash with Juno, my first-ever girlfriend, the name Ruth became an asphyxiating vise, immobilizing me.

Ruth means familial loyalty at all costs, whither thou goest I go, fidelity to what they want for me—a respectable career, a good husband, preferably Jewish, a tree planted in Israel in my name, belief in the system, a life tied up in bows, in knots. A noose that is strangling me. All of why I left Chicago and came here. I feel it in my chest, my back, my heart.

I felt like I would suffocate or terminally stiffen, except Juno patiently, arduously massaged my back, my feet, my chest all over, every knotted muscle, every congested inch, until my chest and back and heart started to relax enough for us to make love and fall asleep.

The next morning we planned the ritual to discover the new name that should be mine. Juno's circle of women friends brought flowers and together we burned incense, smoked some gentler weed, and used the *I Ching*, the Chinese Book of Changes, for guidance. We threw dozens of hexagrams— *The Creative, The Receptive, Waiting, Biting Through, Holding Together, Splitting Apart.* We meditated over the simple lines, translating thousands of years of human experience from a vastly distinct society and culture into a lexicon of our own. I had no idea where it was all going, what I believed and what I didn't, but I loved reading the texts, listening to other women's tales of joy and pain, and reinterpreting them in the context of yin and yang, the inner and the outer, backward and forward.

At one point, a woman named Francesca, turned to me, put her hand on mine, and said earnestly, *You are very wise about people, very sage!*

That's it! Juno declared, the light of magic shining in her eyes. *Sage is your name. Wise but in need of healing, and your gray-green eyes—it is all you.* At first I hesitated because, of course, I wasn't really sage but had just been using my academic intellect to deconstruct meanings, as if I were writing a paper for Asian literature. But Juno and the others convinced me that *Sage* wasn't a static concept. It was a name that I could grow into, who I could strive to be.

Each time I told my name-changing story it varied a little depending on who I was telling it to. When she was little, Anise loved to hear the version that ended with choosing *her* name. I was eight months pregnant and Brooke and I had just finished planting some anise herbs in our garden. We had read that anise possessed multiple healing properties that could not only help ease my chronic congested cough but would also increase my milk supply during nursing and offer a cure for baby colic.

As we were sitting quietly, inhaling the melded fragrances of our abundant herbs and flowers, Brooke suddenly suggested that we throw the *I Ching* to help us figure out the baby's name. I hadn't turned to it for guidance in years, but we had been through the name books again and again and still hadn't come up with the right one.

We threw the hexagram *The Corners of the Mouth/ Providing Nourishment.* The Judgment read, *In bestowing care and nourishment, it is important that the right people should be taken care of and that we should attend to our own nourishment in the right way.*

After she read the passage, Brooke's face lit up. *How about Anise? She will nourish us and we will nourish her.* It was perfect.

Anise used to throw her arms around me and declare giddily, *Me and mommy are two healing herbs. We will keep the whole world healthy forever and ever!* Now she seemed to think that the *I Ching*, herbal healing, and the name Anise were all white hippie appropriations.

Why would you want to take the I Ching *from another culture and turn it around for your own purposes?* she accused one day. I couldn't explain, in any way that would make sense to Anise, that the *I Ching* had helped fill my aching need for ancestral wisdom and guiding magic. And that, in some indescribable way, it had became a gateway to learning from revolutionary cultures around the world.

I left Juno, whose brand of magic became too self-serving for me. I started singing with a women's band and going to meetings of the newly formed socialist feminist Women's Union. There I met Jamie—tough, cute, and practical but with a belief in the invincible power of rebel witches. She introduced me to the people who had just formed Uprising—Maxine, Brian, Luba, Cassandra. I began visiting brothers at San Quentin with Cassandra, before she was arrested for the first time in 1976. Before she miraculously managed to escape from prison two years later.

Ours was the magic of Che and Fidel in the Sierra Maestras. Of Vietnamese peasants downing B-52 bombers.

Ours was the wisdom of Marx, Lenin, Mao, and Ho Chi Minh. Forward-thinking optimism rooted in dialectical materialism: a scientifically based prophecy that revolutionary change was inevitable. A visionary picture that I believed in and proselytized for. Until there were too many arrests, too many betrayals, disappearances, and deaths. The lens began to flip and in place of magic realism all I could see was a trick-box of illusions that no sleight of hand could ever transform into an American reality.

After I left Uprising, when I got the job at Hanover, I gladly immersed myself in tangible parameters and trained my mind to always search for measurable objectives and identifiable outcomes. We called it *magical thinking* when someone pitching a fundraising event claimed that we could raise hundreds of thousands of dollars in one easy evening if we only could get a certain band or speaker to anchor it. We gently encouraged them to always start with more limited but realizable goals.

When I finally sat down to concentrate on Rahim's fundraising suggestions, after the Hanover retreat, I expected to find the kind of magical thinking that often overtakes people when they think about making money, especially when they have had little access to it all their lives. I had forgotten Rahim's capacity to surprise me. Yes, one or two of his ideas were on the outer edges of plausibility, but most of them were grounded in clear, well-thought-out possibilities. Contacting the large circle of former donors to Uprising. Holding house party fundraisers with his extended family and their friends. Persuading Hanover to sponsor a large fundraising event that could reach out to a broader set of people in the Bay Area to raise money and confront the media distortions head-on.

These were many of the same ideas I had been mulling over in my mind. Common-sense tools for organizing political support and raising money that he had developed sitting in his cell, without the help of PowerPoint Venn diagrams.

On my visit to the jail the following weekend, Rahim and I engrossed ourselves in plotting and planning a step-by-step fundraising campaign. Rahim was fascinated by the sequencing and framing techniques that I had developed over the years at Hanover. I was pleased at the common ground we seemed to share when it came to raising money. When the guard announced that the visit was over, I realized that neither of us had looked at our watches once.

Do me one favor, Sage, he said right before I left. *Talk to Maxine about our plan. She's helping with outreach and has some interesting ideas. It would be really good for the two of you to connect.* I agreed before I could think about what I was committing myself to. Before I realized how skillfully Rahim had sequenced our conversation to close with this specific ask at the very end.

I'm not sure I can do it, I complained to Brooke as we were gardening later that day in our weekly Sunday ritual.

I told Rahim I would, but I just can't see myself planning anything with Maxine after all that's happened.

Don't you think it's time you put all that behind you? The irritated snap in Brooke's voice surprised me. I glanced over and I could see bright red blotches dotting her face, signaling how upset she was.

I don't think you understand how painful a break it was. How rigid and moralistic and judgmental they all were, with Maxine leading the pack. You don't get it because you never were involved with a group like Uprising. And besides, you're oblivious to the negative side of people.

My words hung in toxic knots between us. I waited to see if Brooke would walk away, as she sometimes did when we had a fight, not wanting to continue on my terrain of wordy, hammering arguments.

Instead, she moved over close to where I was hunched on my knees, aimlessly yanking at the weeds.

Sage, I'm not questioning any of that. Her voice no longer had its brittle edge. *I work all the time with an awful lot of rigid, self-righteous doctors, so yes, I know about judgmental people. I realize that it's not the same thing because you loved the folks in Uprising. And I think you still love Rahim. I'm trying not to be jealous because I know that he needs your support. But if you want to give that to him you have to get over being so damn self-protective.*

She stopped. I wasn't angry at her anymore. I was grateful. Grateful that she was a person who didn't sharpen her criticisms into a piercing sword. Grateful that she had named out loud the confusion of love I felt for Rahim that I couldn't name for myself.

Okay, I'll think about it, was all I could manage to say. I resumed plucking the weeds with a little more kindness.

The next week I went to court for the first time. It was a routine hearing for the defense to present a motion for Discovery, hoping to obtain documents from the prosecution and the FBI that might contain some hidden material that could help exonerate Rahim. In 1996, Black Panther leader Geronimo Pratt's conviction had been overturned after twenty-seven years in prison, based on evidence that had been concealed until it was finally uncovered in the prosecutor's files. The key witness against Geronimo at his trial had been an FBI informant, and the state had repeatedly lied to cover up this fact, legal grounds for overturning his conviction.

I remembered the shock of excitement I felt when I had heard Geronimo was free, decades after I had first worked on his case. Geronimo had always maintained his innocence, had declared that he had been targeted by COINTELPRO and was framed for a murder that he hadn't committed. In Uprising, we had supported his truth, his fight against the combined forces of the FBI, the Los Angeles DA, and the courts. So when his conviction was thrown out, when the picture flipped and he was no longer a criminal but a victim of the corruptness of the U.S. judicial system, I felt a surge of happiness and vindication. For a moment, I was even sorry that I wasn't sharing the news with all the other people who had believed in Geronimo for so many years.

Now here I was in court, surrounded by people who believed that Rahim was also being framed. I had talked cordially on the phone with Maxine about outreach plans before the hearing. Luba and many of the Panthers I had worked with closely years ago all greeted me warmly. Still, I felt awkward and out of place, uncertain about my right to be there. Until they brought Rahim into the courtroom. In his orange jumpsuit, he stood out like a brazen banner amid the muted grays and beiges of the walls and furniture.

Rahim raised his fists in a greeting to us, despite the heavy manacles that weighed them down. Our side of the room stood up in a silent salute, while the other side, which was filled with San Francisco cops, FBI agents, and Homeland Security officers, glared straight ahead, unwilling to even admit the presence of our opposition in this bastion of their power.

Our gesture was too much for the judge who pounded his gavel loudly and threatened to empty the courtroom if there were any other displays of defiance that threatened the security of his courtroom. I waited tensely, half expecting someone to take up the gauntlet that the judge had thrown, as might have happened in the old days. But everyone sat down quietly, with not even a smirk at the absurd claim that anyone's safety was at risk. Except of course, Rahim's.

I was relieved when George, one of the team of radical lawyers who had come together to defend Rahim, insisted that his shackles be taken off during the proceedings. The judge beckoned the lawyers for the defense and the prosecution to approach him, and for ten minutes the hushed voices argued back and forth.

What possible justification can they have for keeping him shackled in court? It's so degrading! I whispered to Brian, who was sitting next to me.

Security concerns can cover everything in this day and age, Brian whispered back. *You know, Rahim could have concealed a gun in the leg of his pants and as soon as the shackles are off, presto, you have an uprising.*

I laughed, and for the first time in many years, I felt glad that I had once conspired with these people to upset the rule of law.

Finally, the huddle was over and we had won. Rahim's shackles were removed. Ten minutes later, after the defense had presented the motion for Discovery and the Judge had agreed to consider it, the next hearing date was set and Rahim's shackles were carefully replaced for the walk back to his cell.

The rest of the week, I looked forward to my Sunday visit with Rahim. The evening after the hearing, I described the courtroom scene in detail to Anise. She had gone to court a few weeks before with her friend, Antwon, who was being charged with marijuana possession and resisting arrest. I thought she might appreciate my description of the day's courtroom absurdities. I was hoping that she would offer an exchange account of her experience in court with Antwon, but she just listened intently and didn't say much.

As I stood up to clear the table, Anise asked abruptly, *What was your relationship like with Rahim back in the day?*

I took a deep breath and started out carefully. I couldn't think of anyone I was close with now, besides Brooke, whom I had talked to about Rahim. It wasn't a subject that I could compress into easy sound bites.

The factual details seemed most manageable. I explained how I had originally started visiting San Quentin with Cassandra Bridges. But then she was arrested and I stopped visiting until 1978 when Black prisoners at San Quentin were being attacked by Klan prisoners who were backed by the guards. Seven years after George Jackson had been assassinated inside San Quentin, things had only gotten worse. Uprising was asked to help support the Black prisoners. Rahim was one of the leaders inside and I was a representative of a coalition trying to publicize what was going on in the prison.

So did you only talk about politics? Anise interrupted.

Well, we talked a lot about politics. But we talked about many other things also. Books especially. We started with books like Soledad Brother, *but then we discovered how much we both loved James Baldwin, Alice Walker, and Toni Cade Bambara. Rahim introduced me to C.L.R. James and Walter Rodney—someday you should take a look at their books. I introduced him to some lefty white women authors like Tillie Olsen, Nadine Gordimer, and Judy Grahn.*

We didn't only talk about the books. We wrote letters about them, or mostly Rahim did. Long, fascinating letters that pulled together concepts from dozens of different books, fitting them all together into his vision. He always concluded with the possibilities for change contained in each book. Rahim was incapable of ending a letter, or a visit, stuck in a hopeless pit.

I was about to stop there, but something about Anise's hungry look made me go on.

I would read Rahim's letters late at night, just before going to bed. I used to keep a little notebook by the side of my bed. When I woke up after an intense dream, I would jot down the images. Sometimes I would write a song or a poem, which I would send him. We both believed that art was part of our political path forward, that politics should never be some dry, uninspired set of dogma. Though sometimes it was hard to hang on to that feeling, especially when the guards and the Klan were breathing down the prisoners' necks inside, and we were getting harassed constantly on the outside.

I was spinning my tale from buried fragments that I didn't realize were still inside of me, fragments that reverberated in my ears like someone else's story but that I knew were, in the realest sense, true. Anise was gazing at me as if she were hearing my voice for the first time.

Wow, Mom! That sounds amazing! Could I read the letters? I'd like to meet Rahim sometime. How come you never talked about him before he landed back in County?

My stomach began to knot up. Before I could think of a meaningless apology, a diversionary excuse, Anise's cell phone rang and for once I was glad that her calls took precedence over everything else that was going on in our common space.

There were so many, many reasons that I had never told Anise about Rahim. I had told Brooke about him only because I was still getting his letters when she and I moved in together. Rahim had been very important to me, I explained carefully to Brooke. He had taught me so much about Black history, about prisons, about literature, about myself. But he couldn't accept that I no longer wanted to be involved with Uprising's work. I had rejected the militancy, the clandestine activity that they all thought were the mandatory next steps forward. Rahim wanted to continue the debate even after my decision had been made. He was convinced that I would change my mind, that *he* could change my mind.

Brooke had listened closely, trying as she always did to translate my different life experience into terms that made sense to her. She could see that he had been a real mentor to me. But if he couldn't accept who I was and my life choices, maybe it would be best to disconnect with him for the time being.

We left it at that. I didn't want to tell her anything that could fan the flames of jealousy. What good would it have done, at that early stage of our relationship, to describe the point in my life, a few years before, when all week long I would look forward to my visit with Rahim? To recall the notebook I kept by my bed strewn with slices of dreams, scraps of poems, snippets of inadmissible desires? To reconstruct how, when we were together in the visiting room, the hours disappeared in a cocoon of ideas and imaginations that we wove between us—a heady but platonic connection whose only overt physical aspect was the brief officially sanctioned hug that marked the beginning and the end of each visit.

When my then-girlfriend Jamie accused me of loving Rahim more than I loved her, I self-righteously denied it. When Jamie and I broke up, I knew that tangled among all the reasons it didn't make sense for us to be together, was the inchoate mix of feelings that kept Rahim and me writing and calling and visiting week after week for years.

Soon after I told Brooke about Rahim, he stopped writing. A while later, I burned all his letters. By the time Anise was born, Rahim was buried in an unnamed crypt that almost never cracked open. How could I explain to Anise that his reappearance at 850 Bryant resurrected stories, ideas, and feelings that had mummified inside of me? How could I make clear that I hadn't talked about Rahim because, for all intents and purposes, I had forgotten who Rahim was?

After the court hearing, I pushed myself to schedule a meeting with Ron, Hanover's executive director, to propose a fundraiser to support Rahim's defense. At my initiative, Hanover had recently started a new criminal justice fundraising track. So far, we had funded a program for teenage girls at risk and a stop-the-violence community event in Bayview–Hunters Point. I knew that a fundraiser for Clarence Jackson, accused cop killer, was a stretch beyond anything originally envisioned in the carefully worded objectives for the criminal justice track, so I carefully outlined my talking points beforehand. If I hadn't known Ron well, I might have missed the flicker of irritated disbelief that crossed his face as soon as I mentioned the name *Clarence Jackson* and explained that I thought that his wrongful accusation offered Hanover an opportunity to support a very important local case of injustice.

That's such a high-profile case, Sage. I'm not sure that we want to get involved in anything with that type of publicity. You know how our donors are.

I had anticipated his argument about publicity and was ready with my reply.

But the media drummed up the publicity to create a negative atmosphere. They want to prevent people from getting involved and understanding the real facts of the matter.

The real facts? What makes you think you *know the real facts, Sage?* The sarcasm in Ron's rapid-fire response was a departure from his usual earnestly sincere manner. It made me want to go over and shake him, but instead I shot out words that weren't in my script.

I know him. I knew him in the seventies and I think he is being framed, thirty years later, because he was a Panther and the government needs to justify ramping up their antiterrorist campaign in the wake of September 11.

For a moment I thought the look of comprehension on Ron's face was an indication that my personal acquaintance with Rahim had helped shift the conversation in a positive direction. *Oh, Sage. I hadn't realized that you knew Mr. Jackson. Usually your instincts are clearer about what is possible and what is impossible for Hanover and our specific donor base, so this makes more sense. I understand where you're coming from, but Hanover's mission stresses alternatives to violence and no matter what you and I may think, support for this case, with the San Francisco Police Department on the other side, is not a good fit for us.*

The blandly familiar justifications ricocheted crazily through my head. Why had I thought for one minute that I could convince Hanover to support Rahim? Ron was right. A month ago, before I had visited Rahim, I would have been crystal clear about why this could never happen. But Rahim had addled my sense of reality, had bisected my vision between the mandates of the dominant development world and the upset challenges to those rules from a subterranean, alternate universe where people in need claimed rights to available resources.

I don't think it's so cut-and-dry, Ron. Remember, some of the donors that I brought to Hanover used to support the Panthers, and I bet if we reminded them of the history of COINTELPRO and government frame-ups they could see beyond the corporate media spin on this story.

I was going further out on a limb than I had ever planned. But what could I do, short of occupying Ron's office with Rahim's family members, friends, and the active cohort of former Uprising members? I needed to remind Ron of the role I had played in bringing many of the former Uprising supporters into the Hanover donor network. I wanted to imply that I could, potentially, go beyond the usual decision-making structures and bring my proposal directly to them.

Ron's face was bleached and strained. *You're upset, Sage, and I don't think we'll get any further with this today. Let's schedule a time to discuss this again next week and examine the options more calmly. Now, I would really appreciate it if we could move on to our appeal letter, which was our main agenda item for today. This is an excellent letter, as always, but I do have a few minor tweaks that I'd like to suggest.*

As I waited for Rahim to come out to the visiting booth the following Sunday, I planned to start by telling him that Anise wanted to meet him. I would save the report on my discussion with Ron till the end. They brought Rahim out ten minutes late and his face, through the smeared glass, was rutted and troubled. Still, he pushed out a welcoming smile for me.

When I asked him what was wrong, he seemed surprised that I had noticed anything going on.

My nephew, Roland, came by yesterday. First time I've seen him since he was a baby. Just got out of SQ a couple of weeks ago. Been in and out of juvie for years and after he turned eighteen caught an adult case.

He was going to leave it at that, but I asked whether Roland had any support network.

My sister's mainly given up on him. Says she's tried too many times before to talk some sense into him. But how can you give up on someone who's just twenty years old? He's a smart kid, understands a lot about the system, knows about Mumia, Leonard, and the other political prisoners—something I made sure of in my letters to him.

He sees what they're trying to do to me and understands why. But it doesn't mean anything 'cause he doesn't believe anything can change.

I started to say something, but there was no stopping his unusual dirge, pent up beneath the bubble of plans and ideas for years.

Half the boys Roland went to high school with are in prison now. Most of the others dead or dodging gunshots every day. He looked straight at me, told me he respected me as one of the OG's who tried to do something back in the day, but nothing like that happening anymore. When I told him it was up to him to make something positive happen, he just looked at me like I was some demented fool. When I suggested he hook up with my defense committee, he nodded just to make me stop hammering at him.

Sage, I'm surrounded by young people in here without a glimmer of awareness, without a sliver of hope. All they know is their hustles, their survival game, and who am I to tell them that there's anything else out there when I haven't been out on the streets since I was younger than they are? The greed and violence of the empire comes home to roost—not in the way Malcolm envisaged it, but penetrating our communities with vengeance and despair.

We had been on a similar jagged, dejected edge before. But in the past Rahim was the one pulling *me* back, insisting that we didn't have to fall off—there were means of getting around it, passageways and channels that others had started, that we could extend deeper, longer, and stronger. We might not reach the light at the end of the tunnel in our lifetimes, but the effort would be intrinsically worth it.

I don't have the luxury to choose despair, Rahim used to say, implicating the privilege that, in the years that followed, allowed *me* to walk away from him and everything else, seem-ingly unscathed.

Yet I wanted to tell him, I had not been able to walk away entirely. I thought of the poster, hanging above Anise's bed—*R.I.P., Rest In Peace*—the words read, and below the words were the pictures of her two high school friends. A brown face and a tan face clowning for the camera at a football game the afternoon before they were shot. Anise was beside herself when she heard the news. I tried futilely to comfort her, but I also wanted to know what had happened, how it had come to be that two friends of hers were killed on a Saturday afternoon after a football game.

Was it drugs or gangs? I asked stupidly, adopting the labels assigned by the police and the media to justify such inexcusable happenings. Anise had lashed back at me between her sobs, *All of the above or none of it, does it really matter, Mother? They're dead and the cops can't fix it and no one but their friends really cares!*

I went to the funeral with her because I did care and I had to show it somehow. But when she hung the poster over her bed, I couldn't control myself. I didn't want their goofy, expectant kid faces suspended just above her head, insinuating themselves nightly into her dreams, into my dreams. When I suggested, carefully, that at least she could move the poster to the other side of the room, she refused.

You might think that distance makes things easier, Mother, but I need to keep them close and present. I want to remember them and what happened always.

Rahim's face was sagging, drooping toward despondency. Telling him about Anise's friends wouldn't help. I had to break the anguish of this moment.

I sat near some really cool kids from the Bayview in court the other day. Their teacher was a young brother who explained everything that was going on to them. He was well informed and the kids seemed engaged, wanting to learn the history. They loved it when you raised your fists coming into the courtroom. They stood up proudly with the rest of us.

Really? That's good! Rahim's eyes brightened, and I relaxed a little. *I'd love to be able to talk to them, understand what they think of the case, help them comprehend a little more about this setup on me and how it connects to their lives. After all, they have to see the connection to themselves. Otherwise it doesn't mean anything, won't help them figure out how to organize.*

His mind was ticking away again. Plans, plots, possibilities. After twenty-eight years living in dungeons, he hung on to this indomitable capacity.

I got the teacher's name and number. He was eager to help and we talked about possibly doing a house party fundraiser for you. I'm sure they'd want to visit you! And by the way, Anise says she'd like to meet you too.

Together we managed to end the visit on a forward-looking note, the way Rahim always wanted.

I drove home up Harrison and across Cesar Chavez where, even on a Sunday morning, groups of Latino men congregated on the corners, flagging down the cars that drove past, hoping to pull in a few hours of work this weekend. On one corner where I was stopped for a long red light, I saw that the cluster of people included women and children. When I looked more closely, I could see that they were gathered around a street altar.

I couldn't see the picture clearly but I assumed, from past experience, that it had been lovingly put together for some young man who had been shot—by the police, or a drive-by, or some random corner fight.

Every year it seemed like the shootings multiplied exponentially. I read about them in the Chronicle over my morning coffee and heard about them on KPFA as I drove to work. I reviewed them in grant narratives submitted to Hanover, proposing innovative solutions that would clean up the violence, just like the newest Clorox derivative miraculously removed stains.

I had loved this area of the Mission when I was in Uprising. Jamie and I had lived just a few blocks away on Treat Street in a bright yellow house with burgundy bougainvilleas cascading down the front staircase. Our neighbors' daughter, Araceli, used to come over to our house every day after school and complain about her strict parents and confide about her secret boyfriend. Until her parents forbade her to visit the *lesbianas* next door. There were lots of problems, but few shootings.

Once I passed Mission Street and wound my way up the hill into Noe Valley, the clusters on the corners were all people waiting in line in front of the various popular brunch spots. Many Sundays, Brooke and I would be on one of those lines, making small talk about our gardens and our greenhouse renovations or which of the many varieties of omelets, created with sustainably raised eggs and organic cheeses and vegetables, we would order. The cages at 850 Bryant were just a couple of miles away. The altars in the Mission were down the block. Most of the people on line would easily agree, if ever asked to comment, that the disjunction was appalling. But what could *we* do about it? Our despair, and our hope, was deeply entombed within a mountain of alternative goods and services. Besides, there was hardly any chance we would be asked to comment.

This was Brooke's one Sunday a month to work at the hospital, but I was hoping that Anise had come back from sleeping over at her girlfriend's house, or wherever she had really been. When she was out on a Friday or Saturday, which was often, I couldn't stop myself from chanting silent magic mantras to keep her from disappearing, to shield her from the horrors that befell too many of her friends on weekend nights. This time she wasn't home, but there was a message from her on the house phone, reassuring me that all was fine and she would be back later on. The house was empty and I couldn't face the list of chores that was taped up on the refrigerator.

As I grabbed my jacket, I noticed that my copy of the *I Ching* was lying sideways on the orderly shelf of books above the hall table. Had Anise been covertly searching for some ancient wisdom that could help her navigate the conflicted streets of San Francisco? I put the book in my bag, along with a bagel, some grapes, and my water bottle, and got back in the car.

I drove till I reached Lands End at the outermost edge of the city. This was the spectacular point at the tip of the continent where ocean touched earth. Here, waves broke furiously, threatening the cliffs that towered imperviously above. Here, submerged rocks pierced unsuspecting ships, dooming future journeys, and casual slips could catapult oblivious walkers down the sliding rock face. Here, I had my final conversation with Luba about my decision not to go underground.

Empire's End, we used to call it jokingly. The site where the westward grab for land and gold on the U.S. mainland had to terminate because it had reached the vast unconquerable expanse of Pacific Ocean. Except the empire inexorably found ways to expand beyond the western land limits. Luba and I needed to go to a place where the drama of our discussion would be put into perspective. A place that we both loved. Still it was the most difficult talk I ever had.

We had gone over the issues many times before. When Luba first asked me to be part of a collective that would go underground, I hesitantly said yes. I could understand the need to produce IDs and to develop a network of safe houses to protect fugitives. In 1978, Cassandra had gotten a furlough from prison and never returned. In 1979, a Puerto Rican political prisoner, Guillermo Morales, had climbed out of a window at Bellevue Hospital in New York where he was undergoing treatment. A few months later, Black Panther Assata Shakur had escaped from a maximum-security prison in New Jersey. They had all disappeared into a protective clandestine web. These were audacious examples of the types of actions an underground collective might help with, actions that would not only symbolize but could also actualize liberation. Yes, I could see the theoretical potential of such a collective.

We began to meet, to train in clandestine techniques, to debate various models, to analyze successes and failures of different groups in a long preparatory process that would culminate some point in the future with our subterranean submersion.

Long, charged meetings and laborious, tense trainings began to take over more and more of my life at the same time as I continued my public work with Uprising, made connections with our resourced supporters, and lived with Jamie.

Jamie would wonder where I was and what I was doing away from our home so much of the time. I came up with ridiculous cover stories that were also part of honing our clandestine methodology. But no matter what I told her, she believed that my frequent disappearances were in some way connected with Rahim, and after a while I no longer had the energy to convince her otherwise. At some point we broke up. Even though I was visiting Rahim less in this period, I couldn't deny that he was centrally involved in our secretive plans.

When I did get to visit Rahim, our conversations were now more guarded and narrowly focused. I was the person designated to discuss our plans and progress with Rahim, while other people liaised with different prisoners and other organizations. I was supposed to glean input from Rahim's experience and perspectives that I could share with the rest of the group. But as time went on, it was my gnawing questions and doubts that uncontrollably erupted during my visits with him.

Was our project sustainable in the current political climate? Weren't we too out of touch with the social reality of the country and even the Left? How could the collective be so arrogantly certain about the project when such huge problems were staring us in the face?

Rahim seemed to have infinite patience with my concerns.

It's good that you're questioning all these things, Sage. It's because you have such an active, demanding mind—a quality that is needed in this work and that I have always appreciated in you. These are all important issues that we can figure out together.

Yet none of his answers ever satisfied me, and all of my uncertainties continued to incessantly churn through my demanding mind. Rahim only got irritated with me once when I mentioned to him that I was going to throw the *I Ching* to help figure out whether I was meant to do this type of work.

That's a cop-out, Sage! For a Marxist dialectical materialist to use three coins and hexagram magic to make one of the most important decisions of her life, it's not worthy of who you are.

I snapped back that hexagram magic was more useful than Mao's *Little Red Book* when it came to figuring out political strategy relevant to the United States in the 1980s. The comparison polluted the air between us. It was one of the few visits where we didn't end on a positive note.

A week later, Rahim was abruptly shipped three thousand miles away to a prison in Pennsylvania to serve out another rigged sentence from that state. Perhaps a guard or snitch had overheard our whispered plotting and decided they needed to break up this conspiracy in the making. Or perhaps the timing was purely coincidental. Either way, without Rahim my misgivings began to consume me. I became a shadow of gloom, a specter of doubt, eroding the unity and purpose of the collective. I heard myself picking apart every idea, disparaging every rule, interrogating every plan. Ronald Reagan was the president. Eleven Puerto Ricans were in prison charged with seditious conspiracy. The disastrous Brink's bank expropriation in upstate New York had resulted in deaths and arrests. How could we go up against such daunting odds?

Luba voiced the impatience of the group with my repeated doomsday warnings. *We can't keep debating these issues in the abstract forever. We can name the dangers and try to learn from past mistakes. But we owe it to ourselves and the Third World movements we work with to test out our vision in practice.*

At night, alone in my bed, I couldn't sleep. Jamie was gone. Rahim was gone. I couldn't draw the line between my political objections and the knot of fear that had taken over my gut. In a meeting with Maxine, she accused me of using political rationales to cover my cowardice.

If you aren't up to making the sacrifices, just say it. Don't try and paint it over with elaborate rationalizations. Do you think the people who liberated Assata were sure their plan would be successful? There aren't any guarantees in this kind of work.

I resented her self-righteousness, but she was at least partly right. I couldn't face the prospect of clandestine exile. I didn't think I could survive decades of living in a cage. And I needed some type of guarantee that I wouldn't be sacrificing so much for nothing.

Each day, I expected the group to tell me that I had to leave. But they wanted the burden of the decision to be mine. Finally, I told Luba that we needed to talk and she suggested that we meet out at Lands End. I had prepared all my reasons, my many arguments about the direction the collective was going and why I felt that I couldn't be part of the project any longer. She cut me off, saying that I had expressed my disagreements enough already and it wasn't surprising that I had decided to leave.

Then, watching the waves explode fiercely in the brilliant sunlight, our discussion unexpectedly took a more cosmic turn.

We talked about the far-reaching realms of human possibility—ordinary people winning unthinkable victories against military juggernauts like in Vietnam, Cuba, Zimbabwe, and Nicaragua. And we talked about the meaning of defeat and the losses closer to home—the disintegration of so many Left groups, the narrowing of the vision, the many friends who were now in prison or on the run.

Luba said that she couldn't make a decision based upon a win vs. loss tally or the existence of a roadmap for success. *Traveler, there is no road. The road is made by walking*, she quoted one of our favorite verses by the Spanish poet Antonio Machado. Underneath the husky sureness of her words, her voice cracked with emotion.

One of the hardest things for me is wondering whether I will ever be able to have a child, she confided.

I told her that I had thrown the *I Ching* to help figure out whether, in fact, this path was the right one for me to walk on. I had gotten the hexagram *Splitting Apart*. When I read the Judgment, *It is not cowardice but wisdom to submit and avoid action*, I knew I was making the right decision. I thought Luba might jump on me like Rahim had done. Instead she confessed that she was also thinking about throwing the *I Ching* but so far hadn't done it.

At some point, as the sun was streaking blood red over the ocean, Luba realized that we hadn't yet discussed the concrete details of what *splitting apart* would mean in our situation. So she officiously laid out the plan that had been devised for this contingency. My differences meant that I could no longer be part of Uprising on any level.

So that's it? I asked weakly. *After working together for eight years, I'm now banned for life?* I tried to argue that I still wanted to be part of the work somehow, but Luba wouldn't hear of it. Security required that I distance myself from the collective, the organization, and everyone in it. I should develop a cover story that I was leaving because of my need for personal space. *At least*, Luba added with a strained laugh, *the cover story will be partially true.*

My life was cracking apart and my heart was rupturing. From inside a blinding mind fog I heard myself laugh bitterly. The absurdity of the situation was unspeakable.

I cut myself off from Uprising as I had been instructed, and for the first year I hardly knew why I was getting up each morning. Rahim's letters only made things worse. He wanted me to visit him, needed to understand what had happened, had to hear from me directly, not second- and third-hand from Maxine or Brian. He sent me beautiful haikus and drawings from other prisoners meant to inspire and energize me, but instead they sank me deeper into the quicksand of guilt and blame.

It wasn't until I met Brooke that I began to take real steps to reshape my life. In the last letter that I ever wrote to Rahim, I told him about meeting Brooke. I also told him that I was surer than ever that I had made the right decision. I found my job at Hanover, started a lesbian gardening group with Brooke, and seriously took up yoga.

A while later, Chloe called me with a tentative apology. The organization recognized that there had been problems with the way I had been treated. They wanted to get together and talk about it. They hoped there was a way we could work together again. I managed to tell her no politely, but when I got off the phone I had to do yoga for an hour before I could loosen the knot in my chest and breathe normally again.

The night after Chloe called, I dreamt about Luba. I was watching her plant seeds in a lush garden behind a pretty yellow house. I was a little surprised to see her gardening, since she never had struck me as the horticultural type. When she turned around and stood up, I could see that she was very pregnant and I felt a wave of happiness that a baby was going to be born, until I remembered how angry I was at her.

Then I heard a pounding on the door of the house and I knew for certain it was the FBI. For a split second, I was worried that somehow I had led the FBI to her. I wanted to warn her but it seemed like she already knew because she had lit a match and her gorgeous garden was burning. What will happen to her baby now, I desperately wondered. I woke up sobbing and was relieved to hear Brooke talking to the delivery guys who had been banging on the door with our new garden furniture.

I almost called Chloe after I read that Luba and her collective had been placed on the FBI's ten most wanted list in the summer of 1986. They were wanted as part of a conspiracy to help a Puerto Rican woman escape from prison. The newspaper article said that the FBI had been trying to find them ever since they had managed to evade a sting the year before. However, the article went on, the FBI had arrested another co-conspirator, Cassandra Bridges, in Miami. Bridges had been a wanted fugitive for eight years, ever since her escape from prison.

I wanted to call Chloe and ask what more she knew about what had happened, but I knew she wouldn't answer any of my questions. I wanted to scream at her that this was the inevitable, logical outcome of their arrogant vision and misguided project, but the words sounded hollow and vengeful even when I said them to myself.

Before we went to bed, I described to Brooke the last time I was with Cassandra, the day before she was first arrested in 1976. We had just finished a visit at San Quentin and were walking to the car when she stopped abruptly and looked back over her shoulder toward the guard tower. *I can feel their guns trained right on my back*, she said stoically. The next day, she was arrested for buying guns for the Panthers.

Luba and her son Nick returned to San Francisco in 1995 after they surfaced in Chicago and resolved their case. When I got the invitation to their welcome home party, I decided to break my vow of distance just this once. I got there late and Luba was addressing the crowd, explaining the circumstances of their return. Their collective had miraculously eluded the FBI all these years, but they had finally decided there was no political point to remaining underground. They had successfully negotiated their surrender several months before. Two of the collective members had gone to prison but the rest of them were able to resume their public lives under the terms of the deal without implicating anyone else. Luba looked older, but she sounded unrepentant. She still wanted to figure out how to be a radical activist at this stage of her life.

She seemed genuinely happy to see me. *I've been haunted by our last conversation at Lands End*, she said when I went over to say hello. *Let's get together and talk*, she suggested before we were both separated by the crush of the party. I wondered what her thoughts were about our conversation. I wondered how she had managed to hang on to the same political commitment all these years. I tried to imagine what life was like for her, returning to San Francisco with a kid and the other members of her collective in prison. She left me a few messages, but I never called her back.

I bumped into her now and then, but didn't spend any time with her until Bush invaded Iraq in March 2003. Anise insisted that I skip work and go out with her to demonstrate. *You can't just hate this war in private, Mom!* she urged. *We have to get out in the streets or it won't mean anything.*

When we got downtown, the first people we bumped into heading toward the Civic Center congregating point were Luba and her son, Nick, whom Anise knew from high school. I wanted to turn around and run home, but I couldn't do that to Anise. As a makeshift affinity group, we swarmed across the city, chanting our anger at the faceless, looming skyscrapers and evading the police, the visible representatives of our oil-thirsty government. We didn't acknowledge the awkwardness or the irony of the situation, but I could tell that Luba was as glad as I was to be on the streets together again, now with our children, bracing for the slaughter to come.

Now I was walking aimlessly across the accessible pathways that had been constructed at Lands End to help tourists and other walkers more easily navigate its cataclysmic geography. The precipices were still there, but they had been disguised as scenic overlooks with decorative railings. It seemed less likely that one misstep would condemn the walker forever, but was it so?

For the past twenty years, I had structured my life deliberately and carefully, trying to ignore, or at least distance, the myriad pitfalls, the multiplying cages, the meaningless massacres, because I had no healing answers to offer, no sage models to proffer. But, serendipitously, Rahim had reappeared and I was now reaching out to make contact through plexiglass, raising my fist with former comrades in court, waging battles that might cost me my job, and sharing long-disappeared memories of poetry and visions with my daughter.

The fog was rolling in, thick and indecipherable. I got back in the car. The *I Ching* was lying on the seat where I had left it. I wanted to wrap up the day with a breakthrough prophecy, a clairvoyant road map that would point me toward a life-altering resolve. But I couldn't pick up the book.

I sat in the car and watched the waves attack the cliffs blindly, persistently, doggedly, until my phone beeped with a text message from Anise. *Where r u?* I turned on the engine and headed back home.

CAMOUFLAGE—
MAGGIE
2007

IF HE HADN'T STUMBLED CARELESSLY AGAINST ME AS I WAS RUSHING TO CROSS THE street, I might never have noticed him. I was late for my shift on the Ortho ward and already irritated that Gordon had been too busy skateboarding to let me know he wouldn't be home after school. So when I felt the man's body weight slump onto mine, I almost shoved him rudely away before I saw his dayglo-orange uniform and the chains shackling his feet. If I had pushed him, he would have crumbled downward, helpless, on the pavement below.

Sorry, Miss. Clay here seems to have lost his balance. The man in the crisply ironed olive green uniform and buffed black shoes was tugging on Clay in a clumsy, misplaced effort to get him upright on his feet. Clay was staggering, trying to stabilize himself, but I could tell immediately from his labored breathing and the sweat rolling down the dark wrinkles of his face that the stumble was caused by more than his chains.

I think he needs to sit down, not stand up, I said and began to help Clay settle himself on the curb of the sidewalk. When the guard seemed to hesitate about following the instructions of a small, non-uniformed woman regarding his prisoner, I added in my most commanding voice, *I'm a nurse*, and flashed my ID badge at him. *This man may be having a heart attack. We need to call the ER across the street to come get him.*

That seemed to shake Mr. Olive Green up a little. I wasn't sure about the heart attack, but I imagined that this burly guard wouldn't want to explain a death on his watch.

Okay, I guess. He has an appointment with some other department. He fumbled for a paper in his pocket. *Maybe my partner has the paper. He went to get some food at the cafeteria, which is why I'm here by myself. We usually escort the inmates in teams, you know.* He was explaining this to me as if I were the supervisor he might have to justify things to back at the jail.

Neurology. Clay's breathing had calmed down enough for him to talk. His voice was gravelly but surprisingly deliberate. *I have an appointment with the neurology specialist because I've been having trouble with my balance lately.*

Abruptly, I realized that I hadn't talked directly to the man himself before he spoke. He was an orange-suited inmate and I had chosen to communicate with the commander in olive green instead. I appreciated that Clay wanted to take authority over his own condition.

Thank you. Can you tell me what has been happening lately?

I didn't want to do an intake interview. But, now that I had heard his voice, I needed to know what he had to say. Despite his distress, Clay quickly described his history of severe headaches, visual impairment, nausea, and increasingly frequent falls that had been ignored for more than two years.

He left the accusation of malpractice unstated. I was drawing my own conclusions when the ER team arrived.

Thank you, Miss—

Rafferty. Maggie Rafferty.

Only when Clay grabbed my hand to say goodbye could I feel the clawing panic beneath his sharp clinical observations.

I will check on you later, Clay, I told him as the guard was pulling him away. *I work in orthopedics, but I'll try and come down and see how you're doing later on.*

By now, I was very late for work. I knew that Belinda, the nurse I was supposed to relieve, would be drumming her fingers in exasperation even while she continued to cover for me. I started to cross the street again.

Watch where you're going! I spat furiously at a skateboarder who nearly collided with me as he sailed recklessly through the crosswalk, his camouflage pants and punk orange hair billowing in the wind.

You don't give a shit about anyone but yourself! I yelled at his receding silhouette, trying vainly to slow his arrogance down. He wasn't only risking his own skin. There were those who weren't privileged to move about freely as he could. Those tied down by canes, walkers, wheelchairs, and chains. But his eyes were riveted on the next thrilling slope ahead, and his thrusting army-booted foot had already propelled him way past earshot.

As I made my way through the crowded hospital hallway, filled with nurses who were getting off their day shifts, I tried to shake the image of Clay's chained feet. In orthopedics I had come to appreciate the importance of feet as the bedrock foundation for the rest of the body. Walking through the hospital corridors, I often found myself speculating on the size, shape, and muscle tone of the vast array of feet that stood beneath the fancy Nine West heels, the chic Dr. Martens boots, the athletic Nikes, and the utilitarian Keens. A cool shoe might well conceal a gnarled and desperate foot. But there was no way to disguise the chains that entangled laceless, sneakered feet.

When I got to the break room to hang up my coat, I noted that Candelaria, the unit clerk, was wearing yet another pair of Payless super-sandals that were certain to destroy her back and her feet sooner or later. As usual, she was poring over the astrology section of the paper, trying to find an ordained path out of her repeated, predictable heartbreaks.

Where have you been, Maggie? Everyone's asking for you at the desk 'cause you're never late. Gemini are supposed to have an unexpected encounter today. Is that what kept you?

She giggled suggestively. I wanted to go over and shake some sense into her. If she spent less time looking at magical astrological forecasts for solutions and more on owning her fatal mistakes when it came to men, she would, I was sure, get much further.

My son was late getting home, was all that I said in return.

Belinda had waited past the end of her shift to give me her report. She was the one person on this ward I could rely on to be there when I needed her.

What's going on, sweetie? Must be something serious to make you late!

She listened closely as I described my encounter with Clay.

Shackles, so appropriate for these guys who can hardly put one foot in front of the other, she responded, shaking her silver hair angrily. *I hear that in the ICU there are twenty-four-hour guards paid triple-time standing watch over prisoners on life support. A great use of taxpayer money! We should really get a petition going about the shackles. It's obscene!*

I appreciated Belinda's bluntness and outspoken attitude though, as usual, she was taking it further than I meant to go. She seemed to invite a constant fight, like Gordon's *Challenge Authority* T-shirt, which he insisted on wearing to school despite my efforts to convince him that this would alienate his teachers, even in his alternative charter school. When he brought me a button that said *Question Authority, But Not Your Mother,* I had to laugh. I realized that he would only stop questioning my authority if he figured out more hidden ways of getting around it.

I don't know about the petition, I answered Belinda, *but I want to try and make sure that the people in the ER aren't intimidated by Mr. Olive Green and his impressive badge and see to it that Clay gets the treatment he needs.*

What's his last name? Maybe I can check on his status on my way out, Belinda offered.

I almost cried when I realized that I had never gotten this simple, crucial piece of information. Was Clay his first name or his last name? In the tumult of the moment, I had forgotten all of my professional training about procuring necessary data. Belinda tried to make excuses for my omission and I swore that I would go search for Clay personally in the ER as soon as I could take a minute from the floor.

When I finally made it down to Emergency on my break hours later, I tried to describe Clay to the unit clerk at the desk.

A prisoner. Elderly. African-American. He was having trouble breathing. Wearing an orange jumpsuit. The description blurted out before I realized how hopelessly generic it was.

The clerk scanned the computer records, disinterestedly.

Since they signed the new contract with SF County Jail, we're getting more inmates all the time. Several today before my shift began. None of them named Clay. All of them discharged already.

Clay must have been a nickname. It was the officer who called him that and I hadn't even questioned whether it was the name *he* wanted to be called. It could have even been a taunt—feet of clay—assigned by the guard to humiliate the stumbling man. I had repeated it without thinking. Now I had no way to identify him, no way to ever find him again.

That night, I dreamt about Bobby. When we first broke up, after Gordon was born in 1991, Bobby would flit winsomely before me at random moments. While I painstakingly helped a hip patient adjust to crutches after surgery, Bobby would appear with his scraggly ponytail (a beguiling cross between a hippie and a biker), and I thought I could hear his melodic, beseeching voice whispering in my ear.

Bobby had fine hips and a workhorse back, but that didn't keep him from using *me* as a crutch when he stumbled home, drunk and raving, from the bars on Haight Street during the final years of our affair. When I first met him, his guitar rhapsodies and healing hands had bewitched me. After waitressing all day and going to nursing school at night, Bobby would cradle my weary feet in his inspired hands, touching the precise reflex points that could release my pain, while humming "Early Morning Rain," our favorite Gordon Lightfoot song.

Unlike my father, who had been a raging, brutal bull when he got drunk, Bobby became a pied piper after a few drinks. My father yelled ancient Gaelic curses at all the real and imaginary foes who had victimized him throughout his life, while Bobby strummed magical incantations, infusing all the furious, sad, and scared victims who cared to listen to him with his harmonic power.

Over time, Bobby seemed to lose the capacity to transform *their* fury and fear. Instead, he began to absorb it all into his core. Maybe it was the homeless vets he hung out with who mixed their agent orange–induced disabilities, their PTSD, and their endless war stories with alcohol to produce a fatal potion. Or maybe it was some hidden genetic flaw, the same one that had warped my father and might even be silently hibernating inside of me.

But really, I believed that it was the nights he spent in County Jail, down at 850 Bryant, that put him over some invisible mental edge. He had gotten caught up in one of the crazy drug war stings that swept the Haight while I was pregnant. One of his PTSD-twisted buddies had fingered Bobby as a way of helping himself. I bailed Bobby out as quickly as I could and hired a lawyer to prove that there was no way he could be involved in the absurd cross-border conspiracy they had implicated him in. His charges were dropped, but his other friends weren't as lucky.

In the year after Gordon was born, Bobby's melancholy harmonies turned into discordant dirges about government plots and planetary destruction. His apocalyptic night terrors kept me awake more than Gordon's voracious feedings. COINTELPRO, CIA conspiracies, international torture rings, government surveillance, genetically poisoned foods, global deforestation. Grains of terrible truth sprinkled amid paranoid delusions, but at a certain point I no longer cared to distinguish which was which. I had a job to get to in the morning, piles of homework to finish, and a new baby to nourish.

One night, Bobby woke me, hysterical, just as I was dozing off while nursing Gordon. *We need to put a hex on them, Maggie baby. An ancient Irish curse. Stop them from fucking up the planet any more. We have to do it to make the world safe for Gordon,* he pleaded. Desperate for sleep, I began to push Bobby out of the house. As I shoved him down the stairs, into the windy fog of Downey Street, everything I had plugged down inside me for months heaved up at him.

He was the one who was poisoning Gordon, I screamed. I hadn't escaped my father's booze-drenched house in San Jose and worked my way through nursing school to end up with a crazy, pathetic, hallucinating drunk who would destroy my child. Gordon would grow up whole and free of torment.

It was a dreadful, hurting, unforgivable scene. Even while I was yelling, I swore that I would never live through one like that again. At some point, Bobby looked up at me, and for that moment he was sober and clear.

You're right, Maggie. Gordon doesn't deserve this. I'll stay away.

Once he was gone, I became a forward-focused laser. Work and Gordon were my only anchors. After a while, I even succeeded at banning all apparitions of Bobby, first from the hospital and then from my sleep. At some point, I bumped into one of his friends on Haight Street who reported that Bobby had moved to New Orleans, had found some steady music gigs, and had been clean and sober for a few years.

Occasionally, Gordon would ask about his father, and I would always make it clear that he could look him up someday if he wanted. For my part, I thought we were both better off without him. And Gordon, who was skateboarding his way through life, didn't put his feet on the ground long enough to pursue a father he had never known.

That night, after Clay stumbled at my feet, I wandered through Golden Gate Park with Bobby, as we had countless times when we first got together, exploring hidden pathways, discovering new exotic flowers, weaving fantasies about our future. At one point Bobby tripped on the tendrils of a gorgeous orange flower that had overstepped the soil bed and was spreading out onto the pathway. When I leaned over to smell the blossoms, he hissed hysterically,

They're not what they seem to be. They look innocent and safe, but they're nonnative weeds that the government has encrypted with surveillance devices.

I tried to calm him down, to persuade him that this was just a flashback to his old paranoid state, but as I was trying to placate him, I could see that the iridescent orange flowers were multiplying uncontrollably before our eyes.

In the light of day, I began to see orange everywhere. Orange shrouded men, and occasional women, proliferated in the crammed corridors of the hospital. Aged men with creased faces and soiled suits who, like Clay, struggled to keep themselves balanced against the willful tugs of their guards. Large, bold men who tried to stride purposefully as if there were nothing binding their determined feet. Pregnant women whose engorged feet pushed and swelled from the tongues of their undersized, frayed sneakers, their eyes blindly accusing everyone in their path. While hospital staff, patients, and visitors painstakingly looked around or through them, my eyes were riveted on the fear-coded fluorescence of their orange marking.

At night, the TV tube's flicker transfixed me with an unrelenting lineup of orange jumpsuits. No names, no faces, just the outline of men's bodies branded in orange, accompanied by a mantra of official reasons. Detained at Guantánamo for terrorism reasons. Tortured at Abu Ghraib for intelligence reasons. Drowned in a jail cell by Katrina's floodwaters for natural disaster reasons. I began to keep a log in my nightstand, documenting all the virulent variants of orange that were infecting the planet.

Orange had been one of my favorite colors—the burnished orange of the Golden Gate Bridge. The party-bright orange of the San Francisco Giants. The happy, carefree orange of the California poppy. A color too brashly bold for my wardrobe but one I could secretly paint on my toenails, hidden to everyone but Bobby and me. Gordon was conceived by the light of an orange-scented candle that Bobby brought me when he moved into my house. And just before I bumped into Clay, I had let Candelaria convince me to have my colors read by a color specialist friend of hers one evening during our dinner break. Surprisingly, the woman claimed that my dominant aura was orange, although I had never admitted to anyone that I liked that color.

The apricot in you makes you thoughtful, and the pumpkin gives you great self-discipline, but you need to access your bright power orange to bring out the vitality that is buried deep inside.

She encouraged me to surround myself with orange aromas and accessories. I was skeptical, but still I hennaed my hair to bring out its auburn highlights, sprinkled turmeric in the stir fry meals I cooked for me and Gordon, and planted bright marigolds in my bedroom window box. Now I began to regret these small changes. Instead of offering me private, energizing pleasure, orange was tying me to a universe of alarm and loathing.

When I walked into the break room one evening at work and saw Candelaria crying convulsively, my impulse was to turn around and walk out stealthily before she saw I was there. Whether it was the scuffed tennis shoes she was wearing in place of her usual wannabe elegant sandals, or the undammed wrenching of her sobs, something stopped me from fleeing. I sat down next to her and put my hand on her shoulder.

What's going on, Cande? I asked, my voice clipped and professional.

She looked up dazed, as if she had forgotten that anything could interrupt her grief. For a split second she hesitated, scanning my face to see whether I could be trusted with the answer she was about to give. Then her words came gushing out.

It's my sister, Celestina. Last week they denied her parole for the third time. Then yesterday, while she was out in the yard, one of the guards said something nasty to her about the Parole Board not wanting man-killers like her on the streets, and she began scream-ing back at him. So they sprayed her all over with orange crush and put her in the hole. She finally was able to call my mother today. She said that they were threatening to put her on suicide watch if she didn't stop screaming and crying.

My mother is usually the calm one, but now she can't stop screaming and crying. She keeps saying this is all wrong and we have to figure out something to do, something to make the Parole Board understand that Tina shouldn't be in there anymore.

I couldn't believe what I was hearing. Somehow, I had tripped again into a parallel universe filled with guards, yards, holes, and—had I heard her right?—a spray called orange crush. And ditzy, luck-starved Candelaria had a sister who was one of its inhabitants.

What's orange crush? It wasn't the place to start, but I couldn't stop the question.

Some stuff they spray on the girls in there when they're out of control. It's like pepper spray but much, much stronger. It makes them bright orange all over and stays on the skin for a few days. If you try and wash it off, it burns you worse.

I pictured a woman who looked like Candelaria, her streaming, dark hair embedded with orange chemicals, writh-ing on the ground, unable to escape from her smoldering skin.

Why did they call her a man-killer?

The question sounded accusatory, even though I hadn't meant it that way. But Cande seemed glad that I wanted to hear the story.

She didn't kill anyone! She left her boyfriend 'cause he kept beating her up. She was scared he would hurt the kids. He found out where she was and started leaving notes in her mailbox saying he would kill the kids and she would be responsible for their deaths. So finally she asked some friends to shake him up a little, try and make him stop. They went and shot him, but it was only in the legs and he was out of the hospital in a couple of days. Still, they arrested her and she got convicted of trying to kill him. She never even was near him the day it happened, and she got a seven-years-to-life sentence.

That doesn't seem right, I said cautiously. It was always hard to tell what was truth and what was dramatic embellishment in Cande's stories. It didn't make sense that a woman in twenty-first-century California could get a life sentence for a murder that hadn't even happened.

Which is it? Seven years or life?

It's all up to the Parole Board. She's already been in there ten years, and they've turned her down three times already. If they don't want to let her out, she may never be with her kids again!

I put my arms around Cande, trying helplessly to soothe her, and I caught the scent of orange blossom oil, which the color therapist had recommended to settle the nerves.

Maggie, could you talk to my mother, try and calm her down? Cande pleaded. Before I thought about it, I said yes.

It's a bad joke, this system they call justice, Amapola had declared to me as soon as I had introduced myself over the phone. I had imagined that her mother would be an older version of Cande—talkative, endearing, and hopelessly confused. Instead, Amapola laid out her case against the system with clear, documented authority.

Before all of this, she explained, *I believed in the system. When the neighbors complained to me about the cops who patrolled our neighborhood like* zopilotes, *I thought they were just trying to protect their bad kids, who were into drugs and gangs. When the daughter of my best friend at work went to jail for drug trafficking, I couldn't believe that it was just the boyfriend's fault, even though I didn't argue with my friend about it.*

So when they arrested Celestina, I was worried but trusted that once the lawyers and the jury and the judges knew the truth, it would all work out. They would see how she had been beaten, stalked, and harassed by this bruto and put him into prison, not Celestina, who had never been in trouble with the law or drugs before she met him.

The lawyer I hired, and mortgaged my house for, slept through half the trial. He never called any witnesses about Celestina's character, none of the teachers from the beauty school Tina was attending, none of the priests from our family's church, none of her many friends from Whittier, where she had grown up and lived all her life. But the prosecution brought all Javier's buddies from the construction company where he worked. He made it sound like Celestina was a crazy, wild dope fiend who was just jealous about an affair Javier was having. In fact, Javier was the one who had introduced Tina to drugs in the first place and was always madly jealous even when she just walked down to the corner store.

The jury never even saw the pictures that I had taken when Tina was black and blue after one of Javier's beatings. The judge said they weren't relevant to the case at hand. My lawyer assured me that the most that Tina could get was five years. When I heard the words "seven to life," all my faith evaporated, poof!

I was blind but now I see, as they say, but in my situation it didn't work the way the Bible meant it to.

Now she could see that the judges, the lawyers, the Parole Board, maybe even God, were all part of the conspiracy to keep her daughter locked up by concealing the truth. She had tried legal appeal after appeal, but Celestina was still in prison. Now she knew that she had to rely on herself and her family. Recently she had discovered an organization that worked with women prisoners, Unshackled Women. They seemed as outraged as she was by this so-called justice system. They promised to work with her to get her daughter out and all the other women who were victims of the same cruel set-up.

When she heard that Celestina had been sprayed with orange crush, Amapola had tried to call the warden at the prison. When she couldn't reach anyone, she wrote a letter.

How can you burn a woman because she has lost her faith in freedom? How can you scald her with an orange chemical that leaves her skin blistering and then throw her in a hole and let the poison consume her? What kind of human beings are you?

So what can we do now? I asked her on the phone, swept into action by her scathing condemnation. Among Ama's long list of things we could do was the Parole Board's monthly public hearing, where loved ones and others could plead their case to the commissioners.

Please come with us. It would mean so much to Cande, and you and I could get to know each other better. I couldn't say no. I had to get to know this woman who was on a mission to uncover the truth. A woman whose name, *Amapola*, was a bright orange poppy.

I expected Belinda to applaud me when I asked her to cover my shift so that I could go up to the Parole Board with Cande and Amapola. We were sitting in her apartment on Ashbury surrounded by her dogs and candles.

Just know what you're getting yourself into, Maggie, she cautioned. *Honey, I love you, but I know you keep your boundaries tight. If you're going to start stretching them, you have to be prepared to deal with unexpected consequences.*

Then she told me about a woman from her past who had asked for her help hiding an envelope with information about political refugees from Central America. The woman was very courageous, someone Belinda admired deeply. Belinda agreed to help, but when the woman disappeared suddenly and the FBI came to Belinda's door looking for her, she almost betrayed her friend before she turned the FBI away.

What happened to the woman? I asked, not exactly sure what the story had to do with me. Belinda sighed. *No nosy questions, Maggie. Just think about what I said.*

When I told Gordon that I was planning to go up to Sacramento to try and convince the Parole Board that a woman should be let out of prison, he stared at me as if I had announced that I was getting back together with Bobby.

That's cool, Mom, he said, choosing his words carefully, as if the wrong one might crack my resolve.

He went to the door and picked up his skateboard, and I thought the conversation had ended. But he put his board down suddenly and came back into the kitchen where I was preparing my evening meal to take to work.

You know, I went to court a few weeks ago for my friend Jabari. Some bullshit case about how he had violated a gang curfew when he isn't in a gang and didn't even know about the curfew. Luckily, the basketball coach and some of the teachers from school all showed up at court and told the judge how it was all a mistake and what a good kid Jabari was, and they dropped it. He could have ended up in juvie for no reason. That would have been it for him—his basketball career, everything.

I started to ask why he hadn't mentioned any of this to me before now, but I swallowed the nosy question before it slipped out.

I'm glad it ended up okay for your friend, I said. *Maybe it will work out that way for Celestina and her family.*

Sure, I hope it does too, Gordon called as he picked up his skateboard and slid out the door.

The plush chairs and commanding quiet of the Parole Board hearing room were a welcome relief after the two hour car ride where six of us were crammed into Cande's old, overheating Ford Focus along with enough junk food to feed an army. I had hoped to have some time in the car to talk with Amapola about our presentation to the Parole Board, but the constant clamor of Celestina's three kids made this impossible.

When I was first introduced to them, I had to choke down a laugh—Angelita, Angelique and Angelo. Clearly, Celestina had hoped that the karma of angels would envelop her kids. Sadly, the hoped for karma had not been enough to safeguard her against her boyfriend's punishing abuse. In the car, Angelita, the youngest who was ten, prattled nonstop about what she planned to do with her mother once she got out of prison.

First, I'm gonna take her to the new McDonald's that just opened down the block. You know, she's never even been to this one, but I told her all about it and about how Grandma takes me every Sunday and I get a Happy Meal. Then we're gonna go to Payless. They have the cutest sandals there now, either in turquoise or cinnamon, and she would look so hot in them. You know, she can only have tennis shoes in the prison and those awful baggy jeans. Last time we visited, we planned what we would bring her to wear when she was getting out once she got her parole date.

Angelita's words froze, when she realized that the parole date had not been granted and that's why we were now all driving up to convince the Parole Board to change their minds. But within a couple of seconds she was back on track, imagining the capris and halter tops that they would get at Target in the exact color to match the sandals.

Finally, Angelique who was twelve, told her to shut up, she was giving everyone a headache, and Angelita punched her. Angelo, the oldest, threatened to make them both stop talking for good if they kept it up.

They're just nervous because this is their big day to speak in front of the Parole Board, Cande apologized for her nieces and nephew. Amapola ignored most of it, and only occasionally looked up from the pile of legal papers she was poring over on her lap.

As we waited for the Parole Commissioners, surrounded by the huge oak columns of this lofty chamber, I began to worry that we hadn't planned how to present ourselves to the Board in our speeches or our clothing. I had been careful to wear pale, nondescript colors that blended with the muted, orderly hues that dyed the walls and carpeted the floors of the hearing chamber. But Angelita's brilliant lime capris, Angelique's hot-pink sundress, Angelo's bright-red T-shirt, and even Amapola's tangerine-flowered blouse defied the understated balance of the chambers. The commissioners might take one look at their clothing and dismiss everything they had to say.

Finally, they filed in wearing their prescription black, gray, and beige suits and sat down behind the long, massive mahogany table on the raised dais in front of the room. One commissioner kept fiddling with his phone; another couldn't seem to keep his eyes open, while his colleague scanned the people seated in the chamber with an unblinking stare. The one woman commissioner kept examining her impeccably polished nails. All of their faces were frozen in expressions that probably were meant to represent impartiality.

The head commissioner explained in an automated monotone that they welcomed public comment but each person would be strictly limited to three minutes. Each group could have a maximum of six presenters.

Remember, please abide by the three-minute rule, he chided before the first speaker even had a chance to open her mouth.

Two groups of family members and supporters made presentations on behalf of their prisoners before Celestina's turn came. One man had a twenty-five-to-life sentence for having killed a pedestrian while high on meth. He had served thirty-three years. His lawyer scolded the Board angrily.

Mr. Baldwin has not had a single disciplinary in thirty-three years. Do you know how hard that is to achieve? He has taken every AA and NA class the system has to offer, and he's the president of his AA group at Corcoran. Still, you tell him at each Board hearing that he needs to take more drug rehabilitation classes. There's nothing more he can do!

The other man had a third strike with a twenty-five-to-life sentence for stealing a video. His family had just found out that he had liver cancer, with less than a year to live.

Please, grant him compassionate release. Let him die with us at home, his father pleaded to the commissioners, who nodded perfunctorily at the end of the man's passionate entreaty.

The scene made me remember my father's constant complaints, when I was a child, about the bureaucrats whose offices he cleaned at the San Jose Sheriff's Department.

They look like humans and talk like humans, but they are aliens who have taken over human bodies and sucked out all their vital organs so there is nothing left but a glossy, hollow shell. A torrent of bitterness from a sour, failed man, I thought at the time. Now his description hit the nail on the head.

Amapola had asked a woman named Luba, who worked with Unshackled Women, to begin the testimony about

Celestina. Her opinion wouldn't seem tainted by family bias, Amapola whispered to me. Luba was wearing muted colors, and her summary of Celestina's story was clear and concise. Still, her husky voice was laced with muffled fury. I pictured her pulling out a cleverly concealed gun and shooting purposefully and precisely, shattering the airless bell jar that hung over the dais into a million incandescent shards of glass.

Next, Angelique talked about all the ways her mother had tried to help her get through life even while she was in prison. *If she was out here with me, I know I could really be a better person in so many ways*, Angelique confessed and then started to cry.

The woman commissioner said, *Thank you, dear. I'm sure it must be very hard for you*, and we all gratefully took this as a sign that Celestina's story had gotten through to at least one of them.

Angelo testified that he remembered when Javier would beat his mother and he would try to push him away, but he was only four and was unable to stop him. It seemed like Angelo might break down also, but Amapola put her hand on his arm, and he thanked the commissioners for their time and sat back down. Then Amapola described how her belief in the system had been shattered by the trial, but even after that she had still tried to work through the courts with no result.

Please restore my faith in the possibility of justice, she begged and tapped Angelita, who seemed to be lost in her own world, to make her presentation. She read from a paper with the words she had carefully prepared.

My mother knew she was going to prison when she had me. She named me Angelita because she needed another angel to watch over her. I've tried to be her guardian angel since I was little.

Sometimes at night when I say my prayers I picture myself flying through the bars on her window, picking her up in my arms, and flying out of there with her. Maybe that's wrong because you still think she needs to be in prison, but I know she's a good woman and I just want to protect her and bring her home.

For a moment there was profound silence. Then the woman commissioner broke the spell. *Thank you, dear. I'm sure it must be very hard for you,* she said. This time I realized that the phrase was simply a canned recording she cued up at moments like these to stop us from seeing that beneath their pressed suits they were all naked monsters.

How dare you pretend that you're listening to us? was all I could think of saying as I got up to make my presentation. But before I could get to the microphone, the head commissioner announced that we had run over our time and they had to end the presentations. He thanked us all and they began to file out the door with robotic precision.

We had three minutes each for six presentations and I'm the sixth person. I've come all this way, and I think you owe me the courtesy of listening for three more minutes to why this woman deserves to be free. I was shouting into the microphone, my voice shrill against their receding backs. I could feel Amapola's hand on me trying to calm my shaking body.

Maybe they all have to go to the bathroom bad, Angelita said. Her foolish, joking excuse was more than I could bear.

I need to go to the bathroom, I muttered as I hurried away.

I sat in the stall a long time. My body was burning up as if I had been sprayed with orange crush. They had humiliated, manipulated, battered us with their disdainful silence. We only had words to fight with—righteous, passionate, sorrowful words—that had bounced off their black, gray, and beige suits. What could possibly dent their flawless armor?

Through the crack in the stall door, I noticed a sliver of beige and heard the tap of the perfectly matched tan heels that the woman commissioner was wearing. Before I could plan what I would do, I opened the door and walked up to her as she was washing her hands at the sink. When she saw me standing still and quiet, she grew pale beneath her powdered skin.

Can I help you? she asked in that voice that oozed sweet concern while dashing all hopes for relief. There was nothing reasonable I could say in reply.

And then it happened. I began to chant my father's Gaelic hex. Countless times I had listened to him heave the curse at his bosses, his neighbors, his dead wife, my mother, as I sat silent in my room, grateful that the curses weren't being launched at me. If I had tried deliberately to remember the words I wouldn't have been able to, but now I recited them with complete certainty.

Go n-ithe an cat thú is go n-ithe an diabhal an cat. Go n-ithe an cat thú is go n-ithe an diabhal an cat. May the cat eat you and the devil eat the cat.

When I asked my father, when he was sober, what the curse meant, he snorted and warned me that it was an ancient Irish secret to be used only against those who truly deserved it, or else it would ricochet back and destroy the person who pronounced it.

Go n-ithe an cat thú is go n-ithe an diabhal an cat, I continued, standing close enough to her that I almost gagged on
the smell of her flowery perfume. For a few moments, it was
a standoff. The chant transfixed her. She was trapped, hanging onto the sink's edge, petrified under the fluorescent light's
glare. Until she realized that there was nothing but mad words
hurling through the bathroom's sterile space to keep her there.

She tore herself away, but her beige stiletto heel caught on
some invisible crack in the seamless floor, tripping her up and
ripping her stockings. Still she kept going, grabbed the doorknob, and lunged through the opening, trying to escape the
chant that had held her captive for a few moments and would
continue to do so if the spell worked its magic as I hoped it
would.

I never told Belinda the whole story, even though she wanted
to hear everything that had happened that day. I did tell her
that I was very angry after the hearing, angrier than I had been
for years. My anger was a bubbling clot coursing through my
bloodstream, but I didn't know how I could help Celestina,
Cande, or Amapola anymore. The problem was a gaping, in-
operable wound, beyond my skills as a simple nurse, a single
mother.

I didn't tell Belinda that I assaulted the lady commissioner
with a Gaelic hex. I didn't tell her that I thought I was teetering
on the brink of the same cliff that Bobby had sailed over but
couldn't let that happen. For Gordon's sake.

With her brass tacks sense, Belinda suggested that one
thing I could do was to donate to Celestina's legal fund. I sent

half my next paycheck to Amapola and a smaller check to Unshackled Women. They seemed to plug away at such efforts without going crazy, and for that alone they deserved to be supported.

I told Cande that I was glad I had met her family and understood what they were up against. But my priority right now, besides work, was to help Gordon get through the next few semesters so he could graduate high school on time. Cande nodded distractedly and shared the latest news. They had let Celestina out of the hole, and her horoscope predicted that the next year would bring a good turn of fortune.

I think that lady commissioner will look into Tina's situation and next hearing they'll let her out, she said brightly.

Gordon seemed mildly glad when I switched up some of my shifts so I could spend more evenings with him. Some of the time I helped him with his homework and some of the time we watched videos about skateboarding, windsurfing, and other thrilling, unfettered obsessions. I began a meditation class in the mornings in Golden Gate Park. I breathed in the early morning fog, allowing it to moisten my inflamed lungs and ease my raspy respirations. When I bumped into orange-suited prisoners hobbling through the hospital corridors, I inhaled deeply and visualized myself in a blossoming valley surrounded by purple velvet mountains. I began to feel calmer, more centered. Until I met Rahim.

After I came back from Sacramento, Belinda saw that I couldn't handle the tangle of shackles that threatened to enmesh my life. So she had been quietly fixing the nursing assignments so I would avoid having to care for a prisoner. But as soon as Belinda went on vacation to visit her mother in LA, Clarence Jackson, SF County Jail prisoner, appeared on my patient roster. I immediately decided to go to Ginny, the head nurse, and tell her some story about why it was impossible for me to deal professionally with a prisoner patient. But Ginny was nowhere to be found and I could see it was time for Mr. Jackson's pain meds. I couldn't stand to see a patient suffer needlessly, so reluctantly I went to administer his meds, just this one time.

I flashed my badge at the man who was conspicuously guarding the door to Clarence Jackson's room, and I deliberately ignored the guard who was sitting in the room's only chair, flipping through the channels on the TV. Clarence Jackson was lying on his side in pale blue hospital-issue pajamas, looking out toward the window where the afternoon sunlight was filtering calmly through the shades. His orange jumpsuit hung limply from the hook on the door.

Good afternoon, Mr. Jackson. My name is Maggie, and I will be giving you your medication after I take your vital signs.

Please call me Rahim, he said in a deep, mellow voice. He rolled painfully over to face me and I heard the rattle of his chains. His difficulty with moving wasn't only due to his back injury. I bent over to help him adjust his position.

Rahim, may I look at your feet? I want to make sure that your leg restraints are on properly.

Hard to be proper when you're talking about chains, he said and laughed before I had a chance to feel bad about using such a stupid word.

When I pulled the blanket back from his feet, I could see immediately that they were swollen and discolored. I turned crossly to the guard who was still playing with the remote.

The restraints are too tight. They are interfering with Mr. Jackson's circulation, and this is bad as he is having surgery tomorrow. They need to be removed right away.

It took the startled guard a minute to fully register what I had demanded.

The inmate's restraints cannot be removed until he goes to surgery. Only once he is in the operating room can they be removed. He recited the rules mechanically from some manual he had memorized.

Well, if they can't be removed, they must be loosened. See how puffy his feet are getting? This is a medical priority. I couldn't remember anything from the long e-mail the nursing staff had been sent about hospital policies for dealing with inmates, but I knew that this wasn't right.

Without acknowledging what I had said, the guard got up out of his seat and began to fumble with his key ring, searching for the one that could release Rahim's strangled feet. I was about to snap at him to hurry up when I looked over at Rahim. He had an amused smile on his face, and when he saw me looking his way he put a finger over his lips to discourage me from saying anything more. Eventually, the guard found the correct key and within a few moments, with my oversight, he had adjusted the chains.

Thank you, Maggie, Rahim said, glancing at my ID badge to make sure he got my name right.

After I gave him his meds, I told him that I would be his nurse till 11:00 p.m. I would check in on him in a couple of hours, but if he had any problems at all, I said, tilting my head in the guard's direction, he shouldn't hesitate to ring the call bell.

It's all good now, he said pleasantly. Then he flashed me a large smile that instantly made me feel calmer.

The rest of my shift was busy with the usual array of backs, necks, and knees, but I didn't forget to look in on Rahim regularly. Each time I checked his feet, I also asked him about his level of pain. I had read his chart and knew that with three herniated discs he had to be hurting.

I'm okay. I've learned to tolerate a lot of pain over the years. I can't let them dope me up too much. They'd like nothing better than for me to become oblivious to what's going on around me. His description was matter-of-fact, not macho. I tried to imagine what it was like to live each day in a cage of pain and not allow oneself the luxury of chemical escape.

How long have you been in prison?

He looked at me a moment, as if gauging what he should say.

Two years at 850 Bryant. Hardly any exercise there. I kept myself in pretty good shape for over twenty-eight years, but these last two have destroyed my back.

He could probably tell that I was trying to process the information, the crushing weight of thirty years, without letting my reactions reach my face.

No, I'm not a serial killer, though they're trying to make it seem like I am, Rahim reassured me. *You probably heard about me when they first brought me back to San Francisco. The evil Black Panther responsible for every crime under the sun back in the sixties and seventies.*

I vaguely remembered Belinda commenting on some story like this. The kind of story that reminded me of Bobby's conspiracy paranoias. The kind of story that usually made me want to change the subject.

Were you a Black Panther? My voice was barely audible so as not to awaken the current guard who seemed to be dozing in his chair. I knew that Rahim heard the question, even though he didn't respond immediately, because the lines around his eyes puckered into deeper creases.

Tell you what, Maggie. If I make it through this surgery, if they don't accidentally, purposely overdose me on anesthetic in the OR, I will tell you some true stories about me.

Oh, you're going to be fine! You have one of the best back surgeons on our team. You need to think positively. Try to get some sleep now. I delivered my nursing mantra emphatically. He nodded and allowed himself to close his eyes as I double checked his legs and straightened up his twisted sheets and blankets.

I was just about to leave the room when I heard a moan. A throttled, punishing lament from deep inside Rahim's chest. Just the other side of consciousness, Rahim's velvet voice could no longer camouflage his anguish.

I'll be meditating for you, tomorrow, I whispered, leaving both men dozing restlessly together in the room.

I tried hard to meditate the next morning. I tried to ease my lungs with cooling vapor. I tried to empty my thoughts and be present with each in-and-out breath. But the siren glare of orange was again overtaking my mind. I could visualize Rahim making it through the surgery. I could imagine us walking through the hallways on the rehabilitative route that I took with my post-op patients. But once he returned to his bed, once the therapeutic respite was over for the day, I couldn't visualize him without his chains. I couldn't envision his release from the confines of thirty-year-old walls. And unless I could do that for him, I wasn't sure what good the rest could be.

Rahim was strong. Within a day after surgery he was able to get up and ambulate for a little bit. I discovered that Belinda had recently won a small battle in the realm of hospital policy when she insisted that post-op inmates be allowed to walk without chains as a necessary part of their treatment plan. I carved out extra time on my schedule to spend walking with Rahim.

We circled round and round, past the brightly painted wall mural of Haight Street, which depicted cute pastel storefronts and rainbow-colored people strolling around without any panhandlers or drunks to spoil the scene. We paused to gaze out the ward's best picture window that boasted a postcard view of the Golden Gate Bridge, the lush green hills of Marin in the distance, and birds soaring effortlessly on the crystal blue horizon. Even though there were two guards trailing somewhere behind us, our conversation fanned out far beyond the circular track around the ward that we had to follow.

Rahim told me about growing up in San Jose, on the other side of town from where I spent my childhood. *When I was in high school, I would hitch up to Frisco almost every weekend to check out the action in the City—the Fillmore jazz clubs, the hippies, the Panthers. I planned to move to Frisco and work my way through San Francisco State, but as soon as I turned eighteen in '67 I was drafted to Nam. Got a bullet in my hip right after I got there. When I was discharged 'cause I couldn't move like I needed to anymore, I came back to the Bay and hooked up with the Panthers right away.*

They helped me make sense of the war, along with everything else. I sold Panther papers, served breakfast to kids, and traveled to build Panther chapters in New Orleans, Pennsylvania, and Chicago. In 1970 I went to Cuba on the Venceremos Brigade. Being in a country that had actually made a revolution blew my mind. When I got back I started working with some of the white radicals I had met on the Brigade, connecting them to the Panther work and also the brothers at San Quentin. There was one woman in particular, Cassandra, but that's another story.

Those early years we were all filled with great hope. Even when Panthers started getting framed, arrested, and killed, we thought these were just temporary setbacks. Even after we understood that the FBI was determined to destroy us with a program called COINTELPRO, we still believed that we could figure out new ways to build the movement.

Somehow Rahim managed to stay alive and out of prison till 1977 when he was framed for the killing of a San Francisco police officer, a conviction he had been trying to overturn ever since. Next they convicted him of being the mastermind behind another officer's killing in Philadelphia, even though he was three thousand miles away when it happened. And now, thirty years later, there was this surreal, post-9/11 cold case. This time he and his supporters were determined to expose the lies and defeat the government's plans to make him and the Panthers a symbol of domestic terrorism.

Bobby's tales of COINTELPRO had been secondhand, formless, and fear-soaked. Rahim's stories were a precise, fierce indictment. Yet he still believed there was a road forward, a path to change, and he began to convince me that there was one too.

There are so many things that can be done! So many tools the movement can use—habeas writs, international tribunals, grassroots mobilizations, direct action, hip-hop exposés, street art manifestos. And now, with the internet, the possibilities are endless! The rhythm of his ideas swept me up even though I hardly understood what he meant by many of them. My own visions began simmering in response, seeking an outlet for action.

While Rahim recovered, I got to know the different guards whose job it was to protect the staff and other patients from him and to make sure, at all costs, that he didn't escape. Most of them were haters who would have been just as glad if Rahim had died on the operating table. But a few, like Carlos, were people who understood that if he hadn't gotten a job guarding prisoners, he might have ended up in prison. They were the ones who took time to make sure, on their own, that Rahim's leg restraints weren't constricting his circulation. The ones who sometimes bent the rules and left the room for a few minutes to hang out with the other guard who was standing watch in the hall, giving Rahim and me a few minutes to talk in private while I checked his vitals and gave him his medication.

During one of these times, I told Rahim about Celestina and the Parole Board hearing. I tried to make the end of the story a joke—me yelling Gaelic curses into the ear of the lady commissioner in a government building john, but he seemed to take it seriously.

Hey, nothing wrong with using folk magic against the man, or in this case the woman. I used to be skeptical of all that but came to learn there are more dimensions to change than any of us can see and name. He paused and looked at me closely. *As long as you don't let the magic mess up your own head.*

Another time, I noticed how one of Rahim's ankles was becoming chafed and red under his ankle cuffs, despite our efforts to make sure that the restraints were loose enough.

These people are such cruel fools, I cried. *How can they think that a prisoner could escape from a hospital?*

Well, it's happened, Rahim replied. Then he told me a story about a Puerto Rican prisoner, William Morales, who was part of a group fighting for Puerto Rico's independence back in the seventies. A bomb he was making blew up and he lost most of his fingers. After he was arrested, Morales landed in Bellevue Hospital, in New York City, where he was being fitted for artificial hands. One day, miraculously, he escaped.

No hands, but somehow he managed to climb down the hospital wall on a rope of elastic bandages he had devised. Ended up in Cuba where he still lives today. That's the kind of story they *never forget no matter how absurd it seems to shackle us when we can barely move. Of course, our side will never ever forget it either. That's the stuff our freedom dreams are made of.*

When I told Belinda the tale of William Morales, her face lit up. *Caramba, that is a fantasy come true!* Then she told me more about the woman from her past who was running from the FBI.

Turned out she was fighting for Puerto Rico's independence too, though she never told me that herself. Found it out from the FBI. Maybe she even knew William Morales. After I sent the FBI away, I was desperate to think of something I could do to help. So I put a hex on them—a crazy mezcla of Puerto Rican swear words and wicca incantations. They never caught her, so I like to think it helped a little.

That night my mind spun off its tracks. Could a hex really work? How did a fantasy become a plot? Did Morales have help? Was a nurse involved? The answers simmered amorphously, taking phantom shape and then dissolving, until at some point they morphed into a tangible plan.

When the doctor announced that Rahim was making impressive progress and should be able to leave the next day, I almost objected out loud. Instead, I accelerated my timetable. All day, between patients and notes and lab results and phone calls, I perfected the sequence. I confirmed that the amiable guard Carlos would be on duty the next morning when I too was scheduled to work. I would tell him that we needed to get in an extra walk through the corridor to prepare for Rahim's discharge. He would unlock Rahim's shackles, as he had many times before, and we would begin our stroll, circling slowly around the hospital corridor while Carlos and the other guard would distract themselves, talking about last night's baseball game or the hottest nurse on the floor.

When they were all mesmerized by the unbroken routine of the ambulatory circles—the repeated, familiar, trodden path that Rahim and I had followed dozens of times before—I would speed it up just before we passed the service elevator. The elevator would be parked on our floor, just as I had arranged, allegedly waiting for surplus storage items to be loaded. I would push Rahim into the elevator, press the close button, and it would descend rapidly, without a stop, to the basement. We would slide out the exit door, which opened directly onto the street, and drive swiftly away in my waiting car. The rest I would figure out with Rahim.

Just before the end of my shift, Rahim commented that I seemed distracted. I told him that I was concerned about Gordon, who had been staying out late without calling for the past couple of weeks, a half-truth that seemed to satisfy him. When I got home, I was relieved to find Gordon practicing skateboard tricks in front of our house.

I have to get this one down before my tournament next week, he told me. I sat on the steps and watched him work on his double kickflips, soaring and landing, landing and soaring, perfecting his brilliant airborne algorithm, until the chill of the night fog began to skew his balance and we both went inside.

When sleep finally came to me that night, it was painted with a warped mural. Chains lying in massive, forlorn heaps next to exploding fields of bright poppies in Golden Gate Park. Gaelic chants scrolled in angry sprawling graffiti across the locked shutters of the upscale stores on Haight Street. Birds drifting blindly across the Golden Gate Bridge carrying wilted, unnamed orange flowers in their pincered beaks.

But suddenly, there was the vision I was searching for. A row of orange suited-men and one woman, her flaming hair sizzling in the wind, gliding across the horizon, in dark relief, on skateboards. Their hands were loosely joined together, and I could tell that they had rehearsed their moves many times as they rolled in from the ocean and Lands End, swooping up and down the hills thrusting their unchained, sturdy feet with poised precision. My heart was bursting as they came closer and closer, and I could see that Rahim was leading the flying procession.

As he came closer, I reached for Rahim's hand to pull him off the skateboard so that I could bring him safely home. But he resisted my tug and for a moment teetered on the skateboard, almost losing his balance, which would have brought all the other skateboarders down with him.

Hands off, Maggie, he commanded in a tone of voice I had never heard him use. *Find a real way to help*, he added, beseechingly, over his shoulder. I tried to run after him, but I tripped. When I looked down, I saw that my own feet were bound by an almost invisible gauze.

Come visit me at 850 Bryant, Rahim suggested, as I helped him put on his jumpsuit the next day to prepare for his discharge. His skin looked flaccid and mottled against the glowering orange. I had stepped back, for now, from the daredevil flight that I longed to execute. But was I ready to accept an impermeable plexiglass barrier between us and coded conversations conducted over a monitored phone as the alternative?

Maybe, was all I could reply.

After all the paperwork was complete, after the guard on shift had signed and dated the form asserting that his prisoner, Clarence Jackson, legal property of the city and county of San Francisco, was ready to be returned to the six-by-ten concrete box at 850 Bryant, we all gathered to watch Rahim shuffle toward the elevator, a guard gripping each of his arms in an immobilizing vise. Belinda was drumming a fierce beat on the counter. Tears were rolling down Cande's face. I stood still, professionally stoic, eyes fixed on Rahim's receding orange back and his shackled feet.

Maybe they would let him get a little more exercise so his back wouldn't freeze up again right away. Maybe he would beat this cold case and return to his cage in Pennsylvania. Maybe, before he left, I would get up early one Sunday morning, pick a bunch of fiery poppies in Golden Gate Park and offer them to Rahim across the plexiglass.

RELEASE—
ANISE
2010

YOUR LIMP WAS THE FIRST THING I NOTICED ABOUT YOU, CASSANDRA, AS YOU WALKED into the visiting room. You limped deliberately toward me, angling your body ever so carefully through the narrow spaces between the tables overloaded with chips, candy bars, and soda. I guess I had expected you, a white woman who had once escaped from prison, to be one of those take-charge striders. Like the towering Drooker woman on the poster on my mother's bedroom wall, tramping fearlessly across the city, hair flowing, arms and legs swinging wide, overshadowing the skyscrapers in the background, stomping through everything in her way. But you stepped cautiously, as if one false move could cause a mass chain-reaction spill—a dangerous cascade of junk food overturning one table and then the next until all the grease and sugar landed—smack!—splattering at the feet of the two imperial guards sitting in command at the front of the room.

When you finally got to where I was sitting in the way back, as far away from *them* as I could get, you said my name, *Anise*, and got it right the first time, unlike most people who make it rhyme with *peace* or *release*. Then you extended your hand in an assured, graceful motion that made me think that you probably had once walked with that same elegance.

You look like your pictures, I said, even though I was thinking how faded you seemed compared to the glamorous woman in the books and magazines I had unearthed at the San Francisco State library. Even in the posed pictures taken in prison, you had looked fashionable—your hair was cropped close and sharp around your high cheekbones, your hoop earrings dangled beneath your sunglasses, and your shirt and jeans fitting just right. You could have been out on the street rather than posing behind bars.

But here, in person, you looked like an inmate, dressed like every other woman in the room with a loose tan shirt hanging shapeless over beige pants. Your hair hung listless down the sides of your head, hiding its striking shape. I wondered whether you were able to get conditioner in prison and how often you could take a shower. Or if you could buy the kind of lotion that could heal the cobweb cracks under your eyes. Not the kind of questions I had come here to ask you. But the pad with the ones I had written down to start this interview were locked in a steel case in the visitor processing room, along with my forbidden pen.

Did you have any trouble getting through the processing? you asked politely after we had formally introduced ourselves. *Not really*, I lied, not wanting to tell you that I had tried to argue with the guard when he said I couldn't bring a pad or pen into the prison. *What could be dangerous about a notepad?* He snapped back that I could either obey the rules or forfeit the visit. I gave up and put the banned pad and pen in the locker like I was told. My friend Shanika used to boast about how she could smuggle in joints, food, almost anything, when she went to visit her boyfriend at juvie. Now my clueless self couldn't even get a lame-ass pen into *this* prison.

You're learning when to give up, my mother had said to me recently, meaning it as a compliment. I almost snapped at her that I was just getting better at camouflage, following in her footsteps. Instead I walked away, proving her point, perhaps.

Honey, don't let them upset you. You'll get used to all their crazy rules, an older Black woman in back of me in the visitor line had advised after my run-in with the guard. She was holding a beautiful, chubby toddler, who was sleeping peacefully despite artificial lights glaring down on him and the suffocating airlessness of the space.

They even enforce the dress code for babies, she confided. Last Easter, she had waited forty-five minutes to be processed because there was only one guard on duty that day even though it was one of the busiest visiting days of the year. When she finally got to the desk, the officer told her that her grandbaby was dressed wrong. At first she didn't understand what he was saying, even though he kept repeating the words stupidly— *beige, he's wearing beige.*

I had just gotten Jamani this cute jumpsuit on sale and never thought about it being an illegal color. As if this tiny boy baby could be mistaken for a grown woman in a uniform! I was so angry I thought I would bust. But then I wouldn't have gotten to see my daughter and she would have been so upset not to see her child on Easter. So I went to Target and bought him something else to wear.

If I had gone all the way back home to find him some other clothes, it would have been too late and we would have missed the visit.

Coretta gave me another piece of advice when we finally got to the visiting room. She probably could tell that I felt like the air was being sucked out of my lungs after each set of electronic doors thudded shut behind us.

Try and get a table at the back of the room. More peaceful that way. Besides, you don't want the guards getting into your business if you can help it.

You thanked me for choosing a table at the back. *Farther from the guardmasters. And it's nice to be close to the childcare room*, you explained. Your eyes wandered toward that brightly colored space where moms and their kids were coloring and doing puzzles. For a moment I wished that I had brought Shanika's baby, Monisha, on the visit with me. Except that Monisha was a fireball and there was no way we would have been able to concentrate on this interview for my senior thesis with her around.

I started asking you the standard biographical openers that I remembered from the list on my pad. You answered with clipped factual statements. Born in Oklahoma City. Father was a high school English teacher, a frustrated writer, hence your name, Cassandra, for the tragic Greek prophetess. Your mother was a housewife, as they called them back then. The most radical member of your family tree was your grandfather who was a Wobbly—*yes, I did know what a Wobbly was*—who died when you were ten, but had time to pass on stories of battles with the police thugs who tried to break up the union. You supported the civil rights movement when you were in high school. Your parents wanted you to go to Oklahoma State but instead you left and went to Berkeley until you dropped out because you were learning much more in the streets than in class.

I was trying to keep mental notes of what you were saying but it all sounded like a dry Wikipedia summary. Instead, I noticed how your left hand kept massaging your leg under the table as you talked, and how the skinny, restless birds, which I could see through the window, were sputtering from one uncomfortable perch to another on top of the barbed wire fence.

What do you really want to know about me, Anise? The directness of your question took me off guard even though it was obvious that we were both bored by the superficial textbook inquiries. When I decided to write about your life, my head had been full of probing questions. But now the overhead lights were frying my brain cells. If I opened my mouth at all I was afraid I would spit out crazy random questions like *what brand of conditioner are you allowed to use* or *how did you get your limp?*

Luckily, just at that moment, Jamani came tumbling out of the childcare room and threw himself, with all of his indestructible eighteen-month-old energy, into your lap. Your face lit up and you hugged him as if you hadn't touched a child for the twenty-five years you had been in prison.

Jamani, honey, I've missed seeing you! Are you having a good visit with your mom? Jamani leapt off your lap and flung his arms around a tall, gorgeous woman with meticulously plaited hair.

Cassandra, I wanted to let the two of you talk, but this boy wouldn't stop calling for auntie Cassie so here we are. Sorry to interrupt.

No problem! I've missed seeing Jamani lately, you assured the woman. At the sound of his name, Jamani bounced joyously back into your lap. You hugged him again and it was several minutes before you remembered that I was there.

Anise, this is my good friend Sage. She's my cellie and one of the people who keeps me from going crazy in this place.

I stuttered, *Nice to meet you*, shaken by the fact that she was named Sage, just like my mother. Now that I was in Sage's commanding presence, I understood better why Coretta had swallowed her rage in order to make sure the Easter visit happened between Jamani and his mother. For a few minutes, I listened to you and Sage exchange comments about the guards on duty.

Hernandez is being a shit as usual, loves getting her hands all up into you when she searches, Sage announced, not seeming to care who heard her.

And Jones is backing her up, not even playing good cop today, you replied in a softer voice. From inside the playroom, Coretta was waving for Sage and Jamani to return.

She needs help finishing the puzzle we started together, Sage laughed. Then she turned quickly and gave me an unexpected hug.

Don't let this one intimidate you, she said and reached over to include you in her wide embrace. *She can be prickly sometimes but she really loves to talk with the youth who come to visit. She also loves KitKats, so you might want to buy her a few to loosen her up.*

Stupidly, I had forgotten about the roll of quarters in the bag that was the only thing I had been allowed to bring inside the visiting room. We got in line for the vending machines, but the first one we tried ate my quarters and no amount of banging on it brought them back. When we finally got back to our table, KitKats and Coke in hand, I couldn't help but mention the disorienting coincidence.

My mother's name is Sage too, you know.

You looked mildly surprised as if this piece of trivia had escaped your memory. Then you confirmed, *Yes, I should have remembered the connection when I introduced you.*

How well did you know my mother? It wasn't one of the things that I had planned to ask you on this first visit, but the serendipity of meeting this other Sage pushed the question out.

You hesitated a few seconds. *Pretty well. But long ago, before I went to prison the first time. Actually, I was with her visiting the brothers at San Quentin the night before I was arrested in 1976. I haven't seen her in person since then.*

When I told my mother that I wanted to write about Cassandra Bridges for my senior thesis, she didn't say much. *Interesting idea*, she offered in her studied, nonjudgmental style and asked me what I hoped to learn from the project. I gave her the bullet points from my thesis proposal—the radical history of the Bay Area, the intersections of feminism and antiracism, the connection between armed resistance movements in the seventies to direct action movements today.

If anyone can tackle all of that, Cassandra can, she commented. When I asked her how well she had known you, hoping for details that would put flesh on the skeleton, she carefully explained that you had visited prisoners at San Quentin together.

Of course, Cassandra took things further than I was willing to. It could have been the opening for the story I wanted to hear, but as usual my mother seemed worried that she might slip and give away some clue that could implicate her in an ancient conspiracy.

Cassandra was very brave but very arrogant. She was a brilliant thinker but had a hard time admitting that she was ever wrong. It was my mother's familiar refrain—a bitter judgment about the people in her shadowy past.

Of course, Cassandra has paid a terribly high price for all of that, she added with a hint of remorse. I resolved to find out the rest from Cassandra herself.

I can't believe my mother has never visited you all these years! The accusation burst out. You tried to make excuses for my mother. *The organization, Uprising, was worried that Sage might be implicated somehow in my case since we had been working together closely. They didn't want her to visit me before my trial. After I was convicted, the first time, I was at a prison on the other side of the country. Then I escaped, went underground and was out-of-touch with everyone for years.*

After my second arrest and conviction, I was sent back to California. By then, lots of my old friends had moved on with their lives. I understood that, couldn't blame them. Several years ago, Sage and Brooke began to send me birthday cards, lovely handmade ones, and a generous amount of money for commissary each year. It was their way of letting me know they cared.

Neither Sage nor Brooke had ever mentioned this to me. I pictured them shoulder-to-shoulder, squeezed together, in their room at night—Brooke cutting *papel picado* patterns for the card, Sage writing the words in the stylized calligraphy she had studied in a class.

Birthday cards! What a token. They probably were Brooke's idea anyway. She helps everyone and anyone. A total Florence Nightingale. But she *doesn't do politics. That's Sage's area of expertise. Which pretty much means that neither of them do much of anything except stuff like cards and money.*

You cut me off.

I was very intolerant of my parents for a long time also.

You tried to make it a matter-of-fact statement, but I heard the judgment loud and clear. *Arrogant is right*, I thought and almost started to stand up and walk out before I remembered that the doors were locked. I was trapped.

Grudgingly, I asked what you meant.

You started off in the same flat monotone as before.

My father was a conscientious objector in World War II. For him it was a noble, moral statement, refusing to fight, despite pressure from his father and all of his friends. He held it up to his four children as the finest stand of his life, before he receded into the halls of high school English teaching.

When I was little, I thought he was a hero. But as I got older, that started to change. When I wanted to go to Mississippi for the Freedom Summer, he wouldn't let me because it was too dangerous. He wanted me to support civil rights by writing school newspaper editorials and poems for the literary magazine. I began to think he was more of a coward than a person of principle.

Your pitch had risen and your elegant hands were punctuating your words in staccato gestures.

After I was arrested the first time, on charges of buying guns for the Panthers, he came to visit me in jail down at 850 Bryant in San Francisco.

Guns, I can't believe it, a daughter of mine buying guns, *he kept repeating.* After I risked so much to avoid fighting? How could you think that guns could ever solve anything?

I tried to defend the principle without admitting anything over the bugged jail phone. It was so absurd, a tragicomic scene. I was trying to communicate through double entendres and coded metaphors, but my father, the English teacher, missed all of the irony. Finally, I told him that if he couldn't support me against the state, he shouldn't come visit me again. He took me at my word.

Before I could ask if you ever made up with your father, one of the guards stood up and began shouting, *Count, all inmates in the visiting room report for count!*

The women all rose up like robots and trooped listlessly out into the cold, outdoor visiting area. For a couple of hours they had been absorbed back into the lives of their children, their mothers, their families and friends. Now they were being yanked away once again.

What had each of them been doing, the moment before their arrest? Feeding their children, ignorant of the loss they would experience the next moment? Crossing the border, drugs in their vaginas? Driving breathlessly through the night, escaping from a man who had ruthlessly ruled their lives? What type of fear had electrified their pulse when they comprehended that they had been snared, ambushed, stung, and from this moment on they would be separated from life as they knew it?

I watched them huddled in the fog. The group portrait could have been a billboard for promoting diversity at my college—young, old, skinny, fat, tall, short, black, brown, yellow, white. Except the black and brown faces overshadowed all the others and there were no rainbow smiles plastered on their faces. You perched awkwardly on a low wall next to Sage, resting your leg. Every woman was frozen in the caged pose they chose to assume until count had cleared.

I thought at first that the beat of your story had been lost in the monotonous bark of count—names and numbers repeated five times a day, sometimes more if there was trouble, you explained. But I was determined to coax the rest from you. Shanika always said that when I was in the right mood, I could get people to tell me almost anything.

You never saw your father again. *Like a soap opera or a Greek tragedy*, you said, trying to make the heaviness lighter. He died of a heart attack a couple of years later, right before you escaped from prison. For a long time, you felt that you had helped kill him.

Every woman in here carries the guilt of the world in her heart, you stated in a tired voice. That too could have been a line from a soap opera, but sitting in the visiting room, surrounded by women who would have to leave their babies, their mothers, their uncles, and their cousins in another couple of hours and return to their cells, it sounded like a reasonable description of fact.

What about your mother? I asked. Your relationship with your parents was no longer a moralistic parable, directed against me. It now seemed like a critical piece of the story I had come here to piece together.

If I tell you everything today, what will we talk about when you visit next time? you joked. Exhaustion fell like a wrinkled curtain across your face. You had had enough of personal revelation for one day.

The specter of guilt enveloped my daytime thoughts and my repeating nightmares after that first visit. In my Gender and the Law class the semester before, I had argued with the professor about women and incarceration. Her presentation was neat and balanced—a multicolored pie chart allocating crime responsibility factors—40 percent to the woman, 20 percent to the family, 20 to the community, and 20 to the criminal justice system. I was furious. From experience I knew that most of the time women were blamed and locked up for survival crimes or shit their boyfriends got them into. She let me rant, but I could tell she was wondering who this white girl was who thought she knew so much about women prisoners.

For my term paper I did a "case history" of LaVonda, a girl from my high school. I hadn't been tight with her, but some of my friends were. She was one of the smart girls, all A's, unlike most of my group. Always bragging about how she was going to be the first one in her family to get to college and the Ivy League for sure. She didn't even party much because she was worried that it would screw up her grades. None of us thought much of it when she started going with this older dude, Alonzo, senior year. We just joked that she better make damn sure he used a glove so she didn't end up pregnant or with HIV and ruin all her college plans.

Then one day, right in the middle of algebra, the cops came and pulled her out of class. We all thought it must be some stupid identity, Black-girls-all-look-alike, mix-up mistake. But it turned out that earlier that day Alonzo had tried to jack a 7-Eleven in Daly City. The sales clerk had been killed and a customer shot. And LaVonda had been sitting in the car outside. When she heard the shots, she ran. Even made it to algebra class. But Alonzo snitched her out.

Sage and Brooke sat up with me that night when I couldn't sleep. Crazy stuff had been happening to my friends since freshman year in high school when Carlos and Darius had been shot and killed after a football game and we never found out what really happened. But before LaVonda, all the heavy drama had been with the guys I knew. Nothing this bad had happened to a girl.

I told my moms I didn't want to talk about LaVonda and they let me be. We played Scrabble and watched crappy movies. Only when I was starting to doze off on the couch, tucked between them like when I was little, I heard Sage whisper to Brooke, *I can't stop thinking, what if this were Anise? She could be the girl waiting in the car.* Brooke whispered back trying to sound reassuring *No, Sage, don't go there. Anise is too smart, too good a judge of character.* Sage shot back at her, *but these are her friends, the people she is with all the time, being white can't protect her forever.*

I went to LaVonda's court hearings a few times. It tore me up to see how sad and guilty she looked, sitting up there next to her fool of a public defender who stuttered every time he opened his mouth. I asked Sage if she would try to find her another lawyer, but before she could try LaVonda took a deal for a seven-to-life sentence.

All my friends were really hating on her now, saying how she had fucked up so bad going with Alonzo and should have known the kind of shit he was up to. Then on top of everything she had taken a lousy deal. Only Shanika saw it differently. Shanika said they were brainwashed to blame LaVonda instead of Alonzo and the stupid lawyer and the fucked-up laws that held *her* guilty as if she had pulled the trigger just because she was sitting there in the car while he went ballistic pumping thirteen bullets into the clerk's chest.

I wrote LaVonda a few times after she was sent to prison but I couldn't stand hearing how much she hated herself for ruining her life and how jealous she was that all her friends were going off to college while she was going to rot in prison for the rest of her life. I kept thinking that it could have been me, sitting in that car, wondering what was taking the dude such a long time to pick up a Coke. Until I heard the shots and realized that my life was about to change forever.

I decided I needed to take some time off from school to do something real that could help girls stay out of the kind of trouble LaVonda had gotten into. Brooke said that she understood and had some ideas about possible jobs. But Sage was angry.

You are not responsible for all the fucked-up things going on in the world. For once Sage wasn't weighing every word carefully.

Fine if you want to take a year off school, but don't do it because of what happened to LaVonda. I knew in part she was right about what was going on inside of me, but I took the year off anyway.

The professor gave me an A on the paper even though it wasn't really the right format for a case study. She wrote a brief note—*Well written. LaVonda's story encapsulates many important themes and could be the basis for a senior thesis (or a blog ☺).* But LaVonda's story was not the one I wanted to write more about.

I was sick of learning about victims of the system. Every cop show on TV had someone like LaVonda in it. If they didn't end up in jail, they had an epiphany and decided to become a cop in order to help others avoid that fate. I wanted to write about a woman who had chosen to fight. On one of the bookshelves in our living room, almost hidden between a book on holistic healing and the *I Ching*, I found a thin pamphlet about women political prisoners. Inside there were moving poems, drawings, and letters from prison. But my heart skipped when I read your statement to the jury after you were arrested in 1986 and convicted of conspiring to help a Puerto Rican woman escape from prison.

I have been found guilty of breaking the laws of the United States government, but I haven't broken any law of conscience or true justice. The real crimes are those which this court has banned from discussion. The United States has maintained a colonial occupation of Puerto Rico since 1898. It has sterilized one third of Puerto Rican women of childbearing age. It is railroading unprecedented numbers of women of color into lockup all over this country under the so-called war on drugs. It is building the largest prison empire in the world. You can judge me and add me to the ever-growing number of women you hold in cages, but I am only accountable to the oppressed people of the world struggling for freedom.

It was the type of speech that I knew my mother hated. *Grandiose, rhetorical, arrogant* were the terms I was sure she would use. But I loved that you were defiant, unrepentant. A white woman speaking truth to power about the intersections of racism and sexism. Yours was the story I wanted to write for my senior thesis. Now I wondered, when you said that every woman prisoner carried the guilt of the world in their hearts, had you too given up on assigning responsibility to the real criminals?

Our visits grew easier. I left my notebook and pen at home and brought nothing but my car key and quarters for plenty of KitKats. Processing became routine. When grandmothers were turned away because their grandbabies were wearing the wrong colors, I handed them a copy of driving directions to the nearest Target. I barely heard the doors click shut behind me as I entered the prison.

I learned to watch the way you walked into the room to gauge the level of your pain.

When you moved raggedly, latching on to the edge of tables as you crossed the room, I knew you would want to focus on me. I told you about my classes and my efforts to write poetry that meant something. I described the music I had been listening to and the best YouTubes I had seen that week. And I told you about Darius and Carlos and how I could never let myself forget how they were killed when they were fifteen for no fucking reason at all.

Then there were the times when I saw you stroll in, hands-free, almost bouncing toward me (whether it was due to a pill you popped or some mystery shift in your hurting threshold I never knew). Then I got ready to listen to the stories I had come to hear.

You described how after you were captured, the second time, you made up your mind to rebuild your relationship with your mother. She had been your emotional anchor growing up, the one whose lap and arms were always there for you. But once you started arguing with your father about things like Freedom Summer and Berkeley, she refused to disagree with him, to stand up for you. She would counsel you to choose your battles with him, to use sweetness rather than vinegar to persuade him. But you were becoming a feminist and the last thing you wanted to do was dance around appeasing the family patriarch.

For twenty years, your mother visited you faithfully, twice a year. You unearthed the many things you had in common— love of gardens, pottery, your brothers' kids—and ignored the rest. When she died two years ago, you pulled every string you could think of to go to her funeral, but they wouldn't let you. You were depressed for months. It was Sage who saved you by suggesting that you create a set of garden pots in your mother's memory. You were just finishing them up now, using a deep amber glaze that you knew she would love.

It wasn't until our fourth or fifth visit that you casually mentioned that you had a date to be paroled in the next six months. I was so surprised that I let out a spontaneous *wow!* You looked around nervously and then quickly explained that the government could snatch back any date with freedom that it dangled in front of you, so you and your lawyers were keeping this information quiet except for your close network of supporters and friends. Any media attention—mainstream or Facebook—could easily backfire and lead to the FBI and police mounting a campaign to deny your release. I joked that I wouldn't tweet a word about it.

I kept my promise and didn't even mention the news to my moms. But I couldn't stop imagining what it would be like when you got out. I would take you to *Philz Coffee* for that super-strong cup of coffee you told me you yearned for every morning that you woke up in prison. I would help you choose a cell phone and we could call each other to talk whenever we wanted. I would share the hidden corners of Lands End where I went when I needed to get away from all the bullshit. After every visit, as I got to the prison parking lot, I could picture you striding out of the gates, leaving your limp and all your other aches behind.

One day when I got to the visiting room, you were deep in conversation with a couple of women. When one of them turned around and called out, *Anise*, I stupidly stumbled over a kid who was crawling on the floor in front of me. Luba and Maggie were mothers of kids from high school, Nick and Gordon. They belonged to the outside world of parents and school activities. They felt like intruders into this intense, sealed space where I spent my weekends getting to know you.

You must have seen my confusion because you launched into an apology about the mix-up in the visiting schedule. In some ways you were glad that we had all been scheduled for the same time because now we could all hang out together. Luba was a very old friend from back in the day. She had been part of Uprising and of course knew Sage, my mother. Luba herself had been underground for many years, targeted by the same stupid sting operation that landed you back in prison. Luckily, Luba and her collective had avoided capture. Since she had come back up to public life, Luba had been visiting you. Maggie was a nurse and started visiting with Luba after she joined Unshackled Women, an organization that supported women prisoners.

You were drawing a Venn diagram of Bay Area radical circles. It made my head throb, just like when we had to make those charts in geometry class. Growing up, every time my mom and I would bump into someone she knew *from back in the day*, there would be a flicker of connection, a few sentences of polite conversation, and then always a quick retreat and my mother's tight-lipped judgment. I was envious of this forbidden clique that my mother had been so close to once upon a time and so deliberately distant from ever after.

Maggie also worked on Rahim's case. You were proceeding with the introduction. *She met him in the hospital where she's a nurse when he was in the orthopedic ward for back surgery. She even organized another nurse, Belinda, to help with the work on his case. We were just talking, before you came in, about what a victory it was when the state finally dropped the charges against Rahim.*

How did you know Rahim? I asked, wanting you to describe something more than crisscrossing circles.

Honey, you said with a laugh, *that man got me into prison and then helped figure a way to get me out!* Then you added quickly, *Now forget you ever heard me say that, Anise.*

Before I could wrap my mind around the implications, Luba jumped in.

We all knew each other one way or another back then—Panthers, Puerto Rican independentistas, and us solidarity folks. I first met Cassandra and Rahim in Cuba when we were all still children. We were on the Venceremos Brigade helping to pick sugarcane for Cuba's impossible ten-million-ton harvest goal in 1970. What a failure, but what an amazing time we all had there! You and Luba exchanged longing glances.

Enough nostalgia, you said abruptly, reprimanding yourself. *It doesn't help give those who weren't around then a clear picture of all the contradictions of that period.*

Luba nodded but continued with the history.

After that, even when I wasn't working directly with Cassandra, we always tried to keep up our connection. It was precious. So many people were losing loved ones to COINTELPRO, prison, death. Or just stupid disagreements that should never have gotten in the way of what tied us together, but foolishly they did . . . Her voice trailed off. I imagined she could be referring to my mother. Suddenly, I remembered the day that my mother and I had spent with Luba and Nick protesting the invasion of Iraq back in 2003.

Stealth bombers, cruise missiles, amphibious marine landings—I had stayed up late with my moms watching the gruesome conquest unfold. It was the first war I was old enough to understand in real time, and I was mad. Nick had told me about an early-morning blockade of the Bay Bridge to stop business as usual on this side of the world while the lives of Iraqis were being turned upside down thousands of miles away. Brooke had to work, but I convinced Sage to come with me.

We ended up in an ad hoc affinity group with Nick and Luba. Together, we shut down the Bay bridge to morning traffic, snaked through the streets of the downtown financial empire, lay down in the middle of Market Street, and did what we could to get our message across.

As the day went on, I watched as my mom chanted at the concrete and glass towers of power and exchanged hugs with Luba when we managed to outrun the police kettles that were threatening to surround us. Her usual cautious restraint was blown apart by the angry energy—thousands shouting all together, *No more blood for oil!* But back home, when I asked Sage about her past with Luba, she just gave me a generic laundry list of causes they had worked for together. The blood and guts of their connection remained shrouded in the usual mystery. Remembering that day, I began to feel better about this unexpected chance to get to know Luba.

It was so great how Rahim managed to bring so many people together around his case, Maggie chimed in enthusiastically. I tried to wrap my mind around her presence in this visiting room. I had been Gordon's buddy when he was a freshman, and from the stories he told me, his mother was super uptight, not the kind of person who visits infamous political prisoners. But now here she was chatting it up with you and praising Rahim, the Panther icon from my mother's past.

There's a magic about him, Maggie continued. *He's a vision-ary who sees the big picture but he's also very concrete and down-to-earth.*

Your fingers tapped rapidly on the table.

I don't think it's good to romanticize Rahim. He has many gifts, I should know, but he damn well made his share of mistakes, just like the rest of us.

I had gone to visit Rahim once at 850 Bryant with my mother. She had described to me her visits with him long ago at San Quentin, one of the few times she told me something real about her past. It made me want to meet him. I could see right away what it was my mother liked about him. He asked me questions about myself and didn't talk down. When I told him that I wrote poetry, he didn't ooh and ahh or ask me to send him my rhymes. Instead he told me to guard my writing closely until I had it figured out so I wouldn't be swayed by anyone else's reactions.

Rahim's energy was riveting, but it reminded me too much of my first boyfriend, Thomas. He was a dazzling spo-ken word artist and the two of us made great plans to poetry slam the country together. But once Thomas went national, he disappeared from my life and I promised myself never again to make the mistake of believing a master word spinner. I won-dered what mistakes Rahim had made that gave your voice that steel edge when you mentioned them. Before I could ask, Luba redirected the conversation again.

Yes, I keep telling people they shouldn't make an icon out of you, Cassandra. It doesn't help to put people up on an unreal pedestal, though I understand why young people especially look up to the two of you. If it hadn't been for Rahim's almost fanatical belief that he could beat these new charges, I don't think we could have overcome all the past differences and worked together as hard as we did. Of course it helped that the state had such a lousy case and a bumbling fool for a prosecutor.

And, Maggie quickly added, *some things that happened were real miracles. Like when the FBI forgot to edit out the paragraph in the Discovery that proved that Rahim was on the other side of the country and knew nothing about the police shooting in San Francisco.*

You had to agree. *We know they make mistakes, but it was bizarre luck that they left all that key information uncensored.*

The three of you went on to discuss the mysterious mix of organizing, legal smarts, and good karma that had brought about Rahim's win. It was the only combination that could ever achieve a victory for a political prisoner in this perversely screwed-up legal system. Listening to you all, I wished that my mom could be here to be part of this deep talk about Rahim and his rare success.

Another time when I walked through the visiting room doors, I saw that Sage, Coretta, and Jamani were there already, working hard on putting a puzzle together. I sat down at a table right next to them and began to help. When you finally made it through processing, you hesitated by the door when you saw the two tables so close together. But Sage beckoned to you across the room and, when you got close, whispered loudly, *It's okay, Cass, Brannan's in charge and you know he doesn't give a shit about the rule that inmates shouldn't sit too close to each other.*

Besides he's too busy eating. She nodded her head toward the mound of chips and candy piled up on the table in front of correctional officer Brannan.

Still, you took a seat on the far side of my table, the farthest possible point away from Sage. I could see you reach down and start rubbing your leg. Once we had gotten something to eat and drink, you seemed to relax a little. You and I worked with Jamani on the puzzle, Coretta and Sage played cards, and all of us listened to Sage's hilarious stories about her job working in the kitchen, while the strains of gospel drifted in from the Sunday church service in the room next door.

Girl, getting up at three to stir up vats of soggy oatmeal and drippy egg mix for eight hundred ladies, I can hardly make it through without gagging. And there's certainly no eating after I see the other wannabe cooks putting their fingers, hands, hell, whole arms into the stuff. And me trying to be healthy, eat vegan even though it's so hard in here. I start imagining killer bacon and real from-the-chicken eggs while I'm mixing this shit up . . .

By the time she got to *bacon and eggs*, Sage was almost shouting to keep from being drowned out by the *saviors and the lords* now thundering through the wall.

Just like them church folks to try and crush our voices with their music, Sage yelled across the table, making sure that you heard her.

Come on, Sage, we have to try and be tolerant of everyone's beliefs, you yelled back. I couldn't tell whether you were being sarcastic.

When they're tolerant of mine, I'll think about being more tolerant of theirs. The song from next door was winding down, and people around the visiting room turned to see who had hollered these fighting words.

It can be really hard in here not to be a church person, you explained to me quietly. *The guards push the church on everyone and the church lines up lockstep with them. They preach judgment— remorse and atonement are the only tickets out of here.*

Sage nodded vigorously and pulled what looked like another deck of cards, out of her pocket. *This is* my *pocket bible*, she said, patting the box tenderly. *If I'm looking for guidance, I'm not gonna ask some white dude on a cross to forgive my sins.*

Before you could say anything, she added quickly, *Let's do a Tarot reading, all of us, right now. Our own kind of Sunday service.*

You looked disapproving, but Sage was anticipating your objections. *I told you, Brannan's in charge and he really doesn't care about anything unless we were to start toking in front of him. It's been such a long time, Cass, since we've read our cards together. Before they let me out and then snatched me back right after this little guy was born.* She leaned over and kissed Jamani, who was napping in Coretta's lap.

To me the Tarot had always been a game my moms played, along with witchcraft-lite and throwing the *I Ching*. It helped them divine what names to choose and what colors to paint the house. The serious decisions in life were taken apart and put together in long, endless talks over the dinner table or in their bedroom huddles at night, scientifically dissecting the pros and cons, coming up with irrefutable reasons to justify whatever their solution happened to be. But now I was sitting in a locked room with women whose jailers seemed to hold the only key to their futures. I could understand why Sage, and everyone else in here, would search desperately for any alternate power that might offer a secret to release.

Your hand below the table was angrily kneading your leg.

It's not about Brannan. I just don't do readings anymore, Sage. Your voice was like stone and it made me shiver a little.

Sage turned toward me. *When I first met Cassandra, we did the Tarot every couple of weeks. Cassandra was the one who suggested my name, Sage, 'cause every time we did a reading, I drew the High Priestess, the wise one. Cassandra believed in my vision and the truth of my readings then. But when I got myself busted again, well I guess that blew it all up. Now there's no redemption for me anymore with her.* She held the Tarot deck out to you. I wasn't sure whether it was a challenge or a peace offering.

I waited for you to take the deck to reassure Sage that you still believed in her, that it wasn't her fault that she was back in prison. Coretta's head was bowed and I thought she was either asleep or pretending to be now that this pleasant visit was disintegrating around her. *Prison visits cook emotions until they threaten to boil over in a sizzling, uncontrollable mess,* my mother had once told me, when she was describing her long ago visits with Rahim. I had thought she was being melodramatic, but now I understood better what she meant.

Enough! you said, and pulled yourself painfully up out of the chair. *Anise and I need some time by ourselves for our interview. We're going to go walk outside for a while.*

I followed you, but I was raging inside. Sage was asking, pleading for something from you, and you just walked away. Arrogant and unforgiving. Outside the sun was shining and there were kids playing. Earlier that morning, I had seen them swinging on the other side of the fence, as the guard escorted us to the visiting room. Up close it was even harder to understand how they kept up their free-flowing movement, pumping vigorously back and forth, unminding of the barbed wire wall surrounding them.

How could you walk away from her like that? I spat out. For several moments you didn't say anything. Your hands twisted relentlessly and it seemed like your mind was pivoting out of range of my voice.

The day after September 11, they put me in the hole. I wasn't the only one. Political prisoners around the country were yanked out of our daily lives and dumped into solitary.

You were ignoring my question and I started to interrupt. But your story was channeling through you with a will of its own. I shut my mouth and listened.

They treated us as if we were an armed and organized fifth column inside the prisons, ready to support the men who had just toppled their towers. As if we might explode the walls of these fortresses from within unless they buried us before we could act. A pipe dream that might have floated across our minds for a fleeting moment as we watched their towers of power crumble. Until we learned how many innocent people had been killed and wounded. Until we realized the inevitable revenge and retribution that was in store for all the other innocent people around the globe.

Before they could strike Afghanistan and Iraq, before they could erect Guantánamo and Abu Ghraib, before they could entrap dozens of U.S. Muslims in their fabricated terrorist plots, they rounded up those of us who were already captives due to our politics.

We found ourselves stripped, alone in dungeon holes across the country, left to reflect on the turbulent history that had brought us to this point and wonder what the future would hold.

You paused, and I tried to make eye contact, but you hardly realized I was sitting there. Your words were discharging hypnotically, round after round, from some underground space. Your hand was mechanically rubbing your leg.

The first day and night, my leg throbbed constantly as the towers detonated in brilliant fireworks again and again before my eyes. The month before September 11, every time I read the Tarot with Sage, I had pulled the Tower card. Now the card's prophecy of destruction and chaos had come true. When I first started reading the Tarot long ago in a commune in the Haight, we thought the Tower card signaled great changes ahead. Out of their *ruin would come renewal and transformation. The signs were all on our side. But lying frozen on my cot, after spending much of the past twenty-five years in the madness of prison life, each time the towers crumbled, the next instant replay resurrected them taller and more menacing than before.*

With each looming resurrection, I was gripped by guilt for all our slipshod mistakes, our over-bold strategies, our love-colored justifications, our stupid captures. And by a raging anger that neither our dialectical materialist strategies or our magical prophetic divinations had enabled us to upend the empire.

I had been in the hole before for much longer and had figured out how to handle its mind-rotting isolation. But this time I was crumbling under the weight of my own judgments. I knew if I didn't find a toehold soon I would not walk out of that hole intact and they would have won.

I was getting scared. I reached out to touch you, to bring you back into the present of a sunny prison yard with children running in the grass and flying carefree on the swings. Maybe that broke your trance.

Don't worry, Anise, we're getting to the turning point of the drama. At some mysterious juncture, I noticed that I was breathing. Despite the war raging in my head, despite all the wars raging around the planet, my breaths continued, in and out, in a slow, vital rhythm. I began to listen to that steady sound and the clamoring mind-noise receded. It was a small revelation, but large enough to rescue me.

When they let me out after a week, I knew I wasn't a changed person, and for that I was glad. I also knew that in some yet unknown way the world had changed and I had to be ready to face it. When the guard came to get me out, he told me straight-faced, We put you there for your own safety, Bridges.

I looked him in the eye and told him calm as ice, That's complete bullshit, a bullshit cover-up lie.

You stopped talking and for a few minutes we sat together listening to the squeak-squeak of the swings.

What about Sage? I had to re-ask the question now. You sighed, but this time you gave me a direct answer.

I tried to explain to Sage that after my experience in the hole, the Tarot and all the other tricks we used to try and game the future didn't work for me anymore. It wasn't meant as a judgment, but I couldn't stop her from seeing it that way. So for a while I read the cards with her anyway, because it mattered to her and I wanted to support her until her sentence was up. But since she got arrested again, it doesn't make sense anymore.

I jumped in. *She needs you to forgive her.*

You sighed again, this time more impatiently.

I don't blame her, but I do hold her accountable. How could I be an honest friend if I didn't? Sure I blame the fucked-up parole system that was waiting to pounce on her and haul her back inside. And I blame her money-hungry boyfriend who entangled her in his drug web again and gave her a baby at the same time. But she could have done it differently. She could have found the wisdom to live up to her name. I still believe she has the power to transform, not only her life but lots of lives around hers. But not by hanging her hopes on cheap Tarot prophecies.

When the buzzer screeched to announce the end of the visit, I moved quickly to get on the exit line. You had told me the first time I visited that you didn't like long, drawn out, sorrowful leave takings and advised me to always try to be near the front of the line for both our sakes. We stood obediently, we visitors waiting to be escorted out into the free world by one of the guards, and you prisoners lined up in parallel formation across the room, waiting to be herded back to your cages.

I was trying to process all that had gone on during this visit, when a piercing wail of *mama, mama, mama* sliced through the orderly silence. Jamani had thrown his chubby arms around Sage's leg and was refusing to let go. Sage and Coretta were both trying frantically to pry his arms loose, but Jamani was clutching with grief-charged strength. Sage was pleading with him between her sobs, *Honey, Jamani you'll see me next weekend. I'll talk to you tomorrow night. It will be okay, sweetie, mama loves you so much, but you have to let go.*

No one wanted to stare, but there was nowhere else to look. Brannan started to get up out of his chair to force an end to this forbidden scene. Against all the rules, you pushed yourself away from the wall you were leaning on and with surprising speed walked over to where the three of them were locked in battle. You leaned over and started whispering into Jamani's ear, stroking his arms gently.

Magically, within a couple of minutes, Jamani stopped screaming and released his hold. Coretta quickly scooped him up and strode over to the visitors' line, turning Jamani's face deliberately toward the swings outside and promising him that they would go to the playground when they got home. You put your arm around Sage, who was crying even more hysterically than before. Clinched tightly together, the two of you staggered across the room to join the line of prisoners.

When you told me that you were sick, a few months before you were due to be paroled, I wanted to throw my arms around you and not let go. I heard you mouth the words *ovarian cancer* through an echo chamber of fear, trying to listen while you calmly described the covert nature of the disease, the symptoms that had been misdiagnosed for years, the usual prison delays in getting to see a doctor, and now, finally, a plan for surgery that would determine the extent of its spread. You were transforming the terrible turmoil inside of you with a dignified, logical response. But I had no zen training to fall back on. Just when you were on the edge of being free at last, fate was fucking with your life for no imaginable reason.

The next week was a blur of tears and nightmares. I had to tell Sage and Brooke what was happening, but the devastated expressions on their faces didn't help. *Isn't there some sort of compassionate release for prisoners who are dying?* Brooke asked before Sage shot her an angry look that was meant to protect me from your death sentence.

I dreamt that I smuggled in some contraband street clothes for you to wear and you skillfully put them on before Brannan looked up from his bag of cheetos. You looked young and stunning in your DKNY jeans, and not one guard realized you were a prisoner as we lined up and walked coolly out of the visiting room door. But a few feet before we reached the prison gates, your disguise began to shred, exposing your khaki inmate uniform for all to see. I grabbed you close to try and protect you, but the bullets went clean through my body and lodged deep inside yours.

I went online and searched for articles about Black Panther Assata Shakur and her great escape from a New Jersey maximum-security prison in 1979, aided by members of the Black Liberation Army. The articles I found described her time in prison and her political asylum in Cuba, but there were almost no details about the action itself. How had she been taken from a prison visiting room without a shot being fired? What kind of brilliant getaway plan was constructed so that this most-wanted woman was never caught?

The next time I saw you, I asked how *you* had escaped the first time. I wanted more than the few facts that everyone knew—*went on furlough, disappeared.*

Some things people don't need to know, even thirty years later, you cautioned me, but I pressed on.

You did it once, I whispered. *Why not try again?*

You shook your head hard and twisted your hands into a coiled knot. I thought you were angry, but then I saw a tear drip down your face.

Anise, you said, uncoiling your hands to take mine, *I know you don't want me to die in prison, and neither do I. But magical thinking isn't going to help. I'm applying for medical parole to get out sooner. I will make it out and you'll get to help me choose a cell phone yet.*

I was in Cuba when I got an e-mail saying you had been granted medical parole and would be released in a few days. You had urged me to go to a conference in Havana—*Latin American Writing and Political Imagination in the Twenty-First Century*, it was called. You gave me a long list of reasons to go.

You'll change your concept of writing. Your Spanish will improve. You will meet people from around the world who are still trying to connect politics and imagination in this age of soundbites and formulas. When I still wasn't convinced, you shifted gears and asked me to go for you since you weren't sure when you would ever be able to visit again for yourself.

Part of me felt like you were sending me away so I wouldn't be there to watch you die in prison, but once I got to Havana I forgot all that and was just glad that you had persuaded me to make the trip. The workshops made my mind tingle and pop. Spanish rhymes started to spontaneously bubble in my head. I loved being in a city where the revolutionary history was not a secret to be coaxed out of a closet or dug out of a cell. It was blasted all over the public space on street names, billboards, and monuments. It was part of conversation and stories that everyone from conference panelists to cab drivers offered up freely. And it wasn't just a pumped-up praise song. There was questioning, debating, criticizing—enough to rock my brain for years.

When I got the message saying that you would be out of prison in a couple of days, a full month before your parole date, I began to cry out of happiness. The e-mail also asked, on your behalf, that your comrades, friends, family, and supporters take five minutes each morning, at exactly the same time, no matter where we were in the world or which side of the bars we lived on, to meditate to help defeat the cancer.

How can I do this? I wondered. You had counseled me against magical thinking, you had rejected Sage's tarot conjuring, but now you wanted us to pray together to ensure your healthy freedom. I had always refused Sage and Brooke's suggestions to drop by their women's meditation circle, not to mention Shanika's many invitations to come with her to church. *I don't do spiritual*, I lamely explained. But now, under these circumstances, how could I not honor your request?

Later that day, I got an e-mail from my mom. *How hard it must have been for Cassandra, with her self-sufficiency and pride, to reach out like this*, she wrote. She and Brooke were planning to get up at five each morning to do their meditation in the garden beside the pyracantha bush whose orange berries were just beginning to ripen. Without debating anymore, I wrote back that I was planning to do my meditation at the Malecón, the crumbling breakwater that stretched across Havana's harbor. I had been told that people still threw offerings across this wall to Yemayá, the Yoruba goddess of the sea. It seemed like the appropriate place for my meditation.

The waves were breaking wildly over the seawall, spraying and splashing uncontrollably onto the esplanade, when I got to the Malecón the next morning. For five minutes, or maybe ten, I stood there—trying to hear the sound of my breath beneath the roar of the waves, dazzled by the sun-dyed crests crashing around me, drenched by the water that showed no respect for the barrier that was meant to contain its freestyle power.

At some stormy, peace-soaked moment, you found me. Together, we slipslided precariously between land and water, trying to construct a toehold where there wasn't any.

Then, one by one, all the other people who were meditating joined us in this borderless space. Sage, Brooke, Coretta, Jamani, Sage, Luba, Nick, Maggie, Gordon, Rahim, Mumia, Leonard, and hundreds, maybe thousands, of others. After all those years of being physically disconnected from so many of the people you loved, you had figured out how to link us up and forge a tough-as-nails lifeline across the barbed wire, the continent and the sea.

You died, two weeks after you were released. You e-mailed me yourself after you got out and told me not to cut my trip short. *We'll have lots of time to talk once you return*, you insisted.

One of your last wishes was that we not hold the usual type of memorial service that could only include those privileged few who could gather together in the same geographic space. Instead, you asked that we each make some time every day—or once a week, once a month, whatever we could handle in whatever format made sense—to remember the millions still trapped in cages.

I began my meditations every morning, religiously. Maybe I expected that each session would bring a replay of that cosmic moment on the Malecón. Instead, after a few minutes of trying to mechanically visualize all the prison doors flying open, my thoughts would return to you, and especially our last conversation before I left for Cuba.

When you walked through the door that last time, I knew right away that your leg was bothering you. You hobbled slowly across the room and when you got close I could see the layers of powder trying to mask the blotches of pain that stained your face.

And so, after a few minutes of attempted small-talk, I blurted out the question that had been spinning in my head ever since I met you.

How did you get your limp?

You looked surprised, and I wasn't sure whether this too would fall under that no-need-to-know umbrella category. Instead you answered,

You're right, Anise, you should know that story. It's not one for your senior thesis or the textbooks, but it isn't a secret either.

Early on, before my first arrest, I was out in the desert doing target practice with Rahim and other comrades. It was the end of a long day and we were all hot and tired but exhilarated because we had all been in fine form, in synch, during our training. I had just finished cleaning my gun when Rahim, who was in a hurry to get to a meeting, leaned over and grabbed it from me. It discharged into my leg. I had left a bullet in the chamber that I should have removed when I was doing the cleaning. Rahim had grabbed it roughly and carelessly. Together we both had violated two cardinal rules.

Everyone was disoriented and worried, but Rahim had to be on time to make his next connection so we all piled into the car and sped back to the city. Rahim and the others were already underground and it would have been too dangerous for them to go with me into the Emergency Room, so they dropped me off close by with strict instructions to get the leg taken care of immediately. To protect them, and collect myself, I limped several blocks to a coffee shop and drank coffee for more than an hour, struggling with my guilt and the pain in my leg, before finally going to the ER.

The bullet was removed, the wound was treated, and for months, maybe years at a time, I've forgotten it was even there. Yet it never fully healed. I never even got a chance to talk with Rahim about what had happened, since a few weeks later I was arrested the first time. But I've heard that he never forgave himself for his carelessness.

Sometimes the pain breaks through at random moments, maybe signifying a memory or a warning that I just can't grasp. And sometimes, its throbbing seems like a cautionary reminder that there is no release from the struggle. Like after 9/11 when I was in the hole fighting for my life.

I watched as you rubbed your leg hard, agitating and soothing the hurt at the same time. Telling the story had not stopped the pain.

Writing this communiqué to you hasn't stopped my pain either, but it is what I need you to know beyond what I represented in my senior thesis. When I showed you my completed paper, you were polite but we both realized that it was an artificial narrative filled with clear theses, exemplary lessons, and predictable conclusions, supposedly drawn from your life. The opposite of what I had learned from you.

This message is a raw jumble, Cassandra, as much about me as it is about you. It is not a long, drawn-out, hushed good-bye but a loud shout-out to you, across the unmappable zones of the universe.

LANDS END—
LUBA
2020

AT FIRST I WASN'T WORRIED WHEN ANISE DISAPPEARED FROM LANDS END. HER PRESENCE there had always been startling, even unsettling, as if I had imagined her into being—the youthful comrade I could share my history with, the daughter I never had.

On some level, I had expected Anise to disappear ever since I first bumped into her ten years ago at Lands End, a few months after Cassandra's death. We were both wandering the lower pathways, through the ruins of Sutro Baths, beside the ocean. In the thick summer fog, I didn't even recognize her. The hood of her sweatshirt covered part of her face and her distinctive long black curls. In the fog-drenched light, her face seemed contoured and porous, not angular and brash as it had looked under the fluorescent glare of the prison visiting room where I had last seen her.

When she called my name, for a minute I couldn't place her voice. When her name came to me, I was relieved. *Anise is full of unpredictable possibilities*, Cassandra had said to me before she died. *You should search her out.* I hadn't found the time, but serendipitously Anise had run across me in the place I went to get away from everyone.

At Lands End I stop trying to map the wrenching borders between life and after-life, past and future, hindsight and foresight. I stop obsessing about the petrifying walls between dispossessed and possessed, incarcerated and decarcerated, occupied and occupier. My mind gets quiet and I can hear the Yelamu Ohlone, who lived at Lands End before they were driven out, chanting, *We are dancing, dancing, dancing, dancing on the edge of the world.** I accept that centuries later I am tottering along with the rest of the planet on the ever-shifting frontier between parched land and consuming sea. The ocean is inching up toward the path where I first bumped into Anise in 2010. Sometimes I imagine that she and her comrades, or whatever they may call themselves, will one day create a submarine base for their spectacular actions in the caverns of Sutro Baths where she and I used to walk and talk about everything for hours.

That first day, when we met by accident, we talked only about Cassandra. Her death was just a few months past, still raw for both of us. We started with visiting room memorabilia. Banging the vending machines that were eating our money to force the release of the last remaining package of KitKats. Maneuvering to avoid the worst of the guards and fantasizing about schoolgirl pranks we could play to mess them up. Finding chairs in the back of the room, close to childcare, and watching

---

* Information about the Yelamu Ohlone from the pamphlet *The Yelamu Ohlone at Lands End*, by Linda Yamane and Jakki Kehl with the Lands End Lookout Ohlone Planning Team, Golden Gate National Parks Conservancy, 2012.

Cassandra's face light up when the son or daughter of one of her friends came rushing toward her. Until for no reason at all the prison closed down the childcare space in the middle of winter and the kids all milled around, threw tantrums, or got into fights from pent-up boredom and heartache.

Anise asked me how Sage was doing. *Not my mother, but Cassandra's cellie*, she added quickly, although it was obvious she wouldn't be asking me about her mother. I told her that since Cassandra's death Sage had changed her name again, this time to Adila, which meant justice in Arabic.

Cassandra's death really shook her, I said briefly by way of explanation, not wanting to go into details about the sobbing phone calls, the grief-filled letters, or our most recent prison visit when Sage explained why she was changing her name to Adila.

I haven't lived up to the name Sage. Whatever wisdom pretends to be, it's not my calling. But justice, that's something I plan to dedicate my life to.

When I didn't reply, Sage/Adila smiled and pressed my hand. *You don't have to believe me yet, Luba, but you'll see. I promise.*

Anise was staring at the ocean.

Adila was in a vision I had on the Malecón in Cuba when I was meditating for Cassandra, she said and glanced over at me to see if I looked skeptical. When I asked her to tell me about it, she described a human lifeline crossing walls and borders, summoning health and freedom for Cassandra. I felt a tremor move through me as she named the people she had seen in her vision—so many of *my* old comrades, friends, and lovers. Anise's fervor frightened me.

Cassandra had that power, to release visions in us. Even though most of them couldn't be realized, I managed to say in a steady voice. Anise nodded. *I brought Cassandra to Lands End*, I confided. *She was so weak by then that I tried to discourage her from going out, but she was adamant, as always. And she was right to insist. It was our best time together before she died.*

I was picturing Cassandra's lovely face, gaunt but exhilarated, shining against the crashing waves, when I stumbled over some pebbles and Anise had to grab me to break my fall. We had wandered into the Lands End Labyrinth, an artist's creation meant to help walkers channel the *chi* of this borderless space.

As we closed in on the center of the Labyrinth, we saw a pile of wilted flowers and sand-covered shells, offerings that visitors had made to whatever spirits they wanted to honor. Anise dug in her pocket and found a small rock that she placed on the top of the mound. Ordinarily I would have passed by without offering up anything. There were too many new age altars scattered throughout San Francisco that drew on ancient traditions without affirming community roots or meaning. But there was something about this moment, standing next to Anise, soaked in spray and memories of Cassandra, that demanded something more of me. I took off one of the amethyst earrings that I had gotten as a gift, years ago before I went underground, from my *curandera* girlfriend, Isabella. I placed it carefully on the pile, next to Anise's rock.

Anise looked at me as if I had lost my mind.

Don't worry, I still have another one, I said and pointed to the remaining solo hanging on my left ear.

Amethyst has protective energy, Anise said. *Or at least that's what my moms have always said. So hold on to that one*, she cautioned me seriously.

When I bumped into Anise the following week, I knew it was a planned coincidence this time. Anise had an agenda. She wanted to hear my stories. Gradually, I realized that I had an agenda as well. For years I had resisted requests for stories, memoirs, or videos that centered on me. But there were so many pieces of my past that I had never processed. So many tenuous, unbelievable threads linking then and now. Sometimes it felt like I had lived an imaginary history. Anise wanted to know and I wanted to tell. And so my stories came out, not in one consecutive marathon telling but in bits and pieces, over the years, as our paths collided and history kept moving on.

That second time we met, Anise started with a question about my son Nick and what he was up to. She had been close to him during high school and for a few years after that, but recently they had lost touch. I told her he had gotten his PhD in climatology a year ago and had gone off to Antarctica to research ice cores, marine sediments, and ozone holes. I wished he were closer to home but understood his drive to be a twenty-first-century *weatherman*. It was a silly joke that most people wouldn't get, but Anise laughed.

Talking about Nick always made me miss him more. I understood, on some level, why he had chosen to live on the geographic margins of the planet, but it made me feel guilty. As if this was the outgrowth of his early years living underground, when he didn't even know the names of my mother and father.

It made me feel as if I had bred distance and disconnection into his genes.

When Anise asked me whether the name Nick had any particular meaning, I could have given her the explanation I gave most people. He was named for two great revolutionary poets—Cuban, Nicolás Guillén, and Black American, Nikki Giovanni. Instead, I found myself revealing that Nick wasn't his birth name. I explained that he had originally been named Alex, for Alejandrina Torres, a Puerto Rican political prisoner. He only became Nick after we left LA. We had to give him an AKA since the FBI knew that Alex was the name on his birth certificate.

How did you decide to have a baby when you were living underground and knew you could be arrested at any minute? Anise asked. It sounded like this was the real question she had wanted to ask me from the beginning.

Anise can draw me out like very few people can, Cassandra had once told me. *Maybe because she has a stake in knowing the truth.*

So I told her the truth, or at least a lot of it. How at thirty-five, at the very same time that I was committing my life to clandestine revolution, I desperately, urgently wanted to have a baby. A biological urge, a desire to see the world through new eyes, a pledge toward future possibility—all of these feelings combined into a fierce craving. No matter how much my collective argued that it didn't make sense, that it could cause security problems, that the timing was bad, I refused to accept their logical reasons. After all, nothing about our situation was logical or reasonable.

I could have chosen motherhood over clandestinity. Gone back to San Francisco where Isabella, who had given me the amethyst earrings, was hoping I would reappear. There were no charges against me or anyone else at that point. But I didn't think I should have to choose. I could make revolution and also have a child like many women around the world had done, were doing. But to make that happen, I had to break our rules. I snuck away to a sperm bank in another part of LA without telling anyone. I told myself if I didn't get pregnant the first couple of times I would stop trying. But, astonishingly, I got pregnant right away.

For the first few months, I kept the baby a secret from everyone. I didn't want to jinx the thrilling process taking place in my belly. Besides, I kind of relished the irony—a life growing invisibly, unknown to even my clandestine collective. When I finally told my comrades, I expected recriminations. Instead, everyone was very happy. Maybe it wasn't rational, but they all wanted a baby in their lives too. The only person who got upset was Belinda.

Anise looked surprised. *Belinda?*

Without thinking, I had blurred the boundary between past and present and brought the person that Anise knew only as Gordon's mother's nurse friend into my story about Nick. Very few people knew that I had known Belinda when I was underground, although it wasn't a secret.

Now I had to explain at least the barebones of my relationship with Belinda. That I met her in LA at the hospital where I had a job as a secretary. That she became a friend at a time when I didn't have any apart from my collective. That my relationship with Belinda was always complicated. I had never quite understood why she had been so upset when I told her I was pregnant. Something about not wanting to bring children into such a screwed-up world. But after her initial reaction, she supported me 100 percent.

I told Anise how very sad it had made me to leave LA without even saying goodbye to Belinda. And how I couldn't believe the amazing coincidence when Belinda turned out to be Nick's nurse when he broke his leg and landed in the hospital shortly after we moved back to San Francisco.

I stopped there. I didn't tell Anise that connecting with Belinda in the hospital was only part coincidence. When Belinda walked into the hospital room that autumn day in 1996, I was trying to position Nick's pillows to make him more comfortable. He was acting stoic as usual, but I knew he was in a lot of pain. When the nurse said his name, *Nick Gold*, her voice sounded disturbingly familiar. I looked up and saw the shock of thick silver hair but still I couldn't believe it was her. Not until I looked directly at her face and saw her green eyes did I realize that some quirk of fate had brought Belinda Murphy and me together again, in a San Francisco hospital room.

Belinda accepted this stroke of luck more calmly than I did. While I marveled at the serendipity, she took Nick's vitals, questioned him closely about the details of his skateboarding accident, and gave him something for his pain. When he dozed off, we went out into the hall to talk.

It's not just coincidence, sweetie, she told me in the sardonic tone that I remembered instantly from the past. *I tracked stories about you for years after I found out from the FBI that your name wasn't Lynne but Luba. When I read in the paper that you were back in San Francisco, I got a job up here. You just found me before I found you.*

I had no idea what to say. Since I had surfaced, there had been many uncanny, storybook flukes that had unexpectedly brought me together with people from my past. But Belinda was someone I never thought I would see again. She had haunted me since the day we escaped from LA. Only frantic fear for Belinda's safety and ours had kept me from calling to let her know that Nick and I were okay. In those first months on the run, I secretly believed that the Guatemalan worry dolls she had given me helped protect Nick and me from being caught.

Belinda interrupted my confusion.

Besides, I needed to get away from the LA heat, she said more sensibly. *The weather up here is so much more balanced.*

After Nick was out of the hospital, Belinda and I got together for coffee. I assumed that the misfires in our past relationship were my fault. I had lied to her about almost everything—my name, my girlfriend, even the date of my birthday. When I did let a little of the truth sneak out, about Puerto Rico or being pregnant, it seemed to cause more roadblocks between us. Now I wanted to be open and speak freely.

When I noticed a Puerto Rican flag tattooed on Belinda's forearm, I eagerly asked her about it. She told me she had gotten it after the FBI knocked on her door and announced that her coworker *Lynne* was mixed up with Puerto Rican terrorists. Instead of scaring her, they made her want to brand Puerto

Rico on her body so no one could ever overlook that part of her identity again.

What did the FBI ask you? I tried to ask the question casually, as if it didn't really matter to me whether she had talked to the FBI or not.

Oh, honey, don't worry. They never got that far. Apparently my bitchy nurse's voice was more than they could handle. After I yelled at them to go away and slammed the door, they never came back. She gave me a sideways glance and added, *I also put a hex on them. That helped keep them away—from me and from you.*

Before I could react, she continued.

I got rid of that envelope you left with me. Roasted it on the beach with just the dogs as witnesses. Then she added half-seriously, *I hope you didn't expect me to save it all these years.*

Of course not! I exclaimed. In fact I had forgotten all about the envelope. It had just been a test, a way for our collective to gauge whether Belinda could be trusted with real clandestine responsibilities. There hadn't really been any sensitive information in the envelope, so it had fallen off my mental list of things I needed to worry about. Now I had to add this to the tally of thoughtless mistakes we had made in that period.

I began to thank Belinda profusely for what she had done, for risking herself, for not betraying us. She stopped me.

I did it for myself and grandma Consuela, no thanks needed, she said pointedly.

I started to tell her about our case, about the Puerto Rican woman prisoner we were trying to help escape when we got caught in a huge sting operation and had to escape ourselves. About the Puerto Rican prisoners who were still inside serving endless sentences. And about Cassandra who had been trapped as a result of the sting and was now in prison in Dublin, not far from San Francisco.

When Belinda started tapping on the table with her fork, I switched gears and asked about her dogs. She happily launched into descriptions of how each of them had transitioned to doggie heaven, except for Consuela, who somehow was miraculously hanging on to life. Recently she had gone to the rescue shelter and gotten a new puppy. She named the puppy Luba.

Luba means love in Russian, she explained as if I wouldn't know this basic fact about my birth name. *Perfect for my new bundle of love, don't you agree?*

I couldn't think of anything to say in response.

I didn't tell Anise any of these anecdotes about Belinda, but as our walks at Lands End settled into a regular schedule, I did describe how hard it had been, when I first returned to San Francisco, to reconcile my nostalgic memories of people from my past with their reality in the present. Many old friends had settled into families and nonprofit-networks-for-good. Others had given up on social change and were concentrating on personal transformation. Still others, like Belinda, held on to a stubborn but solo path for making justice.

Back above ground, I was losing my foothold. A former-fugitive lesbian mother, working as a secretary with a preadolescent son who had a voracious interest in the earth's geography and an uncanny knowledge of radical history. Where did we fit in the topography of the U.S. 1990s?

It was Cassandra who brought me perspective and balance in those years. Cassandra, who loved geography as much as Nick and told him which history books were worth reading and which he should read just so he could know how the other side thought. During our weekly visits, she and Nick played *Where in the World Is Carmen Sandiego?*, and their own version of Scrabble, limiting the words they could place on the board to the scientific category of the day—botany, geography, astronomy, climatology.

Sometimes, I would visit Cassandra by myself. We would start talking about geopolitics, world philosophy, and international poetry, but inevitably we would circle back to our own slice of radical history—the many mistakes, the rare victories, the cryptic twists of fate that had landed her and so many others in prison and kept me, and a few others, free. Cassandra patiently discouraged my survivor's guilt, especially when it came to Joan and the ill-fated phone call that had ultimately resulted in Cassandra's arrest. I doggedly nourished her hope for release, even after 9/11 when she was in her darkest place.

Ironically, it was Cassandra who reconnected me, through a prisoner-driven circuitous route, back to Belinda. I had lost touch with Belinda after a few strained dates where we searched for, but never figured out, our common ground. Years passed and then Cassandra got a letter from Rahim while he was preparing for trial, locked in SF County Jail. He wrote that he had met a nurse named Maggie when he was in the hospital for back surgery. She was an interesting woman and he cared for her a lot, but he was worried about her mental health. He hoped Cassandra might have some ideas about how to help. Cassandra thought of me and the Unshackled Women community that I had been part of since I returned to San Francisco.

When I got together with Maggie, I vaguely recognized her as a parent at Nick's high school. Her son Gordon was several years younger than Nick, but they had friends in common and sometimes skateboarded together. More surprisingly, Maggie remembered me from a Parole Board hearing in Sacramento where I had spoken in support of Celestina, a prisoner Unshackled Women was advocating for.

You were so calm and professional, Maggie told me. *But there was something in your voice that made me think that any minute you might pull out a gun and put a stop to the Board's cruel charade.*

I shivered. Many times as I stood before the Parole Board, I had pushed down just that type of fantasy, a raging relic from my distant past.

When I brought Maggie to visit Cassandra I found out that she was best friends with Belinda, whom she worked with at the hospital. I was surprised but glad. Over the years I had come to accept that the cosmos sometimes unexpectedly restored a little bit of equilibrium to the ragged tilt of human relationships.

Our visits with Cassandra seemed to help Maggie become more centered, especially when it came to Rahim. Cassandra didn't like to dwell on the past, but now and then a story about Rahim from back in the day would slip into our conversation. Then the wildness flitting through Maggie's eyes mellowed as she envisioned him, a young Panther in his twenties, trying to change the world.

When the California charges against Rahim were dropped and he was shipped back to Pennsylvania, Maggie told us she was thinking of going to visit him there and asked us whether we thought that was crazy.

Everything about love and prisons is crazy, Cassandra said sharply. *If you want to see him, go. We'll be here to help you figure it out.*

After our visits with Cassandra, Maggie and I would stop by Belinda's house. The first time Maggie suggested this, I hesitated. After leaving the prison, I wanted warmth and comfort, not the veiled innuendoes and hidden tensions that my time with Belinda usually brought. But Maggie insisted and unexpectedly we started a post-visit routine that turned out to be just what we all needed. With the candles lit and the music playing in Belinda's living room, I would settle into a chair, take a few tokes, and stroke Luba, who was no longer a puppy but was very lovable. While they made dinner, Maggie would recap ludicrous prison visit details, Belinda would make clever jokes, and together we would laugh until our sides hurt.

Anise listened to my stories intently as we wandered off-road, up and down the Lands End cliffs that first year. The concentration in her eyes and the pursing of her lips told me that she wasn't just absorbing all I had to say. She was translating it into some poem or other algorithm of her own. Still, it bothered me that she told me little about herself. None of my prompts succeeded in cracking open her reserve. Until Occupy Oakland.

When Occupy Wall Street started on September 17, 2011, I yearned to discuss it with Cassandra. I wanted to pick apart the significance of this new political moment. Ten years after September 11, 2001, and the decade-long aftermath of counterterrorism and repression, the world had almost forgotten what an uprising looked like. But 2011 had begun with the momentous Arab Spring rebellions and resistance seemed to be sprouting again, even in the U.S. homeland. I wanted to ponder with Cassandra, in a way I couldn't with anyone else, the complicated questions of language—*Occupy, We Are the 99%*. The way these terms seemed to gloss over the contradictions between occupiers and occupied and the vast differences of race, class, and gender within the so-called 99%. At the same time, I knew Cassandra would welcome this new experiment in movement-building with an open heart, as I did.

I hadn't seen Anise for at least a month when we met up at Lands End at the beginning of October. As soon as I saw her, I could tell that something different was brewing. Her face was glowing in the sparkling October light. She almost danced along the road beside me as ideas and plans burst from her mouth.

She had been meeting with a group of people who were planning to launch Occupy Oakland to coincide with Indigenous People's Resistance Day on October 10. Occupy Oakland would build on Occupy Wall Street but would be intentionally different. It would ground its vision in the spirit of anticolonial struggle, in the spirit of the Ohlones whose land they would now be occupying in the service of liberation. They would prioritize the voices of Oakland's Black and Brown community members who had been violently occupied by the police for decades. Together they would reclaim Oakland for the disenfranchised peoples who were now being pushed out by foreclosures, evictions, and gentrification.

Her exhilaration was contagious. Various spoiler alerts occurred to me, but what would be the point in naming them? Anise was on fire and I loved the visionary possibilities even if I could predict the pitfalls. I told her I would come by Occupy Oakland when it took off.

The first time I went to Oscar Grant Plaza I felt the spark. Forty-five years before, the Panthers had shifted everything when they began feeding breakfast to schoolchildren a few miles away from this encampment. Now the diverse group that started Occupy Oakland was carrying forward this tradition with a community kitchen, a children's village, and a medic's tent. The sterile city square that had been called Frank Ogawa Plaza was being repurposed as an insurgent commons, an autonomous zone, open to all.

I hung back, watching how Anise moved deliberately from space to space, engaging in intense political conversation one moment, playing with a group of children the next, intervening in an argument that threatened to escalate into something worse. When she saw me, she sprinted across the narrow pathway, navigating easily between the dozens of tents, sleeping bags, and toys.

I'm so glad you came, Luba, she declared and immediately began to introduce me to dozens of people who welcomed another OG to their blossoming community.

It wasn't until the evening's General Assembly debate about how to respond to the city's eviction threats that my early worries crept back into my head. The Assembly started out strong with passionate speeches that were amplified by the collective voice of the people's mic. But as the speakers' stack kept piling up, more white men began to take center stage, the women who were facilitating lost their grip, and the tone shifted from militant to belligerent. One man kept shouting from the sidelines, *Just let them try to make us leave, we will fuck them up!* and no one could stop him from interrupting.

Anise was only sleeping a few hours every night, but she knew I needed my rest so she had made sure that there was tent space reserved for me. I was very tired, but it was hard to fall asleep. I had forgotten to bring an extra sleeping pad and my back ached from standing all day. At some point someone a few sleeping bags away called out the phrase *I'm on a boat* and it began to ricochet from one ground spot to the next. Was it an existential comment, a prophecy of climate change, a stoned nonsense joke, or all of the above, I wondered? As the phrase was picked up and echoed through the square, my annoyance grew. Was this encampment a serious grounded takeover in the tradition of Alcatraz and Wounded Knee or was it a floating, whimsical bubble that could be shattered by the first police siren? My back was throbbing, I needed my sleep, and I wanted the boat meme to stop.

My irritation turned into nagging worry. Something wasn't right. I had overlooked something very important but I couldn't figure out what it was. Had I forgotten to pick Nick up from school? Had I missed a crucial phone call with our contacts in Uprising? Had I brought my old fake Lynne Rogers ID instead of my Luba Gold one to this occupation? Somewhere a siren went off and a wave of terror ran through me. That was it!

I had forgotten all the most basic clandestine rules. I was sleeping in the middle of a public Oakland square, exposed to the violent impulses of the Oakland police, powerless to escape.

I struggled to wake up, grabbed my backpack, and stiffly pushed myself off the ground before I realized that everyone else around me was sleeping calmly. The siren that had broken into my dream was just one of hundreds routinely disrupting the night, maybe an ambulance or a police car. Nothing to do with our encampment except in the cosmic sense.

I couldn't go back to sleep so I wandered over to a group of people who were telling stories about their confrontations with the police in this same square after Oscar Grant was murdered.

This is our commons, our square, one of the most vocal white men from the General Assembly kept insisting, though no one was disagreeing with him. He put his arm protectively around the woman sitting next to him. *We have to be prepared and be ready to defend ourselves. For Oscar Grant's sake*, he proclaimed, and everyone around him nodded in agreement. I started to ask what he thought that entailed, but something about the enthusiasm of the woman sitting next to him made me feel protective of her also. I kept my mouth shut.

When I saw Anise a couple of days after Occupy's eviction from the square, I could tell immediately that she was running on pure adrenaline. She speed rapped the description of the early morning police raid that had left the camp in ruins, the tent homes flattened despite all their plans for resistance. But later that day thousands of people surged into the downtown streets charging through police barricades and braving a blanketing barrage of tear gas. Over a hundred people were busted and an Iraq War vet had his skull fractured by police rubber bullets. That night they reoccupied the plaza and held a General Assembly of over two thousand people. They agreed to a plan to shut down Oakland the following week by calling for a general strike on November 2.

I wanted to hear what she was thinking, how they thought they could pull off a general strike in less than a week, what were the planned-out steps beyond the general strike, beyond the public occupation that could be torn down by the cops in the wink of an eye.

Anise shook her head vigorously in frustration.

We don't have time to do the analysis, unpack all the dynamics right now, Luba. As you say, the general strike is just a week away. If we lose our focus, we're done!

A week later, as I marched through the streets of Oakland with fifty thousand others, walking, biking, skateboarding, dancing past shuttered businesses to blockade the port as part of the general strike, I thought perhaps Anise had been right. This had been the necessary next step, the massive public claiming of the port of entry to the urban center, the launching pad for more strategic action. I was too stuck in my old-school ways of thinking. I had to put more trust in the intuitive flows of the young.

When Anise called me one morning about ten days later, the urgency in her voice made me rearrange my plans and meet her at Lands End that afternoon. She announced right away, probably as a disclaimer, that she hadn't slept in days. Fatigue flattened her face, and her sentences were disjointed fragments I had to glue together to make sense of the story she was trying to tell.

The period since the general strike had been hard. After the victory, the surge of people's power, it seemed like things could come together, they could rebuild their collective strength, resist the repression, strategize for a sustainable action plan. But instead, all the power trips, unspoken hierarchies, barely concealed divisions began blowing up. Everywhere she turned there was a hidden land mine of racist bullshit, rape culture, and outright piggery. Then a man was shot and killed near the plaza. The city council and the police implied that this was connected to Occupy. Even though everyone knew it wasn't, the incident sent a chill through the encampment. It made Anise wonder how all the human damage from conquest and capitalism could ever be overcome.

Anise was slurring off into abstractions, so I asked her if there was something specific she wanted to talk about. She looked surprised, as if she had forgotten the urgency that had made her call me that morning. She took a deep breath and began again more coherently.

There was this man, Milo, whom she had become friends with over the course of Occupy. At first he struck her as a little arrogant, but most white men had that in them. The thing she liked about him was that he seemed serious. He knew a lot about radical history and international theory. His parents had been antiwar activists in the seventies, or so he said. He learned a lot from their generation. They really tried to make revolution. They didn't just talk about it. The peoples' assemblies were all well and good but that type of public discussion only went so far, he thought.

It wasn't a physical attraction but a mental synergy—synapses firing as they discussed the philosophy of revolution, the meaning of militance, the role of clandestinity. She didn't agree with everything Milo said, but she loved the free-flowing, no-holds-barred fabric of their conversations. She began to seek him out when there were problems she didn't think she could figure out on her own.

Several days ago, just as so many things in the plaza seemed to be imploding, Milo asked Anise to come to a meeting. There were some folks who wanted to do things in a different way, take things to a less public level, he explained. She was interested and told him she would come to the meeting, but at the last minute she didn't go. She wished she could say it was her sixth sense about who he was, but actually she had wanted to go. Instead, she stayed at the Plaza to be part of a women's meeting to deal with a sexual assault that had just taken place.

She didn't see Milo after the missed meeting and briefly wondered where he was, but it wasn't unusual for folks to disappear and then reappear. Then the night before last, just before everyone started to gather for the weekly march through downtown, the word went out that a few people had just been busted for some alleged conspiracy against the OPD. Immediately she assumed that Milo must be one of the people arrested. But when they heard the names, Milo's wasn't one of them. His girlfriend had been busted and a couple of other guys he had hung out with, but not Milo.

People started saying that Milo must have set the others up, but Anise cautioned them not to jump to conclusions. Yesterday, a friend of hers whom she trusted had gone to visit Milo's girlfriend in jail. She tearfully confirmed that Milo had snitched the others out, even though the ideas of what to do to fuck up the police had been all his from the start. No one had seen Milo since the bust.

How could I be so gullible? Anise asked, stiff and self-accusatory. *You would think that some of my mother's cynicism about people would have rubbed off on me*, she said with an acid laugh.

I said goodbye to Anise without offering any wise amulet to ward off her bitterness. All I could think about was my conversation with her mother at Lands End, before I went underground.

When Sage told me that she didn't want to come with us, it wasn't a surprise. She had signaled her withdrawal for quite a while, and our collective had planned for this contingency. Some people were angry at her, some felt betrayed by her lack of commitment, and some, like me, felt very sad. I had wanted Sage to undertake this risky experiment with us not only because she was my friend but because many of her questions were also, secretly, mine. The difference was that I thought such questions could only be answered through practice.

By the time Sage and I met up at Lands End, there was no point rehashing the pros and cons anymore. Instead, as the waves exploded below us, we talked about the global revolutionary victories—Cuba, Vietnam, Mozambique—that had first propelled us both to become involved with Uprising. We pondered the defeats and setbacks that now seemed to be overtaking the wins. Until I remembered I had a job to do and followed the script that the collective had decided upon. I told Sage that she couldn't have anything to do with Uprising anymore.

Sage recoiled as if I had hit her in the face.

So that's it? After working together for ten years, I'm now banned for life? she accused with an acid laugh.

At the time, I couldn't think of anything to say in response. But in the underground years that followed, I wondered time and again why I hadn't told Sage the truth—that I was breaking up inside and couldn't even remember why we had decided that this absolute rupture with her was the best way to proceed. I heard from our contacts in Uprising that Sage had followed our instructions faithfully, removing herself from everything having to do with our organization and its political work. I encouraged people to reach out to her. But by then it was way too late.

When I surfaced and returned to San Francisco in 1995, I was told that Sage wore her bitterness like a flak jacket, repelling all overtures from the old crew. I wanted to talk with her, to apologize face to face for the role I had played. She was polite when I occasionally bumped into her but ignored my calls suggesting we get together and talk.

When the U.S. invaded Iraq in March 2003, I unexpectedly spent the day with Sage when Nick and Anise brought us together in an affinity group. Along with thousands of others, we shut down the Bay Bridge, laid our bodies on the streets, and shouted furiously at the gleaming towers of imperial power. We couldn't stop the carnage that was to come, but running through the streets that day started to heal the twenty-year breach between Sage and me.

I couldn't tell Anise about what had happened with her mother at Lands End. It wasn't my story to confide. But thinking about Sage made me realize there was another story I could share that might help Anise. It was the story that Joan had written, explaining why she had worked with Reynaldo, the FBI agent who orchestrated the sting that landed Cassandra in prison. Joan sent it to me shortly after we learned about her part in the sting operation through the court Discovery documents that emerged in Chicago. *Share this with anyone you want*, Joan had written at the top of the first page.

A month later, Anise and I got together at Lands End. By that time Occupy had been evicted from Oscar Grant Plaza for good, and Milo's name had been all over the papers after he appeared in court as a government witness against several activist occupiers.

Before I could ask, Anise told me she had read Joan's story and had a question for me.

Did you forgive her? She set you up, made you leave LA when Nick was just a tiny baby, and then she asked for your forgiveness. Did you give it to her? Her tone was more demanding than questioning.

I told her that it was more complicated than yes or no. The word *forgiveness* came with too much baggage—Christian binary thinking, simplistic formulas.

That's too abstract for me, Anise claimed, so I tried to explain.

When our lawyers showed us the court Discovery that named Joan as the person on the phone call directing us to go to Miami, I immediately blamed myself. It was that call and the instruction to switch our plans from the Northwest that set in motion all the events of the next ten years. Members of my collective had gone to Miami as instructed and connected with Cassandra there to help plan the escape of a Puerto Rican woman prisoner. Unknown to us, the Miami contacts were really FBI agents who secretly followed my collective members back to Los Angeles. Fortunately, we discovered the FBI surveillance, left LA immediately, and somehow escaped. But Cassandra wasn't as lucky. She was arrested the following year, after the FBI had given up on trying to find us through her. She was convicted of participating in the escape conspiracy with added time for her own escape years before.

I reproached myself for not having recognized Joan's voice on the fateful phone call, until Francis pointed out that it wouldn't have mattered. Even if I had, we would have assumed that Joan was working with us, not against us. Francis wanted to take the blame herself. She was the one who had known Joan since high school. She was the one who brought Joan to Amigos, who lived with her and watched her relationship with Reynaldo develop. Francis hadn't trusted Reynaldo. She should have done more to stop them both.

When Joan sent me the story she had written as disclosure and penance, I began to understand that we all had some responsibility for the road Joan had taken. We had been so full of our righteous rage, our correct political convictions, our determination to push ourselves and others to the limits of militancy that we excluded those who wanted a different role. We failed to see how our harshness, our superior standards, our cliquishness could drive people into the arms of our enemies.

I shared Joan's story with Cassandra. I told Cassandra that I was grateful for Joan's willingness to tell her side, to give us insight into why she followed Reynaldo's game plan. But at the end of the story, when she asked for my forgiveness, as if this were a confession ripe for absolution, it made me angry.

Cassandra responded with the steel-edged tone that she reserved for the thorniest moral dilemmas. *Joan needs to hear what happened on the other end of the phone line. How you felt escaping from LA with Nick in your arms and little more, spending ten years on the run—scared, estranged, helpless, irrelevant. What it meant that she, Joan, thwarted a plan that might have freed a Puerto Rican prisoner. What it meant that she helped put me behind bars, maybe for the rest of my life.*

I decided to go back to Pittsburgh and see Joan. South Africa had developed a Truth and Reconciliation process for its people to come to terms with the perpetrators of the brutal abuse they had suffered. Those who had lived through the scourge of COINTELPRO in the United States had no such tools for working through the enormous damage it had done. No matter that this was just a tiny piece of a mutilated landscape, I was determined to hold Joan accountable, face to face.

It was my first time back in Pittsburgh since we had surfaced the year before. As the cab approached Joan's house, which was eerily close to the one I had lived in with Nick for seven years, I felt a surge of relief. I was only visiting. Finally released from exile, I was no longer trapped by Pittsburgh's rain and dreariness. I could appreciate how friendly a place it had actually been, how it had generously protected us, and how radiant the trees looked when the drizzle lifted and their leaves glistened and glimmered in the sunlight.

Joan had recently had a baby, Sean. Even though I could see bumpy red signs of nervousness on her face when she came to the door, nothing could dim her new-mother glow. She quickly explained that she and her husband George had been trying to have a child for years but hadn't been able to. None of the fertility doctors they visited could figure out what the problem was. Then, unexpectedly, soon after she read that I had surfaced, she had become pregnant.

Joan suggested that we take Sean for a walk so we could talk while he napped. My breath caught when we arrived at a nearby playground. Nick and I had spent countless hours at just this playground. It was Nick's carefree joy sweeping down the enormous blue slide at the center of the park that allowed me to accept landlocked Pittsburgh as our temporary home, thousands of miles away from the Pacific coast and all the people I loved who lived there.

Sitting with Joan and baby Sean and many cheerful children slipping and sliding around us, my determination to talk about damage and accountability with Joan dissolved. Instead, we discussed breastfeeding and childcare challenges. She told me about the work she was doing with mothers who had AIDS, and I told her about Unshackled Women, the organization for women prisoners that was just starting up.

Joan wanted to know what it had been like being a fugitive with a baby. Now that she had Sean it made her even more sorry for the turmoil she had put me through. I offered a few anecdotes that were more funny than painful. I couldn't bring myself to tell her more.

When I was getting ready to leave that evening, Joan asked if it would be okay if she wrote the Puerto Rican women who still were in prison. Sometimes she heard their voices in her dreams, struggling to speak through taped mouths. She hoped that they would forgive her too. I started to say that Cassandra was the one she should really write to, but I stopped myself. I didn't think this was a correspondence that Cassandra would welcome.

By the end of this twisting story, I wasn't sure what point I was trying to convey about forgiveness. But it seemed to satisfy Anise.

Is it okay if I give Joan's story to my mom to read? she asked.

Sure, I replied, hiding my surprise at this suggestion. *Sage would probably find it very interesting.*

For a while, Anise continued to work with the antirepression committee of Occupy Oakland, supporting the many people who had been busted for one thing or another during the six weeks of the encampment. She toyed with the idea of becoming a lawyer, so that she could be more useful in the fight to keep people out of prison, but soon changed her mind. She couldn't relegate herself to such circumscribed effectiveness, she explained.

She began to travel and I would get occasional e-mails with lyrical descriptions of struggles in Palestine, Venezuela, Egypt, JeJu. I began to worry that she would become just another radical roamer, restlessly searching the globe for the perfect insurgent moment, the peak revolutionary experience for this age.

She returned to San Francisco for her moms' twentieth anniversary celebration in the beginning of 2014. I was surprised when I received an invitation and scolded Anise for pressuring Sage and Brooke into inviting me, but she assured me that it was their idea. I had missed the start of their relationship and the years since, but I was glad to be part of their recommitment ceremony. It made me feel strangely young, as if we all still had decades in front of us to figure out what recommitment meant. It was a sweet, hopeful moment before the 2014 death vortex began sucking revolutionary souls into the earth.

Amiri Baraka, Chowkwe Lumumba, Gabriel García Márquez, Maya Angelou, Yuri Kochiyama, Fred Ho, Steve Whitman, Felix Shaeffer, Nadine Gordimer, Hurricane Carter, Chinosole, the Freeman Brothers, Samiya Davis Abdullah, Herman Ferguson. These were the quiet deaths from "natural causes," marked by an outpouring of life tributes and memorials.

Then there was the screaming storm of unforgivable murders that blasted through the camouflage of normalcy and peace. Mike Brown in Ferguson. John Crawford at an Ohio Walmart. Eric Garner in Staten Island. Tamir Rice in Cleveland. Alex Nieto in San Francisco. Aura Rain Rosser in Ann Arbor. Roshad McIntosh in Chicago. Ezell Ford in Los Angeles. A cross-continent death squad of police drilling holes in Black and Brown bodies. The occupying army that had been hidden in plain sight for decades, revealed with chilling clarity by the bullets' red glare.

While in cold-blooded global symmetry, Israel launched Operation Protective Edge against Gaza, massacring children on Gaza's beaches, bombing hospitals and schools to ashes, razing houses to rubble and droning neighborhoods into the ground. Till the Palestinians turned the tide—ricocheting rocks, rockets, and rage from the fiery center of Gaza, signaling to the whole world that their will to resist had not been annihilated.

Out on the cliffs, Anise read to me from the Gazan woman poet Nayrouz Kharmout:

A flame within me, an orange bubble glowing angrily, the din killing me . . . For a grain of sand from the sea of Gaza will not ignite, except as hope in the heart beating under a wave which whets the love of life . . . *

As the sun's rays splintered red against the waves of Lands End, an orange glow burned up the insides of Anise's eyes.

Adila got out of prison at the end of November, the day that the Ferguson grand jury failed to indict Darren Wilson, the police officer who killed Mike Brown. On the way to the half-way house in Oakland, our car got stuck in a massive traffic jam as Oakland protesters stormed the freeway.

A tipping point had been reached and the orange bubble of rage that had been simmering for years barely below the surface exploded on the streets. People around the country were seizing streets, bridges, and trains, raising their arms high— *hands up, don't shoot*—transforming a gesture of surrender into

---

* From Nayrouz Kharmout, *My City Burning Peacefully (Our Gaza Is a Dream of Hope)*, translated by Sarah Irving and published in *The Electronic Intifada*, July 26, 2014.

a meme of resistance. While cars honked and drivers fumed around us, Anise, Adila, and I got out of the car, linked arms, stamped our feet, and shouted until our voices were hoarse and cracked—*Black Lives Matter!*

A few weeks later, when Adila was finally able to get a day pass from the halfway house, Anise and I brought her, Coretta, and Jamani to Lands End for a freedom celebration. We hiked down to the labyrinth and while Jamani ran around the circles searching for sea treasures, the four of us sat on a bench and talked. Adila had a million plans now that she finally was free and determined never to go back. Her energy was so absorbing that I didn't notice that she kept rubbing her right leg until Anise asked her what was going on. She rolled up her pants and showed us a black box electronic monitor wrapped tightly around her ankle.

I can't get this thing to stop chafing, she explained, her voice immediately deflated. *They call it a bracelet but shit, it's just another shackle. And the chafing makes my whole leg hurt.*

They're setting you up in an open-air prison, just like Gaza, Anise muttered angrily. *Cheaper than keeping you in a prison building.*

But before we could dig deeper into this mess, Jamani ran over to Adila and presented her with gifts of shells and sand that he had gathered. Adila threw her arms around him.

No matter, she exclaimed. *I'm out here with my beautiful child and my guardian angels and I can feel the ocean spray. I can't ask for more. At least not today.*

Adila started working with Unshackled Women, and soon I could see that she would take our vision to new places. She brought many other former prisoners to the work. She righteously hustled legislators and donors day and night. And she convinced Anise to throw her restless energy into the most draconian cases—those who were labeled the worst of the worst in the women's prisons. For a while Anise immersed herself in their lives, pushing out the stories, digging through trial transcripts, going to Parole Board hearings and organizing protests at the prison gates. Unshackled Women grew along with the movement against police terror and mass incarceration. A sea change indeed, or so we hoped.

When Celestina was released, Adila, Anise, Maggie, and I were at the prison gates along with Amapola, Candelaria, and all the kids and grandkids. Ten years after we had made our impassioned, futile appeal for her freedom in front of the Parole Board in Sacramento, they had finally decided that Celestina and her family had been punished enough.

We shared a bittersweet meal at the Merced Hometown Buffet, the site of many post-visit and post-release gatherings. While Celestina loaded her plate with free-world food, we traded stories about the Parole Board, orange crush pepper spray, the hole and, most of all, the others who were still left behind.

A few days later, Maggie got a call from Amapola. Celestina was having an allergic reaction to her ankle monitor. Her leg was blowing up with rashes and swelling, but her parole officer refused to consider removing it. Adila flew into action, contacting the assemblywoman from Celestina's district, whom she now knew well, and within a few days the paperwork had been signed and the bracelet was removed.

Good for Celestina, but what about all the others? Anise grumbled.

Of course, we had no answer. Since the Israeli company Secure-It-All had enveloped the U.S. market with its enormous menu of GPS products, Electronic Monitoring, or EM, had proliferated exponentially. Anklets, bracelets, choker necklaces, and even oversized toe rings were marketed as offender-friendly accessories and now occupied Brown and Black bodies at an unprecedented rate. They encircled the legs, arms, ears, and feet of those on gang injunctions and bail, those awaiting trial or deportation, and those who had done their time and were trying to reenter the community. The bracelets had even expanded to youth and homeless people who were deemed *at risk* for crime.

Some companies had started producing lookalike products so that "law-abiding" community members could wear similar styles either in satire or solidarity. Looking at people in the streets, on MUNI and on BART, the only telltale distinction between those wearing the real EM and the wannabe versions was that the people with nonremovable devices were constantly rubbing their arms and legs to alleviate their chafing and pain.

One night, soon after Celestina's monitor was removed, Anise called me. I had gone to sleep early, exhausted from a daylong prison visit. At this point in my life, the visits were more draining than ever. I couldn't figure out how much was a byproduct of my aging and how much was creeping burnout— something I had sworn I would never succumb to.

I was deep into a recurrent nightmare where I had committed a fatal security error that had led the FBI to me, Nick, and our whole collective when the phone's buzz woke me. I saw Anise's number and my heart started racing as it always did when I received a call from Nick at night, before I heard his voice and was reassured that he wasn't in trouble but had just forgotten to accurately count the time difference between San Francisco and whatever corner of the planet he happened to be in.

The Gaza database has been destroyed! Anise exclaimed excitedly. *All the information the Israelis have been gathering on the population since 2014 is gone, no trace at all. What an action!*

For a few moments I thought I was still asleep and dreaming, except my dreams were never so wildly inventive these days. In the aftermath of Operation Protective Edge, Palestinian friends had reported that the Israeli government had escalated its effort to collect information about every aspect of Gazan lives. The information was collected in a new gargantuan database that included intimate details about each family member, which were then used to bribe or threaten people into submission. Now Anise was saying that the entire database was gone. I couldn't quite believe it was true.

But it was. And the scope of the action extended further to databases in towns and villages across the West Bank. While we marveled at the genius of the Palestinian hacktivists, Israel and the U.S. vowed to make the terrorists pay.

A couple of months later, Anise asked to go for a walk at Lands End and told me that she was feeling burnt out and needed to take a break from prison organizing. She had found a job teaching English as a second language in Lebanon and she thought it would be a good experience for her.

I tried to argue her out of the decision, something I rarely did with the many young activists I worked with who were constantly grappling with thorny choices about how to survive and thrive. I was disappointed that Anise was resuming her roaming, her vicarious experience of revolution, just at a point when she had acquired legal and organizing skills that were very valuable to the movement here. Besides, I only saw Nick a few times a year. I wanted Anise close. But she already had her plane ticket. It was one of the few times we parted without resolving a disagreement.

At first I received regular e-mails from her, but then they became sporadic. One day when I was in the office with Adila, I complained to her that Anise seemed to have forgotten all of her political commitments, not to mention her friends.

I don't think that's what's happening, Adila told me dismissively as she continued to sort through piles of prisoner mail. I wasn't satisfied and continued to rant about how we had placed a lot of trust in Anise, mentored her, and had legitimate expectations that she would follow through on what she had started. There were still so many others that we needed to free. Anise was using her privilege as a white woman, picking up and leaving while political prisoners like Rahim were still stuck in dungeons after forty years.

Adila put the mail down with a thump and grabbed me by the shoulders.

Check yourself, Luba! You of all people should be able to figure out what's going on.

I sank back into my chair. In that split second I got it. How dense I had been, how willfully blind to take Anise's cover story at face value. I began to apologize to Adila for being so stupid and was about to break down entirely when she put her hand on mine.

You have a right to miss her. I do too. We just can't talk about it.

A few times over the next couple of years, after the e-mails from Anise had stopped altogether, I was on the verge of asking Adila what more she knew—where did she think Anise was based, and who was she working with? But every time I would be stopped by my memory of Cassandra's pained look, back when we were first together in the '70s, when I would demand information about where she had disappeared to. A few years later, once Cassandra was in prison and I had lost hope of ever holding her again, I was on the other end of a relationship. When my girlfriend Isabella pleaded for information after I went missing for days and later months, I would remind her about the need-to-know principle, trying to ignore the pool of tears that inevitably welled up in her eyes.

Amethyst has protective energy, Anise told me when I offered up my amethyst earring to the Lands End altar the first time I bumped into her there. Whenever I start to speculate or worry about her, I touch the solo that I still wear every day, hoping that some of that energy will find its way to Anise's underground labyrinth, wherever that might be.

November 2, 2019, was the fortieth anniversary of Assata Shakur's liberation from prison. It was my custom every year to spend this day at Lands End, using the time to reflect and resolve. Assata's escape seemed miraculous, even forty years later. How astounding that she was still living free in Cuba, that most courageous *palenque* or *maroon camp*, as Assata had described it.

I thought I had turned off my phone, but all of a sudden it started buzzing and wouldn't stop. I started to worry that something serious had happened and reluctantly took the phone out of my pocket. Luckily, I was near a bench and could sit down when I began to read the storm of messages.

The integrated EM systems governing thousands of electronic monitoring bracelets, anklets, necklaces, and rings in San Francisco had been hacked and destroyed. The hyped, impermeable hardware-software end-to-end tracking network was now incapable of tracing anything. People had begun to cut the bracelets from their legs, arms, necks, and feet. The hashtag #breakthebracelet was going viral and the sheriff's office was trying to get Twitter to take it down.

I drove as quickly as possible to the Unshackled Women office where people were already starting to gather. The sheriff and police chief were in a state of shock. They issued instructions to everyone who had a bracelet to report to the local police station. When no one voluntarily responded to this request, they put out the call for community members to make citizens' arrests of those they thought looked suspicious, those who might have worn a bracelet the day before. The few lone attempts to follow this directive were resisted by angry crowds who forced the "citizens" to stop their harassment.

Dozens of media calls were flooding our office asking how Unshackled Women was responding to the disruption of

EM. The collective met and discussed the situation throughout the day before Adila announced our response.

We welcome the dismantling of San Francisco's EM system, although we have no idea how this has happened. We refuse to co-operate with our own shackling any longer. Anyone who has been liberated from a bracelet will be welcomed at our offices as long as we have room. We consider this space a maroon community and we will try to peacefully protect anyone who joins us. We encourage other organizations, buildings, faith-based institutions, and homes to open their doors as well.

And with that, what the media dubbed the Urban Maroon movement was born. Adila claims that the idea for the maroon community originated just that day as people began to crowd into the office. But I recall the many evenings that Adila and Anise would be walking out to have a cup of coffee just as I was getting ready to leave the office. I remember passing by the Malecón Café on Market Street and seeing them locked in conversation with members of the Black Brigade collective. I remember noticing a book on the table by political prisoner Russell Maroon Shoatz, who had taken on his middle name after escaping from prison twice. I believe the maroon strategy had deep roots.

Within the next several weeks, EM systems in a number of other cities around the country were disabled. Many community groups opened their doors willingly to the many bracelet escapees, although a few refused because it wasn't in their scope of work. In some cities mosques, churches, and synagogues provided refuge to those who needed it and homeless shelters squeezed in extra beds. Formerly braceleted people in San Francisco and Oakland began occupying the vacant offices of start-ups that had gone end-up with the latest inevitable recession. And from the other side of the walls, Rahim initiated an Urban Maroon Marathon campaign. Amazingly, the campaign has already raised thousands of dollars through prison yard walkathons. All of the money has been donated by the prisoners to the maroon communities.

Some city councils have been persuaded to let the maroons exist as long as they remain peacefully self-organized. Other cities have dispersed the communities and there have been some arrests. Of course, not all the formerly braceleted have joined maroons. Some are laying low, keeping to themselves. Others have been recruited by the police to infiltrate and disrupt the maroons. So far none of the urban maroons have imploded or disbanded voluntarily.

Companies are working round the clock to rebuild their shredded EM systems, but ten months later none of them are yet operational. The media focuses on the technological brilliance of the hackers, which is undeniable, but when I am asked to comment I point out the obvious. The EM destruction wouldn't have meant anything if the maroon communities hadn't come together and laid claim to their freedom.

I turned seventy a few days ago on September 7, 2020. Nick came home for the occasion, and there was a wonderful celebration at the Women's Building with comrades and friends appearing from every era of my life. Today I walk at Lands End and notice how the sea is surging up. Someday the paths that I used to share with Anise will be under water. The movement is on a rise, but it may all soon be drowned, burned out, razed as I have seen happen so many times before. Oh how I need someone to keep my calamitous side in check.

When I came to Lands End with Cassandra, just before she died, we found a bench and sat looking at the cliffs and the waves and the Golden Gate Bridge for hours. At one point I couldn't hold it in anymore and started sobbing. I expected Cassandra to shake me and make me stop my self-indulgent pity. Instead she pointed toward the promontory furthest out in the ocean.

Look, Luba. I see the Yelamu dancing at the very edge of the cliff. Daring the occupiers to evict the ghosts from their land.

I stopped crying and hugged her tight. Two days later she died.

Ten years have passed since Cassandra's transition. The sun is glinting fiercely, jetting tantalizing rainbow prisms off the waves. I find myself looking at the promontory where Cassandra had glimpsed the Yelamu. For centuries they gathered salt and hunted seabirds on this very site. Harvested bulbs, seeds, and fruits. Pruned and burned. Preserved a balance with sea and land. Until the Europeans arrived and uprooted it all.

Suddenly, I see their shimmering silhouettes twirling precariously on the cragged face of the rocks. I hear their defiant freedom chant echoing from cliff to cliff—*We are dancing, dancing, dancing on the edge of the world.*

Will the sea have enveloped Lands End in another ten years? Will the Urban Maroon movement even be remembered? Will Anise still be living free in clandestinity?

The phone has started to buzz. Another city's EM system has been brought down. I get in my car and head to the office.

ABOUT THE AUTHOR

DIANA BLOCK WAS A FOUNDING MEMBER OF SAN FRANCISCO WOMEN AGAINST RAPE and the Prairie Fire Organizing Committee. She spent thirteen years living underground with a political collective committed to supporting the Puerto Rican independence and Black liberation movements. Since returning voluntarily from clandestinity in 1994, Diana has committed herself to anti-prison work, becoming a founding member of the California Coalition for Women Prisoners and the Jericho Movement. Previous writings include her memoir *Arm the Spirit* and she is a member of the editorial collective of *The Fire Inside* newsletter, which has been giving voice to women and transgender prisoners since 1996. She lives in San Francisco with her life partner, former political prisoner Claude Marks.

ABOUT PM PRESS

PM Press was founded at the end of 2007 by a small collection of folks with decades of publishing, media, and organizing experience. PM Press co-conspirators have published and distributed hundreds of books, pamphlets, CDs, and DVDs. Members of PM have founded enduring book fairs, spearheaded victorious tenant organizing campaigns, and worked closely with bookstores, academic conferences, and even rock bands to deliver political and challenging ideas to all walks of life. We're old enough to know what we're doing and young enough to know what's at stake.

We seek to create radical and stimulating fiction and non-fiction books, pamphlets, T-shirts, visual and audio materials to entertain, educate, and inspire you. We aim to distribute these through every available channel with every available technology—whether that means you are seeing anarchist classics at our bookfair stalls; reading our latest vegan cookbook at the café; downloading geeky fiction e-books; or digging new music and timely videos from our website.

PM Press is always on the lookout for talented and skilled volunteers, artists, activists, and writers to work with. If you have a great idea for a project or can contribute in some way, please get in touch.

PM Press
PO Box 23912
Oakland, CA 94623
www.pmpress.org

FRIENDS OF PM PRESS

These are indisputably momentous times—the financial system is melting down globally and the Empire is stumbling. Now more than ever there is a vital need for radical ideas.

In the years since its founding—and on a mere shoestring—PM Press has risen to the formidable challenge of publishing and distributing knowledge and entertainment for the struggles ahead. With hundreds of releases to date, we have published an impressive and stimulating array of literature, art, music, politics, and culture. Using every available medium, we've succeeded in connecting those hungry for ideas and information to those putting them into practice.

Friends of PM allows you to directly help impact, amplify, and revitalize the discourse and actions of radical writers, filmmakers, and artists. It provides us with a stable foundation from which we can build upon our early successes and provides a much-needed subsidy for the materials that can't necessarily pay their own way. You can help make that happen— and receive every new title automatically delivered to your door once a month—by joining as a Friend of PM Press. And, we'll throw in a free T-shirt when you sign up.

Here are your options (all include a 50% discount on all webstore purchases):
- **$30 a month** Get all books and pamphlets
- **$40 a month** Get all PM Press releases (including CDs and DVDs)
- **$100 a month** Everything plus PM merchandise and free downloads

For those who can't afford $30 or more a month, we're introducing **Sustainer Rates** at $15, $10 and $5. Sustainers get a free PM Press T-shirt and a 50% discount on all purchases from our website.

Your Visa or Mastercard will be billed once a month, until you tell us to stop. Or until our efforts succeed in bringing the revolution around. Or the financial meltdown of Capital makes plastic redundant. Whichever comes first.

Damnificados
JJ Amaworo Wilson
ISBN: 978-1-62963-117-2
$15.95 • 288 Pages

Damnificados is loosely based on the real-life occupation of a half-completed skyscraper in Caracas, Venezuela, the Tower of David. In this fictional version, six hundred "damnificados"—vagabonds and misfits—take over an abandoned urban tower and set up a community complete with schools, stores, beauty salons, bakeries, and a ragtag defensive militia. Their always heroic (and often hilarious) struggle for survival and dignity pits them against corrupt police, the brutal military, and the tyrannical "owners."

Taking place in an unnamed country at an unspecified time, the novel has elements of magical realism: avenging wolves, biblical floods, massacres involving multilingual ghosts, arrow showers falling to the tune of Beethoven's Ninth, and a trash truck acting as a Trojan horse. The ghosts and miracles woven into the narrative are part of a richly imagined world in which the laws of nature are constantly stretched and the past is always present.

> *"Should be read by every politician and rich bastard and then force-fed to them—literally, page by page."*
> —Jimmy Santiago Baca, author of *A Place to Stand*

Fire on the Mountain
Terry Bisson
Introduction: Mumia Abu-Jamal
ISBN: 978-1-60486-087-0
$15.95 • 208 Pages

Long unavailable in the U.S., published in
France as *Nova Africa*, *Fire on the Mountain*
is the story of what might have happened
if John Brown's raid on Harper's Ferry had
succeeded—and the Civil War had been started not by the slave
owners but the abolitionists.

Sensation
Nick Mamatas
ISBN: 978-1-60486-354-3
$14.95 • 208 Pages

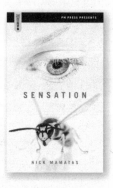

Told ultimately from the collective point of
view of another species, *Sensation* plays with
the elements of the Simulacrum we all already
live in: media reports, business-speak, blog
entries, text messages, psychological evaluation
forms, and the always fraught and kindly lies lovers tell one another.

TVA Baby
Terry Bisson
ISBN: 978-1-60486-405-2
$14.95 • 192 Pages

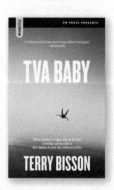

Readers who like cigarettes, lost continents,
cars, lingerie, or the Future will be delighted.
For those who don't, there's always Reality TV.